Cheyenne
IN NEW YORK

Cheyenne
IN NEW YORK
A NOVEL

JACK WEYLAND

BOOKCRAFT

SALT LAKE CITY, UTAH

Visit us at deseretbook.com

Library of Congress Cataloging-in-Publication Data

Weyland, Jack, 1940–
  Cheyenne in New York / Jack Weyland.
    p.   cm.
  ISBN 1-57008-909-4 (pbk.)
  1. September 11 Terrorist Attacks, 2001–Fiction.   2. New York (N.Y.)–Fiction.
  3. Mormon women–Fiction.   I. Title.
  PS3573.E99 C48   2003
  813'.54–dc21

2002151689

Printed in the United States of America
Banta, Nashville, TN

8006-6984

10 9 8 7 6 5 4 3 2

I met my wife, Sherry, in the Sacred Grove right after a testimony meeting for participants in the Hill Cumorah Pageant. I was a full-time missionary and she was a local participant from Queens. She had sung a vocal solo in the meeting. Afterwards I shook her hand and said something profound like, "Nice song." The next time we saw each other was at BYU after my mission. I recognized her and, in a classic pickup line, asked, "Weren't you in the Hill Cumorah Pageant?"

On my mission I fell in love with New Yorkers; that love grew stronger after marrying one of their finest. Sherry has taught me most of what I know about following the Savior's example.

I have always loved to visit New York City, and, now, with my son Brad and his New Jersey native wife, Sara, living there we have more opportunities to do that.

This book is dedicated to New Yorkers. The hearts of people everywhere go out to you for what you have gone through and for the heroes you have given us.

1

On my commute into New York City that Friday in early June, my cell phone started acting up. Just my luck, though, it was working when my mom called to remind me of our annual family get-together at our cabin on Lake Winnisquam in New Hampshire.

"Sounds great, Mom," I said, trying to fake enthusiasm for an event I had no intention of attending. "You suppose we'll have the three-legged race this year again?"

"Don't be disrespectful, Ben. You *are* coming, aren't you?" she asked.

"Oh, yeah, sure, no problem, you can count on me."

"You said that last year and the year before. It's embarrassing to explain why you don't show up to family activities."

"I would've been there last year except for that emergency that came up at the last minute."

"A croquet tournament is an emergency?"

"I came in third, Mom."

"Nothing had better come up this year. Granddaddy is threatening to cut you out of his will if you don't show up."

Any threat involving large amounts of money always gets my attention. "I'll be there, Mom. I promise."

"Is there a girl you're seeing? Someone you'd like to bring?"

"No, not really. I'm not seeing anybody." That wasn't exactly true, but Alisha and I only saw each other maybe once a month. She is an airline flight attendant, and it had been nearly impossible for us to arrange our schedules.

"You need to think about getting married and settling down."

It was a topic I had no interest in discussing. "Mom, you're breaking up. See you tomorrow at the lake, okay?"

Half an hour later, I arrived at the twentieth floor of the Fuller Building on Madison Avenue and Fifty-seventh Street, where I work as an advertising executive at the agency of Crawford, Sullivan, Chafin, and Blunck.

On my way to my cubicle, a cup of coffee in one hand and *The Wall Street Journal* in the other, I spotted a new girl. She was in her early twenties and had long, reddish brown hair and a light spattering of freckles.

She was also, quite possibly, taller than me. I've always felt that girls who are taller than me show a certain lack of respect.

To make matters worse, she'd just plopped a heavy box full of personal items on the desk of the recently vacated, coveted corner cubicle. Ever since Baxter got fired, I'd sent emails to Ross Chafin, my supervisor, begging him to let me have Baxter's cubicle.

"Excuse me, what are you doing?" I asked.

She smiled. "I'm moving in." She had a voice that could be heard five cubicles away. And a big mouth. Oh, I know, mouths are all about the same size, but there was something different about her mouth. Maybe it was that she had full lips. No, that's not it, either.

"Who are you?" I asked.

2

She extended her hand, so I shook it. "Cheyenne Durrant. I'm a summer intern from BYU. Who are you?" She had an enthusiastic grin and a milkmaid's handshake.

"I'm B. D. Morelli."

Long pause. "Your name is Beady?" she asked.

She has no respect for her superiors, I thought. "B period, D period."

She fought back a smile. "Would you like me to call you B period or D period or Beady?"

This girl definitely had an attitude. "I suppose you could call me Benjamin."

"You mean, as in Benjamin Franklin?"

"All right, Ben, then," I said.

"Hey, whatever you feel comfortable with. If you really want me to, I can call you Beady." When she laughed, her entire body got in on the action, which included her voice box. Coworkers stuck their heads out of their cubicles to see if there was a party going on.

I have never cared for tall girls who talk loud. To me it shows a double lack of respect.

She couldn't let it go. "What if your last name was Stare? Then you'd be Beady Stare. Or if your last name was Eyes . . ." Again the laugh. "Beady Eyes!" This time she was joined by four cubicle dwellers.

She noticed I wasn't joining in. "Sorry."

"Call me Ben."

"Okay, Ben, sure, no problem."

So here's where we stood. Strike one: she'd made fun of my name. Strike two: she talked too loud. A possible strike three would be if she turned out to actually be taller than me. That's why I had to find out our relative heights, but she kept bobbing up and down, unloading her boxes and setting her things out on the desk.

"I see you're moving into this cubicle," I said.

"Is there a problem?"

3

She had brown eyes. They were big, too. In fact, everything about her was larger than life–long fingers, a strong handshake, a voice that could be heard a block away, a grin that showed too many teeth. And now she had the nerve to move into what clearly should've been my cubicle.

It was my duty to set her straight. "You're new here so you probably haven't been briefed about cubicle protocol."

"Ross told me to take the one in the corner."

I shook my head. "You must have misunderstood. Ross would never assign this cubicle to a summer intern."

"Why not?"

"Because this is a corner cubicle. It has windows on two sides, and there's very little traffic."

"Oh, I'm sorry, Ben," she said, touching my hand and tilting her head like she wanted to console me. "Did you have your heart set on this cubicle?"

I did not appreciate her patronizing attitude. "Not at all. I'm very happy with my cubicle status."

When she stood erect, it looked like she could be slightly taller than me, but I suspected it was only because she had so much hair. It is a proven fact that many girls have tall hair, but it's the barefeet-to-scalp-height that counts.

I had an urge to reach over and pat her hair down to get a better estimate of our relative scalp heights. However, I decided she might consider my rearranging her hair a little strange. Maybe she'd take it as a New York form of greeting. No, probably not.

"If you'll excuse me, Beady, I need to get moved in."

"Call me Ben." It was more than a request. It was a directive.

"Why are you staring at the top of my head?"

She'd caught me. "Well, uhm, I was just looking at a spider on the wall."

She turned around. There was no spider.

"It ran away," I said.

I couldn't believe what happened next. She actually started to sing, "Eensy weensy spider went up a . . ."

That was it! I'd had it with her. "Excuse me. Here at Crawford, Sullivan, Chafin, and Blunck, we don't sing."

"Well, maybe we should." She looked at her watch. "Whoa, I'd better get going. Excuse me. I need to get some more boxes from my pickup." She started down the hall.

"You know what?" I called after her, "I'm going to check and see if Ross really meant for you to have the corner cubicle."

"Sure, go ahead. See you later."

Don't think I didn't know what was going on. Pretending that she didn't care what cubicle she got hadn't fooled me. I was on to her little game, and I was determined she wasn't going to get away with it.

Ten minutes later I returned from Ross's office. The new intern was standing at the bookshelf, arranging some framed photographs. I checked to see if she was wearing high heels. She wasn't. If she had been, then, clearly I'd have been taller than her. But since she wasn't, I still couldn't be sure.

"So, Beady, what did you find out?"

"Ross wants you to have the corner cubicle," I grumbled.

"Great, then, well, you have a nice day, okay?"

She bent over to place a book on the bottom shelf of her bookshelf. I got beside her and bent over at the same angle, hoping to finally find out if she was taller than me or not.

As we stood next to each other, each bending down, she looked over at me. "What are we doing here, Ben? Playing 'Follow, Follow Me'?"

"What?"

She started singing: "Do as I'm doing; Follow, follow me! . . ."

She had a nice voice. When she finished, she got a big round of applause from the cretins in the other cubicles.

She looked out her window. "This is such a great view!"

5

"Really? I haven't noticed. I'm much too busy to waste my time looking out the window."

She was standing straight, looking down Madison Avenue. Now was my chance to find out how tall she was. I put my hand on top of my head. Now all I had to do was move my hand to her head. That way I'd know who was taller. I was halfway there when she turned to face me. She looked at my hand just inches from her head. "What are you doing?"

"Uh . . . I'm saluting you." I gave her a military salute.

"Saluting me? What for?"

"For . . . many things . . . really . . ."

"Ben, do you have any actual work you do here?"

"Yes, of course. I'm very important here at Crawford, Sullivan, Chafin, and Blunck."

I returned to my cubicle and wrote a memo.

To: File
From: B. D. Morelli
Re: Reasons I hate the new summer intern

    1. She might be taller than me.
    2. She's gotten the corner cubicle.
    3. She talks too loud and sings children's songs.
    4. She thinks I'm a complete idiot.

But that wasn't the worst. A few minutes later, Ross sent me an email about the new intern. I swore under my breath when I read it. Of course, if I'd been her and sworn, the entire world would have heard it.

After gaining some self-control, I went to her cubicle. "Ross just sent me an email. He wants me to work with you and help you get your feet on the ground, so to speak. He asked me to have you follow me around for a few days, just to get the hang of what we do here."

"Great. Sounds good."

I entered her cubicle. "Is it okay if I look out your window? I mean, you're not going to charge me for it, are you?"

"Oh, gosh, Ben, you *are* upset I got the corner cubicle, aren't you? Look, it doesn't matter to me one way or the other where I work. Let's just switch cubicles right now, okay?"

I turned to face her. "That isn't important to me."

"Well, that's a relief. For a minute there I was thinking, 'Boy, this guy must be really shallow and insecure if he's freaked out over something as trivial as who's in which cubicle.'"

"He is hopelessly shallow and insecure!" It was Burroughs, one of my esteemed coworkers, butting in.

She started laughing, and, of course, she had to go and meet Burroughs, my main competitor. As he answered her questions, I found out more about him than I'd learned in the two years I'd worked there. He said he had a wife and two kids and that his wife has a cousin who lives in Boise. Like I cared.

I returned to my slum-dwelling cubicle and pouted. I'm not sure why she got under my skin. It wasn't just because she was tall and had the corner cubicle. It was more than that. Two years before, I'd been the summer intern, full of promise, which was as yet mainly unrealized. She was cutting into my territory. I was supposed to be the brilliant new guy. Not her.

Well, so what? I had more important things to worry about. Like my meeting with Harold Saddlemier, the CEO of Great American Cereals, the best-selling breakfast cereal in America today. I'd been given the account after Baxter had dropped the ball. Great American's market share had dropped in the past three months. And that was the end of Baxter.

With Baxter gone, Saddlemier demanded a whole new advertising approach. What approach? He didn't know. It just had to be new. I'd spent the past two weeks working day and night on it. In a preliminary meeting, Saddlemier told me he liked my ideas. I had hopes of getting him to sign the contract that night during dinner.

If it had been up to me, I'd have ignored the new girl, but Ross sent me another email, directing me to take her to the meeting with Saddlemier.

To help prepare for the meeting, I went out during lunch and bought a pair of shoes with a lift in them to make me taller than the new girl. And some thick, industrial strength mousse to put on my hair to make it stick up more. Two can play the tall-hair game.

I felt much more confident as I approached her cubicle. I was obviously taller than her now.

"Let's go."

She stared in disbelief at my hair, which stuck a couple of inches vertically upward from my head.

"What?" I asked.

She was trying very hard to be respectful. "You've done something to your hair, haven't you?"

"Yes, it's a new style. It's very popular here."

"I see. Well, if you're happy with it, that's all that matters." And then she did the unthinkable. She snickered.

At least she didn't make fun of my new shoes. She did seem concerned, however, when I stumbled stepping into the elevator.

"You okay?" she asked.

"New shoes."

"I see. They're nice. They make you look taller."

"Really? I hadn't noticed."

We went out to hail a cab. She, being the tourist that she was, gawked up at all the tall buildings. "I can't believe I'm here in the Big Apple."

"You realize, don't you, that there's not an actual big apple in this town?"

"I knew that."

"Good girl."

"I'm not a girl, Ben. I'm a woman."

I scowled. "Yeah, whatever."

Just after our cab pulled away from the curb and into traffic, I said, "Look, this is a very important meeting, so I'd appreciate it if you'd smile, be pleasant, but not say anything."

She laughed and then, seeing I wasn't laughing, asked, "Are you serious?"

"I am very serious. I've put way too much work into this presentation to have it ruined by some careless comment from you. So, just for tonight, if you could think of yourself as some mindless, silent, but sexy bimbo, I'd greatly appreciate it."

Her mouth dropped open.

I wondered if maybe I'd been a tiny bit unfair. Appearance-wise, I'd seen mummies in a museum that were less covered up than she was. "You know what? The sexy part is optional. I mean, I wouldn't want to take you out of your game."

She shook her head. "That tells me a great deal about you, Ben, but none of it is very good."

"Look, I don't care if you like me or not. And you don't have to be quiet the whole night. Right now, if you want, you can stick your head out the window and belt out songs to Broadway musicals at the top of your lungs, but once we get in the restaurant and Saddlemier shows up, you need to sit back, relax, keep your mouth shut, and watch a master at work."

I noticed her freckles became more prominent when she was angry, as she obviously was. Again, the least of my worries.

We arrived at the upscale restaurant across from Central Park half an hour early. That was by design. I wanted everything to be perfect for Saddlemier. I needed to relax, though, so I called the waiter over and ordered some wine for us.

"Not for me, thank you. I don't drink," she told the waiter.

9

"Look, just a little advice," I said. "If you want to fit in around here—"

"The reason I was hired is because I'm not like everyone else. I'm a new face. Just ask Ross. He'll tell you. He is hoping I'll give the company a new image."

"You're a summer intern, right? Four months from now nobody will even remember your name."

"Well, one thing for sure, Ben, I'll remember your name for a very long time," she said coolly. "I didn't come here to fit in. I didn't come here to be respectfully quiet. I came here to learn and to be productive."

"Let me tell you something. There's a lot more to this business than you can possibly know. It takes years to learn. But, hey, if you think you can change this company in one summer, then be my guest, go ahead and try."

"Sorry, but trying isn't good enough. It's like my dad says, 'A steer can try.'"

I couldn't believe she said that. "Look, if I wanted Western folk wisdom, I'd have bought a cowboy calendar, okay?"

I drank my wine and ignored her. She didn't seem to mind. She ordered a fresh vegetable tray and happily munched on carrots, celery, and cucumbers. I wasn't impressed. People who like fresh vegetables depress me.

She asked the waiter about his family. I told her to be quiet. She ignored me.

The waiter even showed her a picture of his kids. She said they were adorable. She actually used the word *adorable*.

Saddlemier arrived right on time. Sometimes I think the only reason he made CEO is because he has a thick head of silver hair and a deep voice. Talking to him is a little like talking to Moses.

When he showed up, I did everything short of licking his shoes. I told him how fit he looked and what an honor it was to be in his presence. The only thing I didn't do was introduce the new girl.

"And who's this?" he asked after the maitre d' had left.

I had a brain cramp. I'd forgotten her name. "This is . . . uhh . . . Laramie."

She smiled. "Actually, it's Cheyenne."

I shrugged. "Yeah, right. I knew it was some town in Wyoming."

Cheyenne stood up and gave Saddlemier one of her crushing handshakes. He winced. She told him her first and last name, like she was an equal or something. She was at least three inches taller than him. Poor slob.

"Cheyenne? What an unusual name. Are you from Wyoming?" he asked.

"No, I'm from Idaho."

He broke out into a huge grin. "Idaho? I used to live in Idaho!"

Oh, no! I thought. *She's going to ruin everything.*

She used the flat of her hand to playfully slug the shoulder of the CEO of Great American Cereals, a man whose personal worth exceeded twenty-seven point two million dollars.

"Oh, my heck!," she squealed. "Where did you live?"

"You ever hear of Mountain Home?" he asked.

"Mountain Home? Are you serious? I grew up on a ranch just an hour north of there!"

"Go on!" Saddlemier said, gently tapping her shoulder. "What are you doing so far away from home?"

"I'm a summer intern for Crawdad, Sullivan, Chapped, and Blunt."

"It's not Crawdad," I muttered. "It's Crawford. It's not Chapped, it's Chafin. It's not Blunt, it's Blunck. You did get Sullivan right, so that's one out of four."

They paid no attention to me. "I'll be a senior this fall at BYU," she said.

"One of my buddies from when I was in the Air Force teaches at BYU."

"What's his name?" Cheyenne asked.

11

"David McDermott."

"Dr. McDermott? I can't believe it! He's my adviser!" She playfully hit him again, and he shoved her back.

"Could we all sit down and quit punching each other?" I complained.

We all sat down.

"Would you like a glass of wine to start us off?" I asked Saddlemier, hoping to apply one of the first rules of pitching an idea, which is, a tipsy CEO is a pliable CEO.

Saddlemier looked over at Cheyenne's empty wine glass and asked, "You're not drinking?"

"No, I don't drink. Water's plenty good for me. But you go ahead."

"No, no, I'll have water, too," he said.

Great. Saddlemier was going to be stone-cold sober for my presentation.

They spent the next few minutes talking about the best glass of water they'd ever had. "I remember one time I went hiking with some friends from school," Cheyenne said. "We climbed up to Hidden Falls in the Tetons. By the time we were coming back, we were all so hot and tired, we took off our shoes and soaked our feet in the crick."

"Crick? What's a crick?" I asked.

"It's like a little river," Cheyenne said.

"Oh, you mean creek."

"No, actually, I mean crick."

"It's spelled c–r–e–e–k."

"I know how it's spelled, Beady. But it's pronounced crick. Everyone in Idaho says crick."

"Then everyone in Idaho is a complete idiot."

"I'm from Idaho," Saddlemier said.

"With all due respect, sir, you're not from Idaho. You lived in Idaho for a short time, and then you had the good sense to leave."

"If Cheyenne says it's crick, then it's crick."

12

"Oh, that is so sweet!" she said. "Thank you, Mr. Saddlemier."

I swear she actually said *sweet.*

While we ate, Cheyenne and Saddlemier chatted about Idaho cricks and mountains, while I sulked.

After dessert I tried to close the deal by giving a laptop presentation.

"So that's it," I said, finishing up ten minutes later. "I have the agreement here if you'd like to sign."

Saddlemier turned to Cheyenne. "What do you think about what Ben has shown us here tonight?"

She responded much too quickly. "Boy, it was really good!"

"What did you like the most about it?" he asked.

She hesitated. "Well, gosh, that's hard to say. It was all . . . so . . . so . . ." She seemed to be struggling for the right word. " . . . good . . . I guess you could say. I thought it was a nice touch to have it all seem so . . . well . . . cheesy."

Absolute silence.

"Cheesy?" Saddlemier asked.

Cheyenne hunched her shoulders and gave me a guilty look. "Of course, I mean cheesy in the best possible way."

"How would you change it?" he asked.

I leaned over, put my hand on her wrist and glared at her. "Yes, Cheyenne, what tiny insignificant change would you make?"

"Oh, gosh, I wouldn't change a word."

"Not a single word?" Saddlemier asked.

"That's right."

I gave a sigh of relief and began to relax. Maybe things would work out all right after all.

"How about the visuals?" he asked.

"The visuals?" She cleared her throat. "Well . . . to be honest, I might make a few changes on the visuals."

13

Saddlemier fastened his steel-gray, CEO eyes on her. "Like what?" he asked.

She took a deep breath. "Well, actually, you know what? I'm not sure having a dozen chorus girls in sexy tank tops and short-shorts dancing on a giant cereal box is going to have that much of a positive impact on a young mother trying to decide what brand of cereal to buy."

"They're dancing wheat grains," I said.

"Oh! They're dancing wheat grains! Well, then, that's completely different!" She turned to me and privately whispered, "Dancing wheat grains?"

"Cheyenne, how would you pitch Great American Cereal?" Saddlemier asked.

"Well, I guess I'd try to pitch it from a mother's point of view. I come from a big family. I have one older sister and two married brothers. They all have kids. It's the moms in those families who do all of the grocery shopping. They're interested in good nutrition and having something their kids like that is also affordable."

Saddlemier thought about it, took a deep drink of water, and then nodded. "Ben, I think Cheyenne has a point. I'd like the both of you to work together and flesh out some new ideas, based on what Cheyenne has said, and get back with me on Tuesday. Let's get together in my office about eleven o'clock, and then we'll do lunch."

Half an hour later, we left the restaurant. I walked as fast as I could, hoping she'd get lost. People get mugged in NYC. So why not her?

She seemed to have no trouble keeping up with me. It was probably because of my new shoes.

"You seem kind of quiet," she said after we'd jogged two blocks.

I turned to glare at her and fought to catch my breath. "You want to know why I'm quiet?" I yelled. "Is that it? Well, let me tell you! I'm quiet because I can't put in words how

14

angry I am at you for making a mess of everything! That's why I'm quiet!"

"You don't need to yell. If it's any consolation, I am sorry."

I stopped walking and turned to face her. "You think saying you're sorry is going to fix everything? Well, I don't think so, Missy. You want to know something? I would consider myself very lucky if I never saw you again. But that's not going to happen, is it?"

We started walking again. "Oh, no, that would be too easy! Saddlemier insists we work together, and whatever Saddlemier wants, Saddlemier gets! Well, fine, then, that's just great! Oh, by the way, I hope you don't have anything planned for this weekend because, the fact is, you're coming with me to New Hampshire for a family get-together."

"Great! I like family reunions."

"Well, maybe *you* do, but I don't. In fact, I *hate* family reunions. The only reason I'm going is because if I don't, I'll be cut out of my grandfather's will. This is the way it's going to work. We'll show up long enough for my grandfather to see I'm there, but other than that, every second will be spent working up a new advertising campaign. We'll return Sunday afternoon, go to the office, and work all night, if we have to, in order to finish up what we'll be presenting on Tuesday to Saddlemier. And then, and only then, will we part company and go home and get some sleep. Do you have any questions?"

"Were the dancing wheat grains really your idea?"

"It came to me in a dream."

She shook her head. "Weird dream."

"You know what? I'm sure we'll get along much better if you don't talk."

I dragged her into a coffee shop and used my cell phone to try to reserve two tickets to Laconia, New Hampshire, but they were booked solid. She ordered hot chocolate and

15

started making artistic animal sculptures from the napkins. The manager, originally from Vietnam, loved her work.

A few minutes later, the owner and a few customers were making requests for her to make animals for them. With each one, they applauded. When she turned out a napkin giraffe, they gave her a standing ovation.

"Thank you! You're all too kind. I'd like to sing you a song now. It's about how people say happy birthday in various cultures."

She stood up and began singing. People from outside came in to listen. When she finished, they applauded.

"Would you people quiet down?" I yelled. "I'm on my cell phone here."

"What with him?" the manager asked.

She was even starting to speak like him. "Him having hard day. Tomorrow . . . things better. Things always better . . . morning. As song goes . . ." I swear, she sang a few bars of "Tomorrow."

"He lucky man to have you."

"Thank you very much, but we not married. We just work together. We work at Sullivan, Blinken . . . oh, never mind. We work at an advertising agency." She turned to me and said, "Beady, if it'd help, I can drive us up. I've got my dad's pickup for the summer."

"You think I don't have a car? Is that what you think? I have a car, a perfectly good car. In fact, it's a BMW. So if any-one is going to drive us up, I will be that person."

"Okay. So, are we going to drive up in your car?"

After a long pause, I muttered, "No, we're not."

"Why not?"

"Because it's getting fixed in the garage. No, actually, that isn't accurate. It's waiting for parts to be sent from Europe. By boat . . . once they make them . . . in the factory . . ."

"So you're without a car? That's tough, Beady."

"I've told you before, call me Ben, okay? Ben is my name.

16

And, furthermore, with all due respect, I don't need your help."

She turned her attention to the manager, who asked, "You do elephant for nephew?"

"Of course. I happy to do elephant. But need more napkins."

By the time she'd made five elephants for the customers, I was out of options. "Cheyenne?" I asked politely.

"Yes, Ben."

"I guess maybe I'll let you drive us up."

"Sure, no problem."

She didn't rub it in.

I would have.

2

Cheyenne was staying in a condominium on West Thirty-eighth and Sixth Avenue in the City. The condo was owned by our ad agency for use by summer interns and new hires until they could find a place of their own.

My apartment was in Hoboken, New Jersey, right across the Hudson River from Manhattan. To avoid having her get into an accident in the City or getting lost in Jersey trying to find my place, I got up early and took a train into the City. I got out at Thirty-third Street at 6th Avenue and walked the five blocks to Cheyenne's place. On my walk I phoned and told her I'd be there in ten minutes.

She met me outside her building, wearing faded jeans and a blue BYU T-shirt. Her hair, which the night before had looked brown, now appeared, in bright sunlight, to be a dusky red. She had pulled it back into a ponytail and tied it with a rubber band.

Her dad had loaned her a pickup so she'd have something to drive while she was back east for the summer. She complained that it had taken her an hour to find a place to park it, at the curb, a couple of blocks away. After I called, she'd gone to get it and had it double-parked in front of her condo.

When I first saw it, I started laughing.

"What?" she asked.

"Look, don't even bother to lock it up at night. Nobody's going to steal that hunk of junk." It was a beat-up, rusted-out, ten-year-old Ford with a gun rack over the back window, but no gun, and, of course, Idaho plates.

"Hey, I grew up riding in this truck. In a way, it's a part of who I am."

"Yeah, whatever," I said with a shrug. "I'll drive."

She scowled at me. "I can drive."

"Yeah, yeah. You can maybe drive out on the prairies, but this is no place for amateurs. Gimme the keys."

"I didn't have any trouble getting here."

"Did anyone honk at you?"

"Yeah, a lot of cars did. People here are so friendly."

I held out my hand. "Give me the keys."

I could see she wasn't happy, so I said, "Look, once we get out a ways, we'll switch."

I drove for an hour, then we traded places.

We had a five-hour trip ahead of us, so I thought I'd better clear the air. I told her I felt bad about the way I'd treated her the night before. "Sometimes I'm kind of a jerk."

"It's probably because people have always let you get away with it. Don't worry, though. I'll always tell you when you're out of line." She smiled when she said it, so I couldn't tell if it was a promise or a threat.

She sighed. "I owe you an apology, too. I shouldn't have said anything about your dancing wheat kernels. I mean, you worked so hard on them."

We rode in silence for a minute, then I asked, "So, are we back up to zero?"

"I guess so, except I'm not sure what that means."

"Well, in advertising, when you start on something, you're at zero. Then you work and work, and you show it to somebody, and they shoot it down. So then you're at minus five hundred, and what you have to do is try to work your way back up to zero."

She nodded. "Okay, you're right. We're back up to zero." She paused. "You want to know the rodeo equivalent of being at minus five hundred? An announcer at a rodeo says this after a cowboy has a bad ride." She cleared her throat and then imitated a rodeo announcer. "'He's out of the day money, he's out of the average, all he gets is what you give him. Let's give that cowboy a big hand! Attaboy, Cowboy, good try!'"

My ears were still ringing. "I have no idea what that means."

"*Out of the day money* means he's not going to get money for the best ride of the day. *Out of the average* means when they average his times over the two or three days of the rodeo, that ride is going to count heavily against him. In other words, he's up a crick without a paddle."

I shook my head and smiled. "The sad thing is, 'crick' is starting to sound normal to me."

"We're going to make an Idaho cowpoke out of you yet, Ben."

"Don't count on it."

She laughed. "Whoa! Big words for a guy with no car! You want to walk the rest of the way?"

I nodded my head. "Hmmm, looks like I need an attitude adjustment."

"Looks that way to me, too, Cowboy."

"Let's see what I can do. Crick is good. I can do crick. I can do day money. I can do average. It's all good."

"That's better."

"I suppose you've been to a few rodeos."

"Yeah, sure. In fact, I used to compete in barrels."

Long pause. "You made barrels at a rodeo?"

"No! There's a line of barrels, and you ride your horse in and out of them and then come back as fast as you can."

"Were you any good?"

"From twelve years old to when I turned sixteen, I was the best in Idaho for my age, but then one day I just gave it all up."

"How come?"

"I was good enough that if I had gone any farther, I'd have ended up riding on Sundays."

"So?"

"My dad told me that I belonged in church."

"And you just went along with what he said?"

"I did."

"How come? You're supposed to be rebellious at that age."

"My dad and I are real close." She put her hand on the dashboard like it was her touchstone. "Having his old pickup this summer makes me feel closer to my family. All I have to do is get in, close my eyes, and suddenly I'm home."

"The part about closing your eyes—that's not when you're driving, right?"

She did her best laugh, the kind that makes everyone want to join in. "You are so funny sometimes! You know what, Beady? I'm kind of beginning to enjoy being with you. Isn't that strange? We're so different from each other."

"Really? I hadn't noticed."

A while later, I suggested we stop and get something to eat.

"I made us a lunch," she said. "It's in a cooler in back."

I was stunned. "You made us a lunch?"

"Sure, why not? I thought it'd save us some time, and it's a lot cheaper, too. It's not much. Just some sandwiches, a few carrots, an apple, and a drink."

21

We pulled off at a rest stop and used the rest rooms and then ate, stretching our legs and leaning against her pickup.

"Actually, this is very good," I said.

"Thanks."

"I'm not crazy about carrots though. You want mine?"

"They're good for you."

"Oh, great. Now you've turned into my mother."

"I'll tell you what. We'll munch on the carrots in unison. One big bite. Okay, now we're chewing in unison. One . . . two . . . three . . ."

I couldn't help myself–I ate the stupid carrots.

When we finished eating, we had a contest seeing who could toss our paper bag into the trash receptacle from twenty feet. She won, but she cheated, by doing some kind of fancy hook shot.

We got back into the pickup and took off again.

"What else can you tell me about yourself?" I asked.

"There's not much to tell, really. I grew up on a ranch. I worked with my dad a lot. Most of the time, he treated me like I was one of his sons. But, at the same time, my mom made sure I could cook and sew. She made me take piano lessons. All the way through high school, I sang in choir. Oh, one thing, I taught aerobics for a while my senior year. So when I went to BYU, I got a job teaching aerobics at a fitness center." She reached over and grabbed a CD. "In fact, I'll give you a free demonstration."

The CD was background music for aerobics. In an animated voice, she supplied the encouragement. "Looking good! . . . March it out! One . . . two . . . three . . . four. Looking good! Okay! Step tap . . . one . . . two . . . three . . . four . . . Let's go, you guys! Hips . . . triple . . . okay, now step tap. One . . . two . . . three . . . four . . . March it out . . . You're looking fine!"

My mouth dropped. What I felt was a cross between

amusement and maybe just a little bit of awe. I'd never met anyone so open, energetic, and enthusiastic in my life.

The thing that surprised me most was that I was beginning to like the way she looked. You know how when you go to a movie and get your first huge close-up of an actress you've never seen before, and you think she's not very pretty? But by the time the movie is over, you've decided she's actually gorgeous, and you wonder why you couldn't see that at first? That's the way it had been with Cheyenne. After listening to her talk and watching her facial expressions, I couldn't get over how good-looking she was.

"You know what?" she asked. "If you want, we can pull over, and we'll do the whole routine. I did that on my drive out here, whenever I got sleepy."

"I bet you made some trucker's day when he passed you."

"Oh, nobody saw me. It was in the middle of the night."

"Too bad. Well, you know what? I think we should stop. I think I'd like to see you in action . . . doing aerobics, that is."

She pursed her lips, paused, then shook her head. "You know what, Beady? I'm not sure you're that interested in aerobics." She squinted at me. "You might just want me to put on a little show for you."

"Me?" I asked, trying to sound as innocent as possible. "Are you kidding? Fitness is my life."

"I'm not sure I believe that," she said.

"I guess we'll never know."

"Not likely. Tell me about your family."

I shook my head. "Why do you have to know about my family?"

"Well, because I'm about to meet them."

"How about if you draw your own conclusions?"

"I told you about my family," she said.

"So?"

"Please."

"You want to know about my family? Okay, fine. My dad

23

and my grandfather have absolutely no respect for me. My mother has pretty much given up on me. My aunt and uncle worry that I'm a bad influence on their two kids. When I'm with my family, they drive me crazy, and I can hardly wait to get away. But when I stay away for a long time, my mom complains I never visit. And that's why we're going up there this weekend. Any questions?"

She scrunched up her nose, like someone had just given her a bad-tasting cough syrup. "Actually, I do have some questions."

"When it comes to my family, I don't have any answers."

"These will be easy questions."

"Why aren't you like other girls? Why don't you talk about how unfair it is to have tan-lines or how rotten the last guy was who dumped you?"

"Because I want to know about your family. What does your dad do?"

I sighed. "My dad and my Uncle Eugene both work for my grandfather. My grandfather was born in Yugoslavia. He came here with his family when he was ten years old. He started out as a waiter and then, after a few years, began his own catering business. Now it's called Morelli and Sons Catering."

"Did you ever have any interest in working there?"

"Look, I really don't want to talk about this, okay?"

"Where does your mom come from?"

"A small town north of the City, on the Hudson River."

"How did she meet your dad?"

"She met him when she was seventeen when she was on a vacation with her family in the Catskill Mountains. My dad was twenty, working as a waiter. They saw each other when he waited on her family. My mom had been raised by a protective father. My dad filled the role of the dark, handsome, moody stranger. They started meeting late at night, after her parents had gone to bed."

"Sounds romantic," she said.

"If making bad choices is romantic, then I guess it was."

"Did they get married right away?"

"No. They met secretly for over a year, then she finally told her family about him. They forbade her from ever seeing him again. A week later, my mom and dad eloped. Her family disowned her, and she was never welcome in their home after that. That's it."

"What about your grandmother?"

"She was born in Yugoslavia, never did learn English. I called her Nona. She died when I was in high school. My grandfather used to talk about her a lot, but he doesn't do that much now. That's my family, for better or worse. If given a choice, though, I'd pick worse."

"Why are you so down on your family?"

"I don't see that's any of your business."

I could tell I'd hurt her feelings. I told myself I didn't care. Because I'd gotten up so early, and because I didn't want to talk to her anymore, I took a nap.

We pulled into our cabin by the lake around two that afternoon. My family was down at the dock, swimming or suntanning, or waiting to be taken out waterskiing.

My dad and his brother, Eugene, were working on the boat. Parts of the engine were strewn on the dock. From their grim expression, I could tell things were not going well.

Physically, my dad and Uncle Eugene are carbon copies of each other—black hair, now streaked with gray, lean bodies, and thin faces. Always prepared, always in charge, they are guys you'd trust to take care of every detail of an important family or company reception.

Although my dad and my Uncle Eugene look alike, my dad is more quiet. He's the one who does the grunt work on every job, while Eugene glad-hands everybody and uses his charm to get what he wants.

Uncle Eugene is married to Marilyn. She was born Jewish but was never that strong in her faith, so she converted to

25

Catholicism when she got married, and her family pretty much disowned her—for that and for eloping. Maybe that's why she's always been kind of melancholy. But she's a beautiful woman, and when I was growing up, I had a crush on her. Aunt Marilyn's in her forties now, but she watches what she eats and still has a nice figure. With her high cheekbones and big eyes, she's always reminded me of Sophia Loren.

They have two children. Caleb is thirteen, the best-looking one in the family. He has coal-black eyes, thick, dark hair, and a winning mischievous grin that gets him out of trouble more often than it should.

Their daughter, Emma, is eleven. She's tall and slender and wears glasses because they make her look smart, which she is. I never used to think so, but she will probably grow up to look exactly like her mother.

Emma and I have always been close because when she was younger, I was the only one in the family who'd play Barbies with her. It wasn't that hard actually. Emma would tell me what to say, and I'd say it. From what I'd seen from my uncle and my dad, it was good training for marriage.

We found my mother in the kitchen cooking. She loved food. Maybe that's why she married my dad. But she didn't cook fancy dishes at home, especially if my dad would be eating the food. He was very critical of other people's cooking, and so my mom had learned not to put herself out cooking all day because my father would always find something wrong with it. But when we got together with the entire family, it was different. Then she cooked.

My mom is five-foot-four, fair complexioned, and a little stout, with blonde hair, which should have been turning gray but, thanks to the wonders of chemistry, was retaining its color.

I inherited the Southern European dark-brown hair and olive complexion of my father but the blue eyes and love of art from my mother. Not to brag, but I was a great source

26

of pride for my mother as I was growing up. Since my dad was often gone, she lavished all her attention on me. But when I grew up and moved away, she was, once again, isolated. That's why she loved organizing our yearly family get-togethers and holiday gatherings.

My mother was happy to see me but absolutely thrilled to meet Cheyenne. I'd never brought a girl home to meet my family before and perhaps never would again, after seeing my mother's reaction. She gave Cheyenne a big hug. "We're so glad Ben brought you home to meet the family." The hug was about five seconds longer than I was comfortable with. It was like she was being welcomed into the family. I was sure my mother was thinking *grandchildren.*

"I didn't bring her home to meet the family, okay?" I grumbled.

Cheyenne laughed. "But it's okay if I do, right? I mean, I don't have to be the mystery guest, do I?"

I shrugged. "You can meet my family. Just don't bother to remember their names."

My mom laughed, still holding Cheyenne's hands. "I don't know what gets into Ben sometimes, but I can assure you he was taught better manners than that."

"I can see that."

It was time to secure my position as an heir to my grandfather's money. "Where's Granddaddy?"

Cheyenne smiled. "You still call your grandfather 'Granddaddy'? That is so sweet!"

My mother smiled. "Ben was an adorable child. I have so many stories about him I'm dying to tell you."

"I'd love to hear them all!" Cheyenne said, flashing me a teasing grin.

"Granddaddy, where is he?" I asked, impatient to get that over with so Cheyenne and I could go to work.

"He's in his room, but he's got another one of his terrible migraines. He's been in bed all day."

"Oh, how awful," Cheyenne said.

"I need to see him now," I said, anxious to get the obligatory greeting over with.

We followed my mother upstairs to my grandparents' bedroom. As we entered the room, the shades were drawn, making the room dark and dreary. "Dad, Ben is here with his friend Cheyenne," my mother whispered.

"I made it, Granddaddy. Sorry to hear you're not feeling good. Well, we'll let you rest, okay? That's the best thing. You take good care of yourself, okay?" I turned to Cheyenne. "Let's go."

Cheyenne would have none of it . She stepped close to the bed and took my grandfather's hand in hers. "I'm happy to meet you. Can I call you Granddaddy, too? How are you feeling?"

"Rotten," he said.

"Migraine headache, right?"

He nodded.

"That's too bad. I know how bad migraines can be. Have you ever tried feverfew?"

"No. What is it?"

"Well, it's an herb you can get at any health food store. For some people, it relieves migraines and helps prevent them."

"I've spent a fortune on drugs. Nothing works."

"Would you try feverfew if I can find some?" she asked.

"There aren't any health food stores around here," I said, proud to be poking a hole in this trial balloon.

"Well, it's a common plant. Let me go outside and walk around. Maybe I can find some growing."

My mom and I waited in the kitchen for Cheyenne to return.

"It doesn't bother you that Nature Girl is wandering around the woods picking up twigs and leaves off the ground she's going to give Granddaddy to eat?" I asked.

"She seems to know what she's doing."

28

"Right, that's the way it seems, but I'm not sure it's true."

Cheyenne returned ten minutes later withsome feverfew leaves. She mashed them, added water, and made a paste, which she took upstairs with a glass of water.

When she came down, she said, "Well, I got him to take it. Now we'll just have to see if it works."

"That's so thoughtful of you, to try to help him," my mom said. "But right now come with me, and I'll take you down to the dock and make the introductions."

Mom left me and took Cheyenne outside where she enthusiastically introduced her to my family. I stayed in the house and watched out the window. They loved her.

I sampled the marinara sauce, then went out to join them.

My Aunt Marilyn took me aside. "You got yourself a real treasure there, Ben. I hope you'll both be very happy together."

"Well, actually—"

Marilyn didn't stick around for an explanation.

I went out on the dock to talk to my dad and Eugene. "Need any help?"

"We don't need help," my dad grumbled. He gets tight-lipped and irritable when he's trying to fix something.

Eugene winked at me. We both knew not to say too much to my dad when things were not going well. "Hey, it's good to see you, Benny," Eugene said.

"You, too, Uncle Eugene."

When my dad is working, what you have to do is look interested, but don't say anything. And never offer any suggestions. That's what Eugene and I did for the next few minutes until Cheyenne joined us.

"This is Cheyenne," I said. "We work together."

My dad looked up, glared at her, then it must have occurred to him that she might be my future wife, so he switched suddenly and smiled warmly. "I'm very pleased to meet you," he said.

"Way to go, Benny Boy," Eugene said with a big smile.

29

"It's not that way. Our relationship is purely physical," I said.

Cheyenne looked at me as though I'd lost my mind.

Eugene started laughing. "Really?"

Finally it dawned on me what I'd said. I started to blush. "I didn't mean that. What I meant is professional. We have a purely professional relationship. We both work at Crawford, Sullivan, Chafin, and Blunt."

"Blunck," Cheyenne said.

"That's right, Blunck."

Eugene slapped me on the back. "You're not fooling anybody, Benny Boy. Anyone can see you two are madly in love."

"Actually, we hardly know each other."

"Is Ben taking good care of you?" my dad asked.

I resented the question. It was the kind of question he asked the host at a party, about the hired help—meaning me, when I was in high school.

"Oh, yes, very good."

"Well, that's good. You deserve the very best."

I'd always known my dad could be gracious and charming. I had just seldom seen it without someone paying for the service.

"Excuse me," Cheyenne said. She left to introduce herself to Caleb and Emma while I stood in respectful silence and watched my dad work on the engine.

A few minutes later, Cheyenne returned. "Caleb and Emma are adorable! Guess what? They talked me into going swimming," she said. "You want to join us?"

"No, what I want to do is to get some work done."

"Well, you can do what you want," she said. "I'm going swimming."

I caught up with her halfway up the dock. "I didn't bring you up here to go swimming."

"It won't take long. Besides, how can you be here without going swimming? Look at this lake!"

"Do you realize that fish live in the same water you'll be swimming in?" I asked.

She rested both her hands on my shoulders and looked into my eyes. "Ben, don't be such a grouch all the time, okay? Loosen up. Have fun. This is the only family you're ever going to have. They need to know you enjoy being with them."

"That's just it. I don't enjoy being with them."

She leaned close enough to whisper in my ear. "Fake it then, Beady."

I pulled away. "I'm not going swimming."

She shrugged. "Well, suit yourself. I am." She started on her way to the cabin to change.

"Another thing. I hate it when you call me 'Beady.'"

She turned around and came back to me. "What *don't* you hate, Ben? Look, I promised you on the way up here that I'd always tell you when you were acting like a jerk." She pointed her finger at me. "Well, if you don't go swimming and spend some time with your family, this will be one of those times."

Ten minutes later, wearing an extra large T-shirt over her swimming suit, she ran down the dock and launched herself into the air, shouting, "Geronimo!"

I stood inside the house at the kitchen window and watched her. She was having more fun with my family than I'd ever had. And they loved her.

After a few minutes, I decided I wasn't going to get any work done watching her, so I changed into my swimming suit, and not to be undone, ran down the dock and shouted the same thing and jumped off the dock. Playing Barbies with my niece, Emma, had taught me one thing: just do and say what the girl wants you to say.

Cheyenne swam over to me. "Great jump!"

"Thanks."

We treaded water while Cheyenne got better acquainted with Caleb and Emma. She asked all about their activities in school.

31

"You guys are so talented and smart!" she said after a few minutes. "I never did half the things you're doing in school."

They beamed.

Because Emma was on the swim team, she insisted we race her out to a floating diving platform about a hundred feet from the dock. She won. I pouted a little because Emma was the one who said "Go!" so in my mind that gave her an advantage. Cheyenne told her what a fast swimmer she was and how gracefully she moved through the water. "Like a dolphin," she added.

Emma grinned at that comparison and nodded her head.

When my dad and Eugene finally got the boat working, they took Emma and Caleb out for a trial run. Cheyenne and I were invited, but I told them we had work to do, so they went without us.

She and I swam out to the floating platform so we could talk about cereal. We could hear my mom and Marilyn talking at the dock. "They make such a nice couple," my mom said about us.

"I never thought I'd see the day," Marilyn said. "She'll be a wonderful addition to the family. And their kids will be gorgeous."

"Sorry," I said, not even daring to look Cheyenne in the eyes.

"It's no problem. Don't worry about it."

"Do you want me to put some sunblock on your back?" I asked.

"No, that's why I'm wearing a T-shirt."

"It looks dumb to be wearing a shirt over your swimming suit."

"Don't think I don't appreciate your fashion advice, but, you know what? I think I'll leave the shirt on."

We sat side by side on the floating platform, watching Eugene and my dad give Caleb and Emma the ride of their lives. I realized this was the chance I'd been waiting for.

"Stand up," I said. She did, and I stepped close to her and put my hand on the top of my head, then moved it over hers. Scalp-wise, I was a good inch taller than her. Just as I had suspected, she had tall hair.

"I'm taller than you," I said.

"I know. The reason it wasn't obvious is because you have short hair."

We both got kind of a silly grin on our faces and lay down together on our towels on the floating platform and let the sun dry us off. I may have accidentally placed my hand on hers while we were lying beside each other. Neither one of us moved away from the other, although I'm sure we both considered it.

Just when I was about to fall asleep, I thought about meeting with Saddlemier on Tuesday. That woke me up. "Let's go canoeing. Maybe we can get some work done out on the water."

"I'll go change."

"You don't need to change."

"We're done swimming, right?"

"Yes."

"I burn easily, so I'll change."

"If you let me put sunblock on you, then you won't have to change."

She flashed me a quick, condescending grin as she prepared to do a dive off the platform. "In your dreams, Beady. In your dreams."

We swam back to the dock, and she went up to the house and changed. I wasn't sure her being afraid of getting a sunburn was the only reason. She seemed self-conscious having people look at her in her swimming suit even though she was wearing a T-shirt over it. I'd never known anyone like that before.

She came back a few minutes later in jeans and a T-shirt and carrying a backpack.

33

We paddled to an inlet around the bend, out of sight of the family. "This'll do," I said. "Oh, one thing, to clear the air. I'm afraid my family thinks we're in a relationship and that we're about to get married or something."

"I think you're right about that."

"Sorry."

"Don't worry. I'd never consider marrying you."

That was the last thing I thought she'd say. Ever since my senior year in high school, girls have always wanted to marry me.

"Why's that?" I must have sounded like a fifteen-year-old just turned down by the girl of his dreams.

"Well, for one thing, I would never marry anyone who doesn't share my beliefs about religion."

"Which are?"

So she started telling me what she believed. I'd never heard anything like it in my life. And, of course, I didn't believe a word of it. I mean, who would?

"Do you have any proof that what you're telling me is true?"

"Yes, I do."

"And what is your proof?"

"This."

She pulled it out of her backpack. It was a blue, paperback book called The Book of Mormon. She told me a little about what was in the book and then said, "Read it. Then pray and ask God if it's true, and he'll let you know it is. Then you'll know."

"Just like that?"

"Just like that."

"I don't think so."

"You'll never know unless you put it to the test."

"I have more important things to do."

"No, that's just it, Ben. You don't." She called me Ben as though I were her friend.

Here was a girl from a ranch in Idaho. We had only known each other for a couple of days, and yet, here she was, revealing her innermost beliefs to me. Like I was her friend and she cared about me.

Even though I'd always felt uncomfortable having any kind of religious discussion, I realized that if I wanted to understand her, I needed to know what she believed.

When she finished telling me, she asked, "Any questions?"

"Do you always wear a T-shirt over your swimming suit?"

She shook her head like I was beyond hope. "Do you have any questions about what I've told you?"

I shrugged my shoulders. "Not really. Let's get some work done."

"Of course," she said, reverting back to a more formal arrangement.

We were just getting started when Caleb and Emma, also in a canoe, found us. "Can Cheyenne come out and play?" Caleb asked in a silly imitation of a six- year-old.

"No, we're busy."

"Yeah, right," Caleb scoffed. And then he yelled, "Canoe wars!"

They started toward us. The only way we could avoid being tipped over was to paddle like crazy and fight back.

We'd have fought until dark, but Eugene came in the boat to tell us that it was time for dinner.

As we were about to eat dinner outside on a picnic table next to the house, my grandfather came downstairs. He'd shaved and changed into slacks and a sports shirt.

Granddaddy looks like he could play a crime boss in a movie—chiseled face, dark complexion, steely eyes, with a full head of hair. The truth is, although we didn't talk about it much, he probably did have some Mafia connections. Crime families have parties, too, you know, and they prefer caterers who can keep their mouths shut, which has never been a problem for any of the men on my dad's side of the family.

35

"How are you feeling?" my mother asked him.

"Marvelous! Thanks to that Indian medicine woman Ben brought home. Is she still here?"

Cheyenne waved to Granddaddy. "I'm here."

"You're not Indian. Why did I think you were?"

"Probably because my name is Cheyenne."

"I just know that what you gave me really did the trick."

Cheyenne gave him a big grin. "That's great."

"Such a girl," Marilyn said.

Dinner lasted an hour and a half, after which my dad built a fire for us to sit around. Using the dock for their stage, Caleb and Emma and Cheyenne put on an impromptu talent show for us. Then Cheyenne led us in singing some songs.

When it was over, my grandfather stood up and, in a husky voice and with real emotion, talked about how wonderful it was that we could all be together as a family, and how grateful he was to have Cheyenne with us.

He asked her to say a few words.

"Oh, no, that's okay," she said.

"You must have something to say to us."

She thought about it, then stood up. She thanked everyone for accepting her and for making the day so much fun. She talked about how good the food was and told us what a great family we had and said that she could see how much we loved each other.

Then, after some hesitation, she said, "Today has been so wonderful for me. It reminds me of my own family back in Idaho. And it reminds me once again that families can be forever."

With the firelight flickering on her face and the darkness of the lake and woods behind her, Cheyenne sang a song about families being forever. Her clear voice carried across the water and came back as an echo. When she finished, there was kind of a reverent silence.

"Have you ever heard anything so beautiful?" my grandfather said.

"Ben, you're one lucky guy," Eugene said.

I didn't know what to say. But Cheyenne bailed me out with, "Ben and I will be working together this summer, so basically, we're just colleagues."

"That can change, though, right?" my grandfather asked.

"Well, I suppose so. But you know what? Whatever happens, I'd still very much like to be adopted into this family, at least in the summers when you come back to this place."

"You got it, Sweetie," my grandfather said.

By then it was almost eleven o'clock, and everyone agreed it was time for bed.

"Come back so we can get some work done," I said to Cheyenne as she left with my mom to see where she'd be spending the night.

She returned to the dock twenty minutes later, wearing what I surmised she would sleep in: sweats and a pullover sweater.

We talked about our project for an hour, then she yawned and said, "Well, it's past my bedtime."

"We're working all night," I said.

"I'm not. I need my sleep if I'm going to make it to church in the morning."

"We need to get some work done."

"I always go to church."

"This will be an exception for you then, won't it?"

"Not for me it won't. This morning I got on the Church website and found out I can go to church in Laconia. It starts at nine, so I need to get some sleep. Good night."

"My career is on the line here. You got me into this mess in the first place. How can you just walk away?"

"I'll be more effective for you if I go to church." She put her hand on my shoulder and said softly, "Ben, I really like your family."

37

"Don't bother me. I'm working."

I tried to get some work done but couldn't come up with a single good idea.

At two in the morning, the dancing wheat kernels were starting to look good again, so I knew it was time to give it up.

Caleb and Emma were asleep on the living room floor, and I didn't want to wake them, and I had no idea if my mom had even thought of where I was going to sleep. Finally I just grabbed a blanket and a pillow and went out to Cheyenne's pickup for the night.

I couldn't sleep. I kept thinking about Cheyenne and how well she fit in, the way she was able to make everyone feel special, and the sound of her voice as she sang to us about families. I was amazed at how she was able to do whatever she thought was right, without offending me—even when she went against what I wanted her to do. I'd never met anyone like her.

At two-thirty in the morning, I went to the canoe and retrieved the book she'd given me. Using a flashlight, I picked it up and thumbed through it.

I read the introduction; then the testimony of the witnesses; then the statement by Joseph Smith; then "A Brief Explanation about the Book of Mormon"; then I began with Chapter 1 and read for half an hour before I put the book down and went to sleep.

At eight-thirty the next morning, Cheyenne roused me out. She needed the pickup to go to church. I returned to the bed she had just vacated and fell promptly to sleep. The fact that it was still fragrant with her scent was not totally lost on me, even as tired as I was.

When I woke up, it was ten-thirty. I could hear Caleb and Emma at the dock, having a great time swimming. A few minutes later, I made my way down to the dock and pulled up a lawn chair, too exhausted to say much of anything, just enjoying my family for the first time in a long time. I had to admit that Cheyenne had given me that.

My mother and Marilyn brought two trays of food from the kitchen. I was too tired to pay much attention. Then I happened to look up. Caleb and Emma were each picking their favorite kind of Great American Cereal from the variety packs.

"It's easy to fix, the kids seem to like it, and it's good for them. So how bad can that be?" Marilyn said to my mother.

I remember thinking how strange it was that I had heard what could be our next advertising campaign for Saddlemier.

As I sat there listening to snatches of conversation around me, enjoying the warmth of the sun and the beauty of the lake, I felt like I was back up to zero. But, to be perfectly honest, it seemed like a higher zero than I'd ever experienced before—like maybe I'd gone my whole life thinking that minus 200 was zero.

There was one other thing that I couldn't explain and that made no sense.

I couldn't wait for Cheyenne to get back.

3

After choking down some Great American Cereal, I wandered back into the house and stumbled into the room where Cheyenne had spent the night, crawled into bed, and went back to sleep.

Cheyenne got back from church at twelve-thirty. My mom and Marilyn were in the kitchen fixing something to eat.

The bedroom door was open a little, so I heard Cheyenne when she came in. "Hi, everybody!"

"Did you have any trouble finding the place?" my mom asked.

"No, your directions were great. Can I help out?"

"Oh, thank you, but we pretty much have things under control."

"There must be something I can do. I'll change clothes and then come back."

She came into the room she'd slept in the night before, which is where I was at the time. The drapes were closed, and she didn't turn on the light or look around the room.

I didn't want to embarrass her, so I said, "Hang on. I'm in here."

"Oh, my gosh!" she said. "You scared me. I didn't see you."

"Sorry. Since you were at church, I thought it'd be okay if I slept here. Actually, there weren't any other beds available. Give me a minute, and I'll get out of your way."

"No, stay where you are. I'll change in the bathroom."

She grabbed some things and slipped out of the room.

While she was changing, I found myself wondering what it'd be like to be married to her. I thought it would be very good. For one thing, my family would adore her.

It surprised me that I would be thinking about marriage. I'd never done that before. I'd always thought that getting married is what you do after you've run out of options.

When she went back into the kitchen, I heard Cheyenne say, "Well, here I am, so put me to work. What can I do?"

"How about making a salad?" my mother said.

"One salad coming up!"

I listened to them talk. Nothing amazing, just my mom, my aunt, and Cheyenne, three women working together to feed people they cared about.

I went into the bathroom, washed up, and got dressed. A few minutes later, I entered the kitchen. "Can I help?"

My mom's mouth fell open. "You never help in the kitchen," she said.

"I would like to today though."

"What do you know how to do?" Marilyn teased. "Open cans?"

"Not even that. I'm pretty much a microwave guy."

"Let me see if he's trainable," Cheyenne said.

"Yes, why don't you do that?" my mom said with a silly grin.

Cheyenne found me some counter space. "Okay, Ben, I'm

41

going to have you work here. I'm going to put you in charge of slicing tomatoes."

"With a knife, right?"

"I'm not sure I'll have any tomatoes today," Marilyn said with a smile.

Once Cheyenne showed me what she wanted, it wasn't that hard.

"How's the new guy working out?" Marilyn asked a few minutes later.

"Not too bad. I may keep him on," Cheyenne said.

"We all hope you do, dear," Marilyn said.

It was a little weird being there. You get enough women together when they're in charge, and all a guy can do is go along with what they have in mind.

But I hung in there, and when I finished they all raved about how well I'd cut the tomatoes.

We ate lunch outside on the picnic table.

Over dessert Eugene picked up a copy of the *Sunday Times* and waved the sports page in front of my grandfather. "Did you see this? The Yankees lost . . . again."

My grandfather rose to the bait. "It's June. They can lose in June. But you can be sure they won't be losing in September and October. That's what's important. They'll come back."

"They're past their prime, Dad," Eugene said. "You know a team is old when they're selling Viagra on TV."

"Who won the World Series the last three years? It sure wasn't your Mets," my grandfather declared.

Emma came up from the lake where she'd been lying in the sun after swimming. She spread a towel on the couch and sat down next to her dad.

"Emma, my sweet child," my grandfather said. "Who's the best team in baseball?"

"The Yankees," she said.

"What? My own daughter? What's going on here?" Eugene said, faking outrage.

"Ah, she's such an adorable child, and so very wise," Granddaddy said. "Wise beyond her years. Wiser than her father, even. Such a child."

"Such a traitor," Eugene shot back. He pretended to be trying to push her away.

"Besides, you're getting me all wet," Eugene complained.

"You're already all wet if you're not a Yankees fan. Isn't that right, Emma?"

"That's right, Granddaddy."

The bantering continued like it always did when they weren't working. If they were catering a big party, though, then things could get tense. But it always eased up once the work was done.

Eugene put his arm around Emma and pulled her close. He kissed her on the cheek. "Who's my sweetheart?"

"I am, Daddy."

"You got it, Kid. What else are you?"

"Your pride and joy."

"Yes, that's you, too."

She got up. "I think I'll go take a shower now."

"Don't use too much water."

"You always say that."

"That's because you always use too much."

Emma left, but a short time later Caleb came up from swimming in the lake and pulled up a chair next to his dad.

"How you doing, Son?" Eugene asked.

"Good. This morning I swam from the dock to the platform twenty times."

"Get out of here! Nobody can do that!"

Caleb broke into a huge grin. "I did."

"That's got to be an all-time record for this lake! Dad, can you believe that?" Eugene asked.

"You're getting to be so strong and tall," my grandfather said.

"Flex your muscles and let's see what you've got," Eugene said.

Caleb proudly flexed his muscles.

"Would you take a look at that?" Eugene said, touching the modest bump that was Caleb's bicep. "And that's not all. This boy is in a growth streak. He's eating us out of house and home. In a few months, he'll be taller than me."

"And then what will you do?" my grandfather asked.

Eugene messed up Caleb's hair. "When I tell him to clean his room, I'll have to add 'If that meets with your approval, sir.'"

We all laughed.

Cheyenne and I were sitting next to each other on a bench. We were sitting close enough that our arms and shoulders were touching. She seemed comfortable with that arrangement. I know I was. She leaned into me and whispered, "You've got such a great family! Thanks for inviting me."

Emma returned from her shower and asked Cheyenne if she knew how to put her hair in a French twist.

"I've done it a couple of times for my niece."

"Could you do it for me?"

"Sure, no problem."

While we sat there, Cheyenne did Emma's hair. As she did so, she asked my grandfather questions about his parents. He seemed happy to tell her. I don't suppose anyone in our family, especially from my generation, had ever expressed much interest in his family history.

He told about being born in Yugoslavia and coming to America with his parents when he was young, and how he couldn't speak English, and how the kids in school made fun of him.

"Have you ever written any of this down?" Cheyenne asked.

He looked puzzled. "Written it down?"

"Yes. You know. Made a permanent record of it."

"No. Who would care?"

"Your family. Would you mind if I take some notes? I could write it up and send it to you. You make the changes to make it accurate, and then we can give a copy to everyone in the family. How would that be?"

"Why go to so much trouble?" I asked.

"It's really important to preserve family records."

"Why?" I asked.

"Because our families are the most important thing in our lives."

That was news to me.

Cheyenne kept asking my grandfather questions and writing down his answers. I figured Caleb and Emma would find an excuse to go down to the dock, but they stayed with us.

An hour later, I told Cheyenne we'd better start back to the City. She nodded and went in to gather up her things.

When she came out, Emma said, "Don't go. Stay here another day with us."

"Oh, gosh, I wish we could. I've had such a good time with you and Caleb. Maybe we can do this another time this summer."

"I'd like that. I've always wanted to have an older sister."

"I'd love it if you were my sister and Caleb was my brother."

Caleb was, like me, more reserved. "I was hoping we could do canoe wars again before you left," he said.

"Hey, that was fun, wasn't it?" Cheyenne said. "But, you know what? Ben and I don't stand a chance against you and Emma."

Caleb broke into a big grin.

45

Cheyenne asked for my mom's recipe for marinara sauce, and they went in the kitchen so my mom could write it down.

Then it was time to go. I don't know that anyone was sad to see me leave, but they flocked around Cheyenne like she was a long-lost daughter. There were lots of hugs and kisses as we made our way to her pickup.

"I love your family," she said as we left the gravel road that circles the lake and turned onto the highway.

"They love you, too."

Even though it had been fun, there was a part of me that felt like I'd wasted the weekend. "Have you thought at all about what we're going to present to Saddlemier on Tuesday?" I asked.

"Not much. How about you?"

"I have a few ideas. You want to work on it tonight after we get home?"

"Not really. I'd rather start on it first thing in the morning."

"Why?"

"I don't work on Sunday."

"In this business, you know what they call people who don't work Sundays?"

"No, what?"

"Unemployed."

"I'm hoping I'll be able to get by without working Sundays," she said.

"You won't. Oh, I suppose you'll be able to get by if you're working in some hick town in Idaho, but not if you're in the big leagues."

"Things will work out."

"I really think we should work through the night."

"Let me ask you something, Beady. Was it late at night when you thought of the dancing wheat kernels?"

I couldn't help but grin. "As a matter of fact, it was."

"It's nice you can laugh about it now."

"I'm not exactly laughing."

"What do you call what you're doing?"

"Experiencing mild amusement."

The way she was looking at me made me laugh. "Okay, you win. We'll start in the morning. What time?"

"Six-thirty works for me, but instead of working in the office, what if we take a walk in Central Park and just toss ideas back and forth?"

"Sure, no problem. Also, I have a suggestion that might make your life easier while you're here."

"Okay."

"You're going to be living in the City for, what, three months, right?"

"That's right."

"You spent over an hour your first night trying to find a place to park. That's not unusual. Why don't you let me drive you to where you're staying, then take your pickup out to my apartment? I'll just park it there, and you can take subways or taxis wherever you want to go in the City."

"My dad told me I'd get mugged if I rode the subways."

"I can teach you a few things that will help you blend in with everyone else."

She nodded her head. "All right. Let's do that then."

A few hours later, I dropped her off in front of her apartment building and then drove off in her dad's hammered old pickup, which by then I was really beginning to like.

◆　◆　◆

Walking on the jogging path in Central Park the next morning was embarrassing.

"Good morning!" Cheyenne called out to a jogger coming toward us.

No response.

"Hi, there!" she said to a woman on a bicycle, who passed us.

The woman looked away.

"Actually, you don't have to say hello to everyone you meet on the jogging path," I said.

"Why wouldn't I?"

"The only people who talk to strangers in this town are psychopaths, serial killers, or con artists."

"What's wrong with being friendly?"

Two elderly women with a tiny, yapping dog approached. "Good morning!" Cheyenne said to them.

"She didn't mean it!" I called out.

"I did too."

I needed to get her away from other people before she got us arrested. We went off the trail. She discovered a huge tree with low-hanging branches and insisted we climb part way up. "Let's talk business," I said as we perched on the same branch just inches apart from each other. I had my Palm Pilot, so I could take notes.

"Okay."

"What's the most memorable cereal commercial you've ever seen?" I asked.

"Gee, I don't know. I can't think of a single one."

"You do watch TV, right?" I asked.

"Yeah, once in a while."

"Not every day?"

"No, why?"

"Everyone else on the planet does."

"Really? What a waste of time."

I threw up my hands. "I can't believe you said that."

"Are you saying TV isn't a waste of time?" she asked.

"I'm saying we owe our living to that waste of time."

"I can't watch it all the time, so what do you suggest I watch?"

"Commercials. Pay particular attention to the cereal spots."

"You want to know a secret? What I have for breakfast isn't that important to me. I think that's true of most people."

"What *is* important to you?"

"My family. My faith."

"Do I need to remind you we're meeting with Saddlemier tomorrow? We need to bring him something. So what's it going to be?"

She sat without speaking for a few moments, then said, "What if we focused on promoting families and put the cereal more in the background?"

I tried to be patient. "Well, the obvious reason we won't do that is because we're getting paid by a cereal company."

"After all these years companies have had to sell their product, I don't think anybody really believes that one brand of cereal is better than another. Do you?"

We talked and talked but got nowhere. Finally, a little before noon, we dropped by a deli across from Central Park. It was run by a family of Greeks. I gave Cheyenne some suggestions, and we finally decided on what we'd order.

"I assume we're paying for this separately," she said.

"Yes, we are. Do you want me to order for you?"

"No, thanks. I can do it."

"I'd better warn you. These people can be rude at times, so maybe I should do it."

"No, you order yours, and I'll order mine."

I ordered my sandwich.

"Peekle?" the manager asked me.

It was so noisy in the place, I wasn't exactly sure what he'd said.

"What?"

"Peekle? Peekle?"

"He wants to know if you want a pickle," Cheyenne said.

49

"I know what he said, okay? Look, I'm from New York. I understand people with accents."

"Sorry," she said.

I turned to the manager. "Yes, please."

He looked at me with no comprehension. By then his crew had already made the sandwich and put it in a bag, which meant he was ready for the next customer. "Next!"

"I would like a 'peekle,' if that wouldn't be too much trouble."

The owner grabbed the bag with my sandwich in it and ripped it open, stuffed the sandwich into another bag, threw in a pickle, and slammed the bag on the counter. "There's your peekle! Next!"

Cheyenne was next. I was afraid he'd yell at her, too.

"I'll take a chicken salad sandwich, on wheat bread, with sprouts," Cheyenne said.

"Peekle?" the man shouted.

"Yes, please." She noticed a picture of a large family on the wall. "Is that your family?"

He didn't answer.

"Don't talk to him," I said softly. "You'll only make him mad."

She ignored me. "Mr. Nicopoulos, is that your name? I just want to say you have a beautiful family! You must be very proud!"

His expression brightened. "You like my family?"

"Very much."

The no-nonsense production line came to a stop as Mr. Nicopoulos called his family from the back of the deli and introduced his wife and children and their spouses to us.

"This is great! Can I get a picture?" Cheyenne asked.

We all went outside. I took the picture with Cheyenne standing in the middle of the entire family.

We went back into the deli, and Cheyenne went to pay for her sandwich. Mr. Nicopoulos refused to take her money. Of course, I'd already paid for my sandwich, but did he give me my money back? No, he didn't, even though I was with her, and I had been the one who took the picture.

Mr. Nicopoulos assigned one of his sons-in-law to work the register while he and his wife sat down at a table with Cheyenne and me and showed us pictures of their grandchildren. Cheyenne was totally entranced, laughing as they told her cute things about each one.

A few minutes later, we were eating our sandwiches on a park bench in Central Park.

"This bread is so good! We don't have bread like this back home in Idaho. Let's go tell Mr. Nicopoulos how much we enjoyed his food."

"He knows his product. He doesn't need to be told it's good."

"It would make his day, though, so let's do it."

"Who made you the Happiness Elf?"

"Why not do it?"

"Because we'd have to walk clear across the street."

"It won't kill us. Let's go." She grabbed my hand. I followed.

I couldn't believe his reaction. After Cheyenne complimented him on the sandwich, he gave us a free dessert. Before I let her eat it, I got her far away, deep into Central Park. I was afraid she'd like it so much we'd have to go thank him again and then he'd give her something else, and we'd end up trapped forever in Politeness Prison.

"Now what?" she asked.

"First thing is, I'm going to give you an orientation on living here in the City. You want to take notes? This is going to be very valuable to you. And some day you'll thank me."

I grabbed her hand, and we started walking. "Okay, first, I'll tell you how the City is laid out. Avenues run north and south. Numbered streets run east and west. Next, some

51

important rules. First rule is, never buy a hot dog from a street vendor."

"How come?"

"Okay, you're a street vendor, and it's the end of the day. It's about time to shut down, and you've got one hot dog that's been on the grill all day. What do you do, throw it away or sell it the next day?"

"Throw it away."

"And that, my friend, is why you'd never make it as a street vendor. And why you never buy meat of any kind from a street vendor. Second rule, never open up a folded map of New York City in public. And when you're walking down the street, never look up because if you do it's an invitation to every pickpocket in a five-block radius."

"Oh, like they'd know I was a tourist, right?"

"Right. Never go jogging at night in Central Park and don't jog alone during the day in Central Park, either. Next rule, always take an umbrella with you because if it's raining, you'll never get a cab."

"These are good rules, Ben."

"Okay, your next lesson is about riding subways. So we got to find ourselves a subway to ride. Let's go back to your apartment."

She gave me a suspicious look.

"Don't worry. We won't go in. I just want you to know how to get from your apartment to work and back again."

She lived just a block from the subway she'd be riding on her way to work each day.

We stopped for a minute outside her apartment building. "Okay, pretend it's eight-thirty in the morning and you're running a little late. Walk fast and look like if you don't make it on time, you'll lose your job."

"I'm usually early for most things."

"Look, you want to fit in around here or not?"

She matched my stride and my scowl.

"Walk faster, okay?"

"Do you want me to run?"

"Are you crazy? Running would be the worse thing you could do."

"Why?"

"New Yorkers don't run. We want to look late, not hopelessly incompetent."

"Where does your family live?" she asked again.

"Long Island. My parents live in Manhasset. Eugene and his family live in Great Neck. My grandfather lives in an apartment a couple of blocks from Eugene."

"How come you don't live on Long Island, closer to your family?"

"To get away from my family."

A few minutes later, we were standing in the subway station, waiting for the train. "See that yellow line? You're not supposed to stand closer to the edge than that, but I'd say don't get closer than five feet from the line."

"Why's that?"

"In case someone tries to push you in front of an oncoming subway."

"Does that happen?"

"Usually only a couple of times a year."

The subway came roaring past us and then stopped. And in a few minutes, we were holding onto a metal post as the train rocked back and forth. "Never make eye contact with anyone!" I shouted to her over the roar.

"Can I with you?"

"Yeah, with me, but not with any stranger. That might be hard for you, I know, so you'd better practice. Pretend I'm a stranger, okay?" I stepped away from her.

I stared at her. She looked at me and smiled.

"I'm a serial killer!" I yelled at her.

"For Great American Cereals?"

"Not that kind of cereal. I kill women I meet on subways!"

53

"Really? I didn't know that!"

I went back to her. "Will you stop smiling at me. No eye contact!"

She did the next worst thing. She looked up and started reading the advertising posters.

"Don't read the ads, either! It makes you look like a tourist."

"What am I supposed to do?"

"Look bored. Read a folded up newspaper. Stare through people."

We rode to our stop and then got off and climbed the stairs to the street. I walked her to the agency, turned her around, and then we made the same trip back to her apartment building. The next time we made the trip, we made it as strangers, with me half a car away from her. I even hung back to see if she'd get off at the right stop, which she did.

"You're still a little too friendly, but you're making progress."

"Thanks, Ben," she said as we rode the elevator to our floor. "I appreciate your help."

There was a brief minute in the elevator where we did make eye contact, but I didn't reprimand her.

We went to her cubicle and hashed over ideas. By six everyone in the office had left for the day.

She didn't like anything I suggested, and I thought her ideas were too idealistic. Basically, the problem was I wanted to sell cereal and she wanted to change the world.

At eight-thirty we ordered Chinese, waited half an hour and then went and picked up our order. After we came back, we turned out all the lights in Crawford, etc, and put chairs on her desk and sat there and looked out her window at the lights of New York City while we ate.

It was the second time in as many days I'd wondered what it would be like to be married to her. *This is so weird,* I thought.

"I've got a question for you," I said. "What's the best Chinese food dessert?"

She sighed. "Boy, that's a tough one. I can't think of any."

"Good answer. There aren't any."

"Really?"

"It's a fact. So, when you have Chinese, always drop by another place for cheesecake."

"Does it have to be cheesecake?"

"Absolutely. No exceptions."

"I'll remember that."

I was trying to fish a shrimp out the carton with a pair of chopsticks but was having trouble getting hold of it. Cheyenne wasn't saying anything, but I could tell she was watching me. I looked up at her, and she had this happy look on her face.

"What?" I asked.

"Nothing."

"So, what's that look you're giving me?"

She gave me one of her full-blown smiles—the kind she specialized in. "I was just thinking. It's more like we're friends now, isn't it?" She went to the window and looked out. "You know what?" she asked.

I'm not sure why, but I thought she was going to tell me she was falling for me. Male ego maybe. Or else that I was beginning to think about her that way. "What?" I asked.

"I wish my mom and dad were here to see how beautiful New York City is at night. They worried a lot about me coming here. But that's just because they've never been here."

"Invite them out. They can stay with my folks."

"They'd never come. It's too far to drive, and they've never flown."

"There's always a first time."

"You love it here, don't you?" she asked.

"I don't know. I never think of it that way. It's just where I live. But it's been fun introducing you to the City."

"I'm not sure I could ever get used to it. All the bustle, I mean. Back home I like going outside on a summer night and looking at the stars. It's so quiet there at night. That's what I'm used to. Here it's so noisy."

"You don't notice it after a while."

We put the chairs back on the floor and cleaned up, and then I rested my hand on her arm while I said, "Right now I'd like to take you to the best place in the City to get dessert."

"Will it take very long?"

"No. We'll take the subway."

Half an hour later, we entered Café Lalo on West Eighty-third Street. With its floor-to-ceiling windows and trendy European decor and the long display glass cabinet filled with the most exquisite desserts in the world, it is a dessert lover's paradise.

She and I drooled at each of the desserts and then sat down for service.

"I'll never be able to make up my mind," she said. She looked happy and content to be with me, and that made me happy, too.

"First time here, it's got to be blueberry cheesecake. At least that's one of my favorites."

"Okay, I'll go with that then."

"There are many things I need to tell you about living here in the City."

"Keep going then. I've already learned a lot."

I grabbed a napkin and wrote the word HOUSTON on it, then slipped it to her.

"There's a street in NYC by this name. Pronounce it, please."

Of course, she pronounced like it was Houston, Texas.

"Wrong. If you call it that, everyone will know you're new in town. It's pronounced House-Ton."

"So New Yorkers pronounce it wrong and insist that

everyone else in the world follow along. And you gave me a hard time about crick?"

"Hey, it's our city, we can pronounce things any way we want. Okay, what would you call a geographical area south of Houston?"

"Mexico?"

"No. It's called Soho. The streets north of Houston are called Noho, or also Greenwich Village. Where would you live if you lived in DUMBO?"

"A circus?"

"No, country bumpkin. DUMBO is Down Under the Manhattan Bridge Overpass."

She laughed. "Of course, why didn't I think of that?"

"Okay, a quick review. Where do I live?"

"New Jersey."

I shook my head. "Not New Jersey. Just Jersey. If you say New Jersey, everyone will know you're a tourist."

"I'm not sure I'm smart enough to live here in New York City."

"Actually, I'm not sure of that, either," I teased.

"For that I get a bite of your dessert," she said, reaching over and taking a small bite of my Midnight Chocolate cake on her fork and then eating it.

"Important rule. Never, ever try to take a piece of dessert from a guy from Jersey."

A few minutes later, we were on our way back to the office. It was a beautiful, clear night with the temperature in the mid-seventies.

We entered her cubicle. "It's time to get back to work, isn't it? The world has no use for the drone," she said.

"Where did that come from?"

"It's something my dad says at our place after we've taken a break and it's time to get back to work."

For the next hour, we tried to come up with something we could agree on.

By eleven we still hadn't reached any conclusion. To make matters worse, Cheyenne kept falling asleep. Finally, I told her to go home and that I'd pitch Saddlemier an idea I'd worked up during my senior year at Rutgers.

"Can I see it?"

"No, let's both just go home and get some sleep."

She didn't need to be coaxed into quitting. I sent her off in a cab and then took the elevator to the office, worked another hour, and then took the PATH train back to my apartment.

The next day we met in Saddlemier's office. He seemed very happy to see Cheyenne. "I talked to my old friend David McDermott at BYU over the weekend," he said. "He told me some remarkable things about you, Cheyenne."

"Well, I'm sure they aren't true."

"He says you have an uncanny sense of knowing what consumers want. So what have you two got for me today?"

"I'll be doing the presentation, Mr. Saddlemier," I said.

"I see. Well, I hope Cheyenne here has had a part in its development."

"Not really."

"Then I don't want to see it."

Well, that was awkward, wasn't it?

"Cheyenne, let's just talk," he said. "Tell me what's on your mind." He focused his full attention on her.

"Cereal and families just naturally go together. What if instead of having actors, we had real families?"

"Why would a real family agree to be in a cereal commercial?" I asked.

"We'd pay them."

"Then they'd be just like actors except not as talented or reliable," I said.

"What if we had a contest and the winners got an all-expense paid vacation?" Cheyenne asked.

I objected. "This is getting very complicated. It'd take

58

months to set up a contest like that. And we'd have no guarantee that what we'd get from it would be worth the time and money it'd cost."

For once Saddlemier agreed with me. "Cheyenne, do you have anyone in mind for the kind of family you'd need?"

"Well, my family, of course. Or Ben's family."

"Uh-uh," I said, "first rule of advertising: You can't base an entire advertising campaign on your relatives."

"Why not?" Cheyenne asked.

"Because when they disappoint you, it's harder to get rid of them."

So Cheyenne's idea seemed dead in the water. I must confess I found a certain satisfaction in that.

Cheyenne went to the window and looked out. "You have a great view here," she said.

"I hardly ever look out much anymore. I did when I first moved in though," he told her.

She looked out the window while Saddlemier and I tried to come to some kind of an agreement about the direction we should go.

Suddenly Cheyenne turned around. "I know a family who'd be perfect!"

"Who?" Saddlemier asked.

"Well, you probably don't know them. They run a deli across from Central Park. Their last name is Nicopoulos."

"Nicopoulos's Deli? That's my favorite place to eat!" Saddlemier exclaimed.

"It's my favorite place, too!" Cheyenne called out.

"I eat there almost every day!"

"Ben and I ate there yesterday. I've been dying to know, what are their salads like?"

"Out of this world."

"What's your favorite salad?"

It was like watching a tennis match, listening to them going back and forth. It started with salads and then went on

59

to soups and then dessert. By the time they finished, we were all hungry.

Saddlemier had his driver drop us off at the deli. When we went in, with Cheyenne and Saddlemier, it was like we were family. Except for me, of course. Nicopoulos had not forgotten my "peekle" mistake, but Cheyenne ordered for me, so it went all right.

We stayed at our table all the way through their busiest time, eating slowly, ordering more food all the time, going from sandwiches to soup to dessert. I don't know how many times Cheyenne's voice filled the room. "Oh, my gosh, this is *so* good!" Every time she said it, Mr. Nicopoulos's otherwise grim expression turned momentarily into a tiny smile.

At two-thirty, while his children and in-laws were cleaning up, Mr. and Mrs. Nicopoulos came over and sat down with us.

"I wrote down all the foods I'd love to get recipes for," Cheyenne said, handing him a napkin she'd used as a note pad.

He looked down the list. "This is everything."

"I loved everything. If I'd known food tasted this good, I'd have run away from my home in Idaho long ago."

Mr. Nicopoulos smiled and nodded.

While Cheyenne went with Mrs. Nicopoulos into the kitchen to see how she made one of the desserts, Saddlemier told Mr. Nicopoulos about wanting to use him and his family in a breakfast commercial. It would be shot at the deli, giving him nationwide publicity. In turn he and his family would get a free vacation anywhere in the country.

Mr. Nicopoulos shook his head. "A vacation is not possible."

I totally agreed.

"Why is it not possible?" Saddlemier asked.

"If we're not here for week, our customers will go some

place else. We might not get them back. We have to be open every day."

Okay, that was it. We'd given it a try, and it hadn't worked out. I'd never liked the idea anyway.

I was ready to leave, but as I looked over at Cheyenne, who was in the food preparation area with Mrs. Nicopoulos, I guess I felt sorry for her in a way. She really was a small town girl trying to make it in the big leagues. With ideas like trying to promote the American family while selling breakfast cereal, I was sure she'd never be much of a success. The advertising business is where you'd sell your mother if you could get a good price, not where you applauded motherhood. Cheyenne was behind the times.

I went into the food preparation area to see what I could do.

Cheyenne seemed glad to see me. "Open your mouth," she said.

I did, and she popped a piece of baklava in my mouth.

"Have you ever tasted anything that good in your whole life?" she asked.

"No, I haven't."

Cheyenne looked at her new friend. "Mrs. Nicopoulos, you've been so generous. What can I do for you?"

"Come tomorrow. Say good things about the food. It helps our business."

"We'd like to do something more than that, actually," I said.

I explained our proposal.

"What does my husband say?"

"He says you can't leave. I can understand that you have to be open every day. But isn't there someone else who could run the place for a few days, so you and your family can get away for a very much-deserved vacation?"

Mrs. Nicopoulos furrowed her brow as she thought. Finally she said, "My brother and his family could do it."

"Really?"

"He used to work here, but he couldn't stand the long hours."

"Now what does he do?"

"He works for the post office."

"So he probably has vacation time then, right?"

She nodded. "I'll talk to my husband after you leave."

"What are the chances you'll be able to persuade him to do this for us?"

She looked over at her husband to make sure he wouldn't overhear what she was going to say. "Very good."

On our way back to Saddlemier's office, we told him what Mrs. Nicopoulos had said.

"Work it up for me, and we'll talk in the morning."

Cheyenne and I went back to the office, met briefly with Ross, and then sat in her cubicle and went to work.

It went together easily, and in three more hours we'd finished and were ready to call it a day

"We make a good team, don't we?" Cheyenne asked as we took the elevator to the ground floor.

"Looks that way."

As the elevator started down, she faced straight ahead, giving me a chance to study her more fully.

Being in the advertising business, I'd seen plenty of good-looking women, both in photographs and in real life. Cheyenne wasn't classically beautiful, but there was something about her face that I couldn't get over. She had those freckles, but her skin was soft and smooth looking, except for some faint laugh lines around her eyes and mouth. Even without a lot of makeup, her large eyes were gorgeous, set off perfectly by naturally dark eyebrows and thick eyelashes. I had seen a photograph of her parents in her cubicle, and it was evident that she had characteristics of each—a refined version of her father's strong jaw and nose and the full lips and generous mouth of her mother. I found myself looking at those lips and wondering what it would be like to kiss Cheyenne.

My staring must have made her uncomfortable. She turned to me, and, with a Brooklyn accent, asked, "You lookin' at me? 'Cause if you're looking at me, you're in big trouble."

"You're too much, kid."

When the elevator reached the first floor, we separated and walked as coworkers, strangers really, to the subway.

"You want me to come with you to make sure you make it home okay?"

"I'll be okay. I've learned to look bored and avoid eye contact."

I nodded. "Great, then my work here is done."

Unfortunately, we made eye contact.

"Looks like I need a refresher lesson myself," I said.

"Maybe we can work on that in the morning."

What's going on? I thought. *The first time I saw her I didn't care for the way she looked and now I think she's beautiful? What's with that?*

It was probably making us both worry we might be starting to like each other and neither one of us wanted that, so it was a great relief when her subway blasted past us and then began to slow down.

I waved to her in the bored way New Yorkers do and turned and made my way one level down, to where I'd catch my train.

In a way, it was a relief to be away from her. It felt like I was coming back to the real me. Whatever that was.

4

Our proposal to shoot a commercial in a Greek deli without paid actors, and then to push family values instead of cereal seemed doomed to failure.

Cheyenne and I were asked to present the plan to Hugh Waddell, Great American's vice president in charge of advertising. Saddlemier stood in the back of the room, looking forward to the fireworks he knew were coming.

When we finished, Mr. Waddell asked, "What idiot thought of this harebrained idea?" I wasn't surprised, but I was worried Cheyenne would take it personally. I didn't, though. It had happened too many times before to me.

"It just sort of came together," Cheyenne said.

Hugh stands six-foot-four. What had once been a well-kept black beard is now beset with gray patches, so he always looks like he just came in from a snowstorm. "Well, it can just come apart then. We're not going to do it, and that's it!"

"Hugh, help me understand your thinking here," Saddlemier said.

"Well, for starters, you can't shoot in a deli. The lighting will make everything come out gray and depressing. Second, the actors guild will be all over us for using nonunion actors. Third, because it's not in a studio and you're using amateurs, there may be endless takes before they get it right, so you're going to double or triple the budget. Fourth, the script doesn't say anything about what we're trying to sell, which is cereal. There's not even a voice-over identifying it as our commercial. In conclusion, it will cost us a fortune, it won't accomplish a thing, and we'll be viewed as complete idiots by the industry."

Saddlemier stepped between Hugh and us. "Those are all good points, Hugh. I knew I could count on you to give me a realistic evaluation."

Hugh, usually in a bad mood, nodded, figuring he'd won another victory.

"Even so," Saddlemier said, "I have decided to give this a try, and I'd appreciate your helping to make it work."

"You're overriding me, then, is that what you're saying?" Hugh asked.

"I don't like to think of it that way, but I can see why you might. What I'm telling you is we're going to do one commercial, and so, of course, as always, I'd appreciate your cooperation."

"I'll work with you, sir . . ." He glared at Cheyenne and me. " . . . but I won't work with this punk, Morelli, and his sidekick, Robin the Wonder Girl." He went on to explain in greater detail how young and inexperienced we were. And then he stomped out of the room and slammed the door.

There was a prolonged, awkward silence. Finally Saddlemier said, "Well, that went about the way I expected, but Hugh will get over it."

"Sir, Mr. Waddell could have a point," I said. "We are inexperienced, and the commercial might not do Great American Cereal any good."

"Let's do it anyway and see what comes of it."

Two weeks later, we'd jumped through all the hoops and

65

were ready to shoot the commercial. Crawford, Sullivan, Chafin, and Blunck have a number of freelance crews we call on to shoot commercials for the companies we work with.

Cheyenne and I had no particular duty during the shooting of the commercial, but we were there to make sure it turned out just the way we had envisioned it.

Here's a synopsis of the commercial: It opens from inside the deli, early morning. Mr. and Mrs. Nicopoulos enter through the front door. They start to prepare food that will be served during the day. One by one, other family members come in.

During a time when they can take a break, Mrs. Nicopoulos sits down with a package of Great American Cereal. She pours herself a bowl and starts to eat. She is joined a few minutes later by her sons and daughters-in-law. They talk about the Yankees game the night before. Mr. Nicopoulos comes in and sits down with his family. It's obvious there's nothing he'd rather do than work with his family and serve good food.

He puts his hand on his wife's shoulders. "Another day."

They nod and smile.

He looks at the clock and says, "Let's go to work."

Mrs. Nicopoulos picks up the cereal box and returns it to its place, and the camera zooms in for a tight shot on the label.

End of commercial.

Of course, the Nicopoulos family knew they were getting a free trip out of the deal, so we didn't have to tell them that they should look like they were enjoying eating the cereal, but what you couldn't script is that this was a real family and they did have warm feelings for each other.

When Saddlemier saw the rough cut, sixty-second spot a few days later, he liked it. "Yes, very good! This will be very effective. I'm sure we'll do more of these. Do you have anyone in mind for another family?"

"Well, Ben's family would be good," Cheyenne said.

"Let's not do another family from the New York area," Saddlemier said.

"My sister and brother-in-law would be good," Cheyenne suggested. "They live in Idaho."

Saddlemier began to pace. "If all we use are relatives, we'll run out of them before very long." He stopped. "Here's a question for you two. What if you were to go into a city, visit a grocery store, and hand out samples of Great American Cereal, like it's some kind of a store promotion, while you look for some more families?"

"How many?" Cheyenne asked.

Saddlemier thought for a moment. "Get me six more families from six different areas of the country."

"Aren't you taking a big risk?" Cheyenne asked.

"Very possibly, but, you know what? That's how I got here."

And so, with that, Cheyenne and I took to the road.

◆　◆　◆

Two days later, in Syracuse, New York, Cheyenne and I spent the day at a large grocery store, giving away free samples of cereal and talking to customers, pretending we were your average "have a free sample" persons.

"Hello, how are you doing today?" Cheyenne said to a woman in her thirties. This was about quarter-to-four. We'd been there for three hours.

"Doing good." The woman had one kid in the shopping cart and two roaming the store. She had good features but seemed tired and worn down. She was tall, blonde, and blue eyed. She wore her hair cut short, probably so it wouldn't take as much time to keep up. Looking at her, I figured she'd put on five to ten pounds with each kid. But I could see she'd

67

been a beauty and could easily understand why her husband had been attracted to her.

I was satisfied she could be made to look appealing to viewers with very little effort on our part. She'd look good, but not so good that viewers would think she was an actress we'd hired. I just hoped her husband would be presentable on TV.

"We'd like you to have a free box of Great American Cereal," Cheyenne said cheerily. "What's your favorite?"

"Well, I don't eat it myself, but my kids love it."

"What do you have for breakfast?" Cheyenne asked.

"Spinach dip. I'm on the carbohydrate diet. I've lost ten pounds."

"Well, it's working. You look absolutely great!" Cheyenne said.

It was hard for me to get too involved in these chatty conversations. My one fear about what we were doing was that I'd run into someone I'd gone to high school with. It would be very embarrassing to explain how, after graduating from college, I was giving away samples at a grocery store.

"Take your pick of whatever you'd like. In fact, take two boxes. How many children do you have?" Cheyenne asked.

"Five," she said. "I have two more at home."

"Good grief," I muttered.

The woman glared at me. "Who's he?" the woman asked.

"He's my assistant."

"What exactly does he do?" she asked.

Cheyenne laughed. "Not much, to tell you the truth. Tell me about your family."

She pointed to the baby in the cart. "Well, this is James. He's just six months old."

"Oh, my gosh, he's so cute!" Cheyenne raved. "Can I pick him up?"

The woman, proud of her son, nodded.

Cheyenne picked him up and began fussing over him. "Hello, Baby James, you are such a handsome boy! Yes, you are! Yes, you are, James! Oh, look at that big smile! You're such a good boy! Yes, you are!"

The woman looked around the store for the rest of her family. "And then there's William and Jeffrey." They were nowhere in sight. She put two fingers to her mouth and produced an ear-shattering whistle. Almost immediately her two boys showed up.

"Do you have a husband?" I asked.

She seemed insulted by the question. "Well, of course I do. How could I have all these kids without a husband?"

"Ben, why don't you go out to the van and get some more cereal?" Cheyenne suggested.

The truth is we didn't have a van, and we didn't have any cereal. She was saying that to get rid of me. I left the store.

By the time I came back, the deal had been arranged. "Ben, this is Shannon Rice. We called her husband, Dirk, and they have agreed to talk to us about appearing in a TV commercial for Great American Cereal."

"Shannon, thank you very much. You've got a wonderful family." I sounded upbeat and cheerful. And, in truth, I was. The fact that we'd found our family meant our work was done.

We arranged to meet Shannon's husband and the rest of their family that evening. Cheyenne and I had had a late lunch, so we skipped dinner and drove out to meet Dirk and Shannon in their home. I wanted to make sure their house would be suitable for shooting the commercial.

They lived in a modest home in a housing development about ten miles outside the city. Dirk had a rugged face. If he'd been much of a talker, he could've had a career in the movies. But he let Shannon do all the talking. In fact, she obviously dominated the relationship. He seemed happy enough, though. We sat in the backyard and watched as he played with their kids. He gave them piggyback rides and pretended he was a monster. He had a nice roar. Very believable.

These were likeable people, but the way I saw it, the world was passing them by, and they didn't even know it. I could easily imagine that in ten years he'd be working for the same company, and they'd be living in the same house. The only change is maybe they'd have a few more kids, and she would have put on a few more pounds, and, by then, he'd have lost most of his hair.

They were nice to us, though. And very excited about the free family vacation. They'd been wanting to go to Disney World for years, and now they'd be able to.

By the time we finished, it was eight-thirty. Rather than drive all the way back to New York, I suggested we get a motel. Cheyenne got a worried look on her face.

"Okay, look, let me spell it out for you. We'll be in separate rooms, hey, even on different floors if you want. If that isn't good enough, we can even be in separate motels. I just don't want to drive back tonight."

"Oh."

"It's okay, Cheyenne. People in business do this all the time."

"Okay, then."

Half an hour later, we had checked into a motel. "You want to get something to eat?" I asked.

"Yeah, I'm starving."

"I'll meet you down here in ten minutes, okay?" I asked.

"Give me twenty minutes. I want to phone my folks."

Twenty minutes later, we met in the lobby. "I called my folks but nobody was home, so I left a message," Cheyenne said. "I'm bringing my cell phone with me in case they call."

When the waitress brought our food, I jumped right in, but Cheyenne bowed her head for a moment before she began to eat.

A few minutes later, Cheyenne's cell phone rang. She answered it. "Hi, Daddy . . . Yes, we're staying tonight in Syracuse . . . Well, I thought we'd make it back to New York,

70

too, but Ben thought we should stay the night . . . No, I'm sure that's not what he had in mind . . . Okay, hang on . . ."

She handed her phone to me. "My dad wants to talk to you."

"Hello?" I said.

"What kind of an operation you runnin' out there?" He had a deep voice with an unmistakable cowboy twang, even when yelling over the phone.

"Well, I . . . uh."

"Let me put it to you straight! Are you out to seduce my daughter? Is that why you decided to stay the night in a motel?"

"No, not at all."

"Now I know we haven't met, and maybe I'm barking up the wrong tree, but I'm warning you. Keep your hands off my daughter."

"Yes, sir."

"I don't like the idea of you staying in a hotel together. She grew up being taught to live the law of chastity. Do you even know what that means?"

"Well, laws are enacted by the legislature—"

"I don't mean *laws!* I mean do you know what chastity means?"

"Well, it means . . ." I cleared my throat. I didn't know how to complete the sentence, especially with Cheyenne listening in on the conversation.

"Go on."

"Well, it means not doing certain things."

"What kind of things?"

"Well, uh . . ."

"You're staying in a hotel tonight with my daughter and you can't even tell me what chastity is?"

"Sir, you have nothing to worry about."

"Let me ask you a question. Have you ever kissed Cheyenne?"

71

"No."

"You've never kissed my daughter?"

"No, sir."

"Not even once?"

"No, sir."

"Well, all right, you make sure it stays that way. Don't go thinking that just because you're in New York City and I'm here in Idaho, you can just do whatever you please. Because I'll come out there if I need to. And don't think I won't!"

I chose my words carefully. "I believe you would if those circumstances which you have described ever arose. Nice talking to you, sir."

I handed the phone back to Cheyenne, who promised to lock the doors that night and not let me in, under any circumstances.

She smiled at me. "I take it my dad spoke his mind about you and me."

I nodded. "He was very clear about what he expected from me."

"That's my dad. When I was in high school, he used to be cleaning his gun when a guy he didn't approve of came to pick me up."

"I guess I'd be the same way if I was your dad."

"It used to embarrass me, but now I can see it was good."

"So, if nothing goes before marriage, what about after marriage?"

"My sister Jen is married and has three kids. The oldest is Rebecca. She's six years old. The next is Billy. He's four years old. And the youngest is a girl named Allison. Anyway, one time I asked Jen what it was like to be married. She asked me to guess what was the best thing her husband did to get her into a romantic mood. Well, I wasn't sure how to answer that. So she goes, 'It's when he helps me clean up after supper and puts the dirty dishes in the dishwasher and takes out the garbage and then gets Rebecca and Billy and Allison ready for bed so I can take a leisurely bath. He reads a story to them and gives them a snack and changes diapers. It gives me a chance to relax. And that's when I most want to show him how much he means to me.' She told me that's how it is with two people who are totally committed to each other and to their family."

I nodded. "Thanks for telling me that."

After we split up for the night, I went to the motel bar and had a drink and got into an argument with a guy about baseball. He said the Yankees were past their prime and would never even get to the World Series this year. By the time I went to bed, I was in a foul mood.

At nine o'clock the next morning, I was still sleeping. The phone rang. I picked it up.

"Good morning, Sunshine! It's time we get going." Only Cheyenne could sound that up in the morning.

"I'll meet you in the lobby in thirty minutes," I grumbled.

She dozed off about an hour after we started driving. With her asleep, I was free to study her face. She was a beautiful girl, in a kind of fresh, down-home way, and normally I'd have enjoyed looking at her. But now—after what her dad had said to me—things were somehow changed. Her concept of marriage and family was different from what I had ever imagined. Everything in her world was black and white and totally restrictive.

Looking at her while she slept was like going to a car dealer and spotting an expensive sports car and knowing the price is way more than you can afford. In her case, the price was that I'd have to change drastically. And that was a price I wasn't sure I was willing to pay. I liked my life just the way it was.

I'll be glad when the summer is over and I can get back to my own life, I thought.

That thought was followed almost immediately by, *No, you won't. You'll miss Cheyenne when she's gone.*

I didn't want to think about it, so I turned on the radio and listened to the Yankees game.

Just my luck—they lost.

73

5

On Monday Cheyenne and I met with Saddlemier and Hugh Waddell. Cheyenne started to tell them about Dirk and Shannon Rice but was interrupted by Mr. Waddell. "Why did you pick them?"

"Well, they have the cutest kids, and they're so happy together," Cheyenne said. "Dirk, the dad, has this thing where he's a monster, and he chases his kids around the backyard. It's so fun to watch. The kids giggling and screaming and Dirk always just missing them. Well, it's so cute."

Waddell rolled his eyes. "We have a million dollar advertising budget, and we're wasting it on Family Night in Syracuse?"

Ouch.

Waddell continued. "Harold, with all due respect, this is a complete waste of time and money! And what is it going to do for marketing Great American Cereals? Nothing! Absolutely nothing!"

Saddlemier, always the diplomat, tried to calm Hugh down. "I'm fully aware of your objections, Hugh, but I'd like to do this one, and maybe one or two more, and then we'll run them and see what the public reaction is."

Saddlemier went over to his entertainment center. "Oh, Cheyenne and Ben, while you were out of town last week, we did receive a first-edit copy of our commercial at the deli. Would you like to see it?"

Cheyenne laughed. "As long as we go there for lunch."

So we watched the commercial—Hugh, ever scowling, Cheyenne, delighted by it all. And when it was over, she said, "That is so good!"

Hugh cleared his throat. "Harold, may I make a few comments at this time?"

"Yes, of course, Hugh."

"I took the liberty of showing this to an advertising class at NYU Friday afternoon. I found their comments very interesting. I can summarize them if you'd like."

"Of course, please, go right ahead."

"Sixty-seven percent had no idea what it was we were selling. Some thought we were trying to drum up business for the deli. Some thought it was for a brand of coffee. Others guessed it was for life insurance." He glared at Cheyenne. "I know you're just a summer intern, so let me spell this out for you. Usually, a commercial spot is more effective if the audience knows what's being sold."

"Were there any positive comments?" Saddlemier asked.

"They liked that it was shot in a real deli with real people."

Saddlemier nodded his head and went to the window to look out. "I see. So it wasn't all bad then, was it?"

"No, sir." Hugh went to where Cheyenne was sitting and glared at her.

"Who do you think you are anyway? How dare you waltz in here and treat me like I don't know anything. Well, I know a few things. I know when something is flawed."

I wondered if Cheyenne would stand up. If she did, she'd tower over Hugh Waddell.

75

Without getting defensive, she simply said, "Okay, how do we fix it?"

Hugh Waddell relaxed. He was, once again, in charge. The assault of the younger generation had been turned back. "Let's run it one more time, and I'll show you where we need to make a change."

He ran the commercial until the last few seconds, put it on freeze frame, and said as it would be said as a voice-over in the commercial, "Great American Cereal . . . for the family in all of us."

Hugh could not bring himself to ask us what we thought because he knew it was brilliant.

"It's perfect!" Cheyenne said. "It's just what's needed to tie it off."

Hugh acknowledged the compliment with a nod of his head. "I think with that addition, we could run several of these. And the response would grow with each one."

We all went to Mr. Nicopoulos's deli for lunch, except for Hugh Waddell. I thought it was because he didn't like us, but Saddlemier told us it was because he had an ulcer and was on a very strict diet.

When Mr. Nicopoulos saw Cheyenne walk into the deli, he came out from behind the counter, gave her a big hug, and kissed her on the cheek. "I'm very glad you came back, but this time you have to work for your food. Come with me."

He tied one of his long white aprons on Cheyenne and had her stand behind the counter.

Instead of getting in line, Saddlemier and I sat down at a table and watched the Cheyenne show.

Mr. Nicopoulos coached her. "First, you ask them what they want."

Cheyenne, with a big grin, asked a guy about her age. "What do you want?"

"A date with you," the guy said.

"One date with me!" she called out as if it were a food order.

"No dates!" Mr. Nicopoulos said, wagging his finger at the customer.

"We're out of dates!" Cheyenne said.

"Give me a number two, then," he said.

"Number two!"

"Ask if he wants peekles," Mr. Nicopoulos coached.

"You want peekles?" Cheyenne asked, mimicking Mr. Nicopoulos's accent.

"Yes, peekles."

"Peekles!"

"Very good," Mr. Nicopoulos said. "Now I go take a break."

"Don't leave me."

"You be fine."

Saddlemier and I spent the next fifteen minutes watching as Cheyenne charmed the customers.

"She's something, isn't she?" Saddlemier said.

"Yeah."

"You know, if I were twenty years younger . . ."

I looked at him and smiled. "Actually, sir, to be more accurate, I'd say you'd need to be thirty years younger."

"All right, thirty years. What about you?"

"I enjoy working with her."

"That's not what I'm asking."

"I know."

"Well?" he asked.

I shrugged. "She's not my type." I sighed. "She's a decent human being."

"That she is."

"Whatever she does, she's totally into it. I mean she never whines. She never makes derogatory comments. She's always there—positive, alive, encouraging."

77

"She'd make a good wife," Saddlemier said, watching to see my reaction.

"Yeah, and a great mother. That's what she wants to be. More than anything. I mean not as a side job, either."

"There's nothing wrong with that," he said.

"I know." I paused, then added, "Of course, that's so far from anything I have any interest in."

Saddlemier nodded. "That could change."

"I suppose."

Cheyenne and I spent the afternoon in her cubicle at Crawford, Sullivan, Chafin, and Blunck catching up on paperwork, filling out travel reports, and reporting to Ross about what we were doing for Great American Cereals. He seemed pleased.

I asked Cheyenne if she wanted to go sailing with me after work. She said she had a church activity that night, and so she wouldn't be able to go.

"Would you like to go with me?" she asked. "It'll be a lot of fun. We call it home evening. Families in the church get together every Monday night. Since my family isn't here, I'll be meeting with some friends who are all single and about my age."

I shook my head. "No, that's okay. It's probably better this way anyhow."

"How do you mean better?" she asked.

"It might be better if we don't spend so much time together."

She nodded. "I've been thinking about that, too. I'm glad you feel the same way."

The problem was I didn't feel the same way. I was really starting to like Cheyenne. Only as a friend, though, of course.

I'm not sure how it is for other people, but I'm in a visual business, and I spend every working day thinking about visual images. And so I was beginning to build in my mind—

I'm not sure what to call it—it's like a photo album in my head, filled with pages and pages of mental images of Cheyenne.

Here are three images in my mental photo album from the beginning of the summer:

In the first grocery store we went to, the one in Syracuse, I picture Cheyenne kneeling on the floor to be eye level with a little girl who's maybe four or five years old. She's just talking to the girl, but she's totally focused on what the girl is saying. The image shows a close-up of Cheyenne's face and that of the girl.

Another is Cheyenne asleep while I'm driving. She's turned to the side and is resting her head on her hand, like little kids do. She's facing toward me, and I'm looking at her, captivated by what I now describe as her beauty.

Another scene is the two of us on the subway—me trying to teach Cheyenne to avoid making eye contact. And I'm getting after her for smiling at me, and she's laughing at me, and I realize this is the most fun I've ever had on a subway.

Just being with her. That's all I needed to be happy.

◆　　◆　　◆

The next day at work we tried to decide where we would go that week.

"We could go to Idaho," Cheyenne suggested.

"Why would we do that?"

"Mr. Saddlemier wants us to find people from all over the United States. Besides, I miss my family. I'd like to spend a few days with them."

"Do you have someone in mind who'd be good for one of our commercials?"

"Yes, I do. My sister Jen and her husband, Greg."

"Is she the one who makes her husband clean the kitchen while she takes a bath?"

"He cleans the kitchen as a favor."

79

I scoffed. "Yeah, right."

"Do you want to meet him?"

"No."

"They'd be good in an all-American commercial."

"Why?"

"He's a foreman on a ranch. His hobby is fast draw shooting. He teaches Hollywood stars how to fast draw."

That did look promising. And so, the next day we took an early flight on our way to Idaho. We flew nonstop to Salt Lake City, then took a shuttle to Boise where Cheyenne's folks met us.

I was really nervous as we left the plane and entered the terminal. I remember thinking, *What if her family doesn't like me?* But, then, reality set in. *What does it matter? What parents of the girls I've known have ever liked me? None of them. So why should this be any different? And why should I care anyway? In six weeks, she'll be out of my life for good.*

When we entered the terminal, it was easy to pick out Cheyenne's parents. Her dad was at least six-foot-four with broad shoulders and large, rough, work-hardened hands. He looked like he could play the part of a sheriff in a western movie.

Cheyenne's mom had reddish brown hair like her daughter, only not as long. She didn't use much makeup. And she spoke with an Idaho twang. Even though she looked a bit worn down by the years of being the wife of a rancher, she carried with her an understated charm and elegance that can only come from within. She was not as tall as Cheyenne, but her lips and mouth, eyes, and hair color were very similar to her daughter's.

Cheyenne ran and gave her mom a hug and then her dad. "Well, Mom and Dad, this is Ben."

Her dad shook my hand, nearly crushing my fingers. He stared at me like he was trying to look into my soul.

I said, "Real good," to every question her mom asked me as we made our way to the baggage area.

I figured Cheyenne and I would go to the baggage carousel to claim our luggage, but her father said, "We'll get the bags. You two ladies catch up on the news."

And so her dad and I stood together watching other bags pass by us.

"You behaving yourself with my daughter?" he asked, not even bothering to look at me.

"Yes, sir."

"You sure?"

"Yes, sir."

"Do you know what I'm talking about?"

"Yes, sir."

He stared at me for what seemed like hours. "You're not lying to me, are you?"

"No, sir."

That's when I discovered he had an annoying habit of drawing air in between his two front teeth. I'm sure it was useful when he'd had steak and needed to suck out a stray bit of meat from between his teeth. But there was no need for that now. I later found that he did it whenever he wanted to make a point or change the subject. "All right, then."

A few minutes later, as we headed for their ranch, I sat in the front seat of their extended cab pickup with him. Cheyenne and her mother sat in back and did most of the talking.

Cheyenne lives on a ranch a few miles from Fairfield, Idaho, which is about two hours from Boise.

I sat and listened to Cheyenne and her mom fill each other in on family news and looked out at the sagebrush and the mountains to the north. Her dad told me their ranch is in the foothills of the Sawtooth Range.

Other than that, he didn't say much. He did suck air through his teeth more times than I could count. I felt like yelling for him to pull over so I could open my suitcase and give him some of my dental floss. But, in the end, I decided that wasn't the best way to win him over.

Finally, we turned onto a gravel road in an area that seemed to me like it was at the end of the world. Ten minutes later, we pulled into their place. It was a small house, built probably fifty years ago, shaded by some huge old cotton-wood trees. There was also a large wooden barn and some corrals. The newest structure on the place was a big metal building where Cheyenne's dad kept his equipment.

On the same property, about half a block away, was a newer house with a fenced in yard and a swing set and a tri-cycle. Cheyenne told me that is where Jen and her husband, Greg, lived.

"You'll be sleeping in the barn," Cheyenne's dad informed me as we got out of the pickup.

Sure, that figures, I thought.

"Don't worry, it's really nice," Cheyenne said.

"I'll show you where you're going to bunk," her dad said.

In one corner of the barn, they'd built a bedroom. It wasn't fancy, but it was clean and had a good bed and its own bathroom.

"It can get cold at night, so there's extra blankets in the closet," her dad told me.

"I'll be fine."

"Has Cheyenne told you she's waiting for a missionary?"

"She's waiting for a what, Sir?"

"In our church, the boys go out on missions for two years when they turn nineteen. Cheyenne got to be good friends with a boy in high school. He went on a mission, and she headed off to BYU. We fully expect they'll get married after he returns from his mission."

"When will that be?"

"Sometime in November as I recall."

"What's his name?"

"Justin Whitcomb. His family lives about a mile from here."

"She hasn't mentioned him," I said.

"No reason why she should."

"If he cares about her, why did he leave for two years?"

"You don't know much about our beliefs, do you?"

"No, sir, I don't."

"Well, maybe you should look into it. From what Cheyenne says, you could use something to believe in. I'll leave you now so you can wash up for dinner. We'll be eating in about half an hour."

His words irritated me. Who did he think he was to be passing judgment on me? And what had Cheyenne told him about me that made him think I needed religion?

I was a little perturbed that Cheyenne had never mentioned Justin. I remember thinking, *Good, I hope she does marry him and they never leave this place and they have ten or twenty kids and she loses her figure and becomes domestic and boring. What a perfect ending. Maybe her dad will build her a house next door to her sister and her husband's, so she'll be stuck here for the rest of her life. She'll never know what the rest of the world is doing. That'll serve her right.*

I slapped some water on my face and made my way toward the house, where Cheyenne was waiting for me on a swing hung from a limb in one of the tall cottonwood trees.

"Want to swing?" she asked.

"No."

"Push me, then."

I pushed her in the swing until she was going very high.

"That's enough," she said, laughing at how high she was going.

A short time later, she got out of the swing. "Want me to push you?"

"No."

She looked into my eyes. "You okay?"

83

"Tell me about Justin. Are you going to marry him when he comes home?"

"Did Daddy tell you about Justin? We were good friends in high school, that's all. We did talk about getting married after his mission, but we haven't made any definite plans. We'll just have to see how things go when he gets back."

"If you marry him, the two of you will live around here, won't you?"

"Maybe. Why do you ask?"

"This is the last place in the world I'd ever want to live."

"It's a good place to raise kids."

"Is that all you people think about?"

"No, but if it were, would that be so bad?"

"There's a lot more to life than having a bunch of kids."

"Really? What's more important than family?"

"How about doing something with your life? Or making a contribution to society? Or being respected by your colleagues?"

"I can see we'll never agree on this. Let's go inside. It's probably time to eat."

We went inside and sat in the living room. Cheyenne stayed with me and tried to make me feel at home, but it didn't work out very well. I felt like I was in a time warp. The couch was at least twenty years old. The carpet was shag and a deep brown. There was an old rocker, also ancient. It was like a living room set that you'd find in a museum dedicated to bad taste. They had an old upright piano and stacks of music on a shelf next to it.

There was a coffee table in front of the couch, covered with magazines like *Ranch and Rural Life, U.S. News and World Report,* and a stack of religious looking magazines.

I felt like I was being pulled into a rural black hole.

Cheyenne's sister Jen and her husband, Greg, came in the house. Cheyenne introduced me to them. I stood up and said something trite, like "I'm glad to meet you both."

84

Looking at Jen was like looking at Cheyenne in five years' time. They both had the same hair color and the same silly grin and the same way of pursing their lips before speaking. Jen was not as tall, had darker hair, and seemed a little less outgoing than Cheyenne. But I was sure the camera would love her.

I decided right away that Greg would be perfect for a Great American Cereal spot. Wearing blue jeans and cowboy boots, he was tall and lanky and had a handlebar mustache and a deep bass voice.

We talked for a while, and then Cheyenne looked at me for confirmation.

"They'll do," I said. "Tell them about it."

At first they were pessimistic about being filmed, but they were ecstatic about the chance of having a paid vacation. Jen asked me if they could go to Hawaii over Christmas.

"Absolutely. You make the arrangements and call and tell us the amount you'll need, and we'll have a check sent to you."

Their children had been with their grandfather but came into the living room a short time later.

Rebecca, the six-year-old, was a beautiful girl. She had the same hair color as her mom, just slightly darker than Cheyenne's hair. The next was four-year-old Billy, followed by two-year-old Allison, who looked more like her dad.

I've learned how to do this, I thought. I got down on my knees and said hello. At first they were shy, but a short time later I was making the sound of a monster and pretending to chase them, although I never really moved.

The kids loved it. I looked up at Cheyenne and saw she was surprised and maybe even a little impressed.

I soon found out that Greg was a strongly conservative Republican and had a lot of bad things to say about Bill Clinton. I argued that Clinton had done a lot of good for the country. We ended up debating the issue and enjoying the whole thing. I remember thinking, *He's a lot smarter than he looks.*

Cheyenne had a worried look on her face—like we'd get into a fistfight or something. But that was not the case. We just happened to disagree.

When it was time to eat, Allison insisted on sitting next to me. I made her laugh all through supper and that was fun. After we ate, Cheyenne's dad, a six-term state senator, told some interesting stories about Idaho politics.

We ended up in the living room around the piano singing. Or, at least, they did. I didn't know any of their church songs. We ended up singing "God Bless America." The last time I'd sung that was in third grade. I didn't know anyone sang that anymore except in schools.

The whole thing ended around ten o'clock with family prayer, then they sent me to the barn for the night. I'm a big-city boy, not afraid of anything New York City can throw my direction, but I was nearly scared out of my wits on my way to the barn. I startled some horses in the corral, and they snorted and bolted in the darkness. I'm sure if Cheyenne had known about it she would have died laughing.

Once inside my room in the barn, I couldn't sleep, and so about ten-thirty I decided to take a walk around the place, being careful to stay away from the corral.

I passed Greg and Jen's house and saw him through the kitchen window doing dishes. The bathroom light was on.

I went to the back door and knocked. Greg came to the door and let me in.

"You come to continue our discussion?" he asked with a wide grin.

"Not really. I just thought I'd drop in and say hello."

"Come in." He led me into the kitchen. "You want something to eat? Jen's taking a bath, but I think we have some left-over pie in the fridge."

I suppressed a smile. "You say Jen's taking a bath?"

"That's right."

"Well, I won't keep you then. Can I ask you a question?"

"Sure, go ahead."

"Did you go on a mission for two years?"

"Yes."

"Why?"

"Because it's true."

"What's true?"

"What we believe."

"What do you believe?"

He went to a bookshelf and got another blue paperback copy of the Book of Mormon and handed it to me. "You can keep this. Read it and then ask God if it's true."

"Have you done that?"

"Yep."

"And is that why you live the way you do?"

"Yep."

Down the hall, out of sight, Jen opened a door and called out, "Greg, I'm done, if you need to use the bathroom."

"Ben is here!"

There was a pause and then a disappointed, "Oh."

"I'm going now," I called out. "I know you two have things to do." I started to blush. "What I mean is that I know it's late and you two need to get to bed."

That didn't sound right, either. "What I mean is you both need to get to sleep so you can get up early in the morning. That's what I meant."

Greg walked me to the door.

"There's just one more question," I said.

"What?"

"What should a guy like me do if he started to like Cheyenne?"

"Is that happening?"

"No, not at all. It's just a hypothetical question."

"She'd never marry you if you weren't a member of the Church."

"I know that. So, if it ever happened that I started to get serious with her, what would I need to do?"

"Learn about the Church."

"I'm more interested in Cheyenne than I am in her church."

"With us it's kind of a package deal. And even if you did get baptized, that's still no guarantee she'd marry you."

I shrugged my shoulders. "Well, I just thought I'd ask. I'm not ready to get married, and if I was it wouldn't be to someone who couldn't accept me the way I am."

"I can understand that. It's never easy to change."

"Have you had to change since you got married?"

He glanced down the hall, then said, "If I wasn't married, I'd still be on the rodeo circuit."

"Do you miss that?"

"Sometimes. But it's a rough way to live."

Jen called out from down the hall. "Greg, how long are you going to be? It's getting late."

"I'm going now!" I called out to Jen. "I'll talk to you both tomorrow."

I returned to the barn and stayed awake half the night thinking. How can you admire someone like Cheyenne and yet, at the same time, ignore what makes her the way she is?

At two in the morning, I went outside and looked at the stars. I wished Cheyenne would come out and talk with me.

I tried to think what it would be like to be married to her. I decided that if we were married, and we had kids, sometime during the week, I'd clean up the kitchen so she could take a bath. And I'd put the kids to bed. And I'd put out the cat if we had one. And the next morning I wouldn't rush off to work. I'd stay with her, and we'd talk over breakfast, and I'd help get the kids dressed. And when I got home from work that night, I'd give her a big hug and ask her how her day had gone, and

88

I'd pretend to be a monster and chase our kids around our backyard. And I'd roar and reach out to grab them, but somehow I'd always miss.

It was fun to think about. Half an hour later, I returned to my room and went back to bed and finally fell asleep.

6

I think we have a sleepyhead here," Cheyenne said in a singsong voice a mother might use on her child. She was standing next to my bed, hands on hips.

At first I thought it was the middle of the night and that she'd come to visit me. But then I saw her father standing behind her in the doorway. Sunlight was streaming into the barn.

"You goin' to sleep all day?" her dad said. "This is a working spread, not some dude ranch for rich, spoiled Eastern kids. The world has no use for the drone."

I jumped out of bed ready to put in a full day's work. But then I realized I was in my boxer shorts.

"Is that your underwear?" her dad asked.

I jumped back into bed. "Yes, sir."

"Are you in the habit of paradin' around in your underwear in front of my daughter?"

"No, sir."

"Cheyenne, have you ever seen him before in his underwear?"

"Daddy, that is such a ridiculous question, I'm not even going to answer it." She turned to me. "Hurry up and get dressed, Ben. Breakfast is ready. We're going to help my dad work around the place today."

Cheyenne had me put on a pair of Greg's jeans, a long-sleeved ugly, green work shirt, and a Levi jacket, and a baseball cap from a feed store. When I walked out of the barn all dressed up, she hooted and hollered. "Out of the day money, out of the average, let's give that cowboy a big hand. Woooo! Yeah!"

"I ride tall and lean in the saddle," I said with a Western drawl.

"Let's eat breakfast and then get to work," her dad grunted.

The first thing we did was to go to town for parts for one of his trucks. And then we came back and helped him work on the truck.

Seeing Cheyenne with her dad, I could see where she'd gotten all her cowboy expressions. The things she said that had caught my attention the first time we were together—they were all his. The way she set her mouth when she had something hard to do—he did the same thing. But she didn't suck air between her teeth like he did—he did that enough for both of them.

She had her hair pulled back with a rubber band and was wearing a baseball cap. She hadn't put on any makeup. This was her work outfit for the ranch.

It was obvious she and her dad loved each other, although they never said it. A lot of their talk was about neighbors and friends: who'd been sick, who'd got married, who'd had kids, who'd moved away. Local news. Small-town happenings.

I didn't mind them ignoring me. In a way it was a compliment that in some small way I fit in.

We were about finished fixing the truck when her dad

realized he'd forgotten to pick up an o-ring. "Looks like I'll have to go back in town. You two want to come in with me?"

"I promised I'd help Mom go through my things and pick out what to take to D.I."

I had no idea what D.I. meant, and they didn't tell me.

"I'll go in with you," I told her dad.

He seemed surprised. "Let's do it then."

I was kind of nervous, being alone with him. But he actually sounded interested when he asked, "How do you like our life here far away from New York City?"

I looked out at the rolling, sagebrush-covered hills with the jagged mountains towering in the distance. "I can see now why somebody who grew up here wouldn't want to leave."

"Oh, a lot leave right after high school. But they come back after a few years. This is a good place to raise kids."

"That's what Cheyenne says, too."

He nodded. "Well, it's the truth."

"Can I ask you a question? What if I wanted to learn about your church?"

"Would you be doing it to impress Cheyenne or because you're interested in knowing what we believe?"

"I'm not sure."

He didn't say anything for a while. I studied his face. He looked like he'd spent his entire life outside in the cold and wind and sun. The wrinkled skin around his eyes was like well-worn leather. His big hands, mostly dark, were splattered with age spots.

"I guess you're no different than I'd be. The missionaries will teach you whether you're interested in joining or just curious, or even if you just want to impress my daughter. I have no problem with you learning about the Church."

"Thanks."

"If you decide to join, though, make sure it's for the right reason. If you do it for her, then you'll both end up being the worse off for it."

92

With that said, arrangements were made for me to take the first discussion after supper.

For me the evening was pretty much a disaster.

I figured I'd be taught by guys. I'd seen them in subways in NYC. I could deal with guys.

But these missionaries weren't guys. They were girls not much older than Cheyenne—"Sister" Davis from Sacramento, and "Sister" Williams from Chicago.

They were excited, hopeful, and enthusiastic.

Cheyenne's parents sat in on the discussion.

Sister Davis was cherubic-faced, one of the most sincere people I'd ever met. Sister Williams was new on her mission and seemed bewildered by everything.

This is how the discussion went: They'd present some idea, back it up with a scripture, and then ask me a question. I felt like I was being railroaded into something because the only reasonable answer was the answer they wanted me to give.

I tried to be sarcastically funny with one answer, and Sister Williams looked like she might start to cry. Cheyenne's dad scowled at me and shook his head. Cheyenne looked at her mother, trying to calm her down.

"Seriously, how would you answer that question?" Sister Davis asked.

I gave the right answer, and everyone relaxed.

The rest of the discussion went better. I answered all the questions correctly, and that seemed to make everyone feel good.

But then the hard questions came. "Will you pray and ask God if Joseph Smith was a prophet?" Sister Davis asked.

"Sure, no problem."

"Well, let's kneel down and have you offer the prayer then," Sister Davis said.

"You want me to pray *now?*"

"Yes, if you wouldn't mind."

I closed my eyes and pretended to pray silently.

"Ben?" Cheyenne asked.

"Yes."

"Will you say the prayer out loud so we can join in?" she said.

"Out loud?"

"Yes, that's the way we usually do it."

"I've never done that before."

Sister Davis gave me a recipe for prayers. And then we all knelt down and waited for me to start.

"Father in Heaven," Sister Davis prompted.

"Father in Heaven," I repeated.

"We thank thee . ."

"We thank thee . . ." I looked to Cheyenne for guidance. She opened her eyes and scooted next to me and put her hand on my back. "What are you thankful for?" she asked softly.

"I don't know. I've never thought about it before."

"Are you thankful to be learning what we're teaching you?" Sister Davis asked.

"It's too early to say."

"You can skip that part and go to the asking part," Cheyenne said.

"What should I ask for?" I whispered to Cheyenne.

"Ask him to tell you if what you've been taught tonight is true."

"Will God do that?"

"Yes."

"You're sure?"

"Yes."

I couldn't go on with the prayer.

"What's wrong?" Cheyenne asked.

I didn't want the missionaries or her parents to hear this so I spoke very softly. "I'm not sure I want to know if it's true."

"Father in Heaven wants you to know that it is true," she whispered back.

94

"Why?"

"Because he loves you."

"God loves me?"

"Yes."

"I'm not that lovable."

"You are to God."

I could see in her eyes that she believed God loved me. It was not something I would have ever come up with by myself. But in that one moment, I thought, *If God loves me, then I'll ask.*

I did ask. It only took maybe fifteen seconds. And then I looked up at Sister Davis. "I'm ready to end it."

She told me how, and it was over.

We had dessert with the missionaries, and then they left, after making an appointment to come the next day to give me another lesson.

Cheyenne and I went out to the swing and talked. It was crowded, but we managed to squeeze in together.

"One of us has bigger hips than the other," I said.

"Don't feel bad. I've got some exercises you can do," she teased.

"Actually, I'm not the one who needs those exercises."

"If it's not you, then who else could it be?"

"I have no idea," I said.

She laughed. "Good answer, Beady."

We sat together in the dark, swinging, talking, and teasing each other. I told her I could swing high enough to touch the leaves of the tree. She told me there was no way I could do it and that I was just bragging.

"It ain't braggin' if you can do it!" It was a line I'd heard from her one time when we were arguing who could spit the farthest.

She playfully punched me in the side and jumped off the swing. "Okay, Cowboy, show me what you got!"

As hard as I tried, I couldn't touch the leaves with my feet. Finally, I gave up.

"Out of the day money, out of the average, all he gets is the hand you give him. Let's give that cowboy a big hand!"

"Oh, yeah? Well, I'll show you a big hand!" I jumped out of the swing and chased after her. She ran away from me, screaming and giggling.

I suppose if I'd been able to catch her, we'd have probably kissed. At least I felt like we were heading that direction. But as we ran past the front of the house, her dad opened the screen door and called out, "Cheyenne, it's time for family prayer."

Cheyenne stopped running and said quietly to me, "It's time for family prayer."

"You people must wear God out with all your praying."

We did family prayer, and then her dad asked me if I'd been warm enough the night before.

"I was fine."

"If you weren't, then we've got more blankets. Or you could borrow a pair of my pajamas."

Cheyenne started to laugh. "I would love to see Ben in a pair of your pajamas, Dad. Especially the pajamas with the big potato pattern."

Her dad gave her a stern look, then walked me to the door.

My time with Cheyenne was over, but I couldn't sleep. I saw a light on at Greg and Jen's and decided to call on them again.

I went to the back door and knocked.

Greg came to the door. "Ben, come in."

"I don't need to if this isn't a good time."

"No, come in, we're just doing bills."

I sat down at their kitchen table with them.

"You want some milk and cookies?" Jen asked.

"Yeah, sure, that'd be great."

96

She opened the pantry. "I just have chocolate chip cookies. Is that all right?"

"That's my favorite."

She set the bag on the table and retrieved a gallon of milk from the refrigerator, then got three glasses out of the cupboard.

"I took a missionary lesson tonight," I said.

"How'd it go?" Jen asked.

"Okay, I guess. The sisters are coming tomorrow for another one."

"Good. How do you feel about the things they taught?"

"Why does everyone ask me how I feel?"

"That's how you find out if it's true."

"I'm not used to talking about feelings. I'm a guy, okay?"

Jen picked up a magazine and asked me to read an article, which I did right there at the table. But even while reading, it was impossible not to observe Greg and Jen together as they paid their bills and decided how they needed to spend their money next month.

I guess my parents had done the same thing when I was growing up, but I'd never paid any attention to it. I'm not sure why this was different. Maybe because Jen was my age and looked like Cheyenne. It was all of a sudden the realization they were a family. This was a big deal. This was a major commitment from both of them. They were going to stay together.

They finished their work, and Jen began clearing the table. Greg leaned back in his chair and stretched. I took that as my signal to leave and stood up.

"Mind if I take this with me?" I said, holding up the magazine.

"Sure, go ahead," he said.

I went back to the barn and got ready for bed.

I thought about praying. I knew it would make everyone happy if I did. I thought about reading in the Book of

Mormon. That also would have been a good thing to report the next day when I received another missionary discussion.

But I didn't do any of those things. The reason wasn't because I didn't care. It was because I was afraid God would answer me.

◆　◆　◆

Later that week, back in my apartment in Jersey, I received another discussion.

To tell you the truth, I was a little disappointed by the missionary discussions. I thought it'd be more like when you join a health club. They give you a tour of the facilities. They tell you to shower before you use the hot tub. They tell you what the dues are. They show you how to make a reservation for a racquetball court. You pay a little money, and they give you a membership card. And that's it.

This wasn't like that at all.

Here's what the discussions are like: They give you a little information. And then they ask easy questions. And if you give the obvious answer, they're out of their mind happy with what you say.

But then, and here's the bad part, they ask you to do something. All the elders asked it the same way. It was always, "Will you . . . ?"

At first it was easy. I said I'd read a few pages in the Book of Mormon and that I'd pray. That wasn't too bad.

But then, with each discussion, it kept getting worse.

They wanted me to go to church.

They wanted me to quit drinking. Not that I ever drank much. Mostly just for social occasions. They wanted me to quit drinking coffee and tea. Can you believe that? What's the point of going to work without a cup of coffee to have while you read *The Wall Street Journal*?

They wanted me to live the law of chastity. Not just some

98

of the time, either, like between weekends or holidays. All the time.

Also, they wanted me to donate ten percent of my income.

I phoned Greg in Idaho to talk to him. I told him I'd had three discussions.

"How do you feel about what you've been taught?" he asked.

"They want me to change my whole life. I'm not sure I want to change that much."

"You like Cheyenne, though, don't you?"

"Yes, more or less."

"What part of what the Church teaches would you not want her to have in her life?"

"I'm not sure I know what you mean."

"Well, do you wish she drank beer?"

For a minute, I thought about how much fun it would be to get drunk with Cheyenne, but then something about that turned me off. I couldn't imagine her being out of control and acting foolish. As for smoking, I don't like it when people smoke around me. So that part was easy.

"No."

"Would you like her better if she didn't live the law of chastity?"

Again, a lot of inner turmoil followed. On the one hand, if she was in the habit of sleeping around, then maybe some day I'd get lucky. That would be good. But then knowing she'd done the same thing with other guys, well, that wouldn't be so good.

"Ben, are you still there?" he asked.

"I'm thinking."

He told me that when he and Jen got married, it was, for both of them, their first time. "It's better that way," he said.

"Why?"

"It was like a gift we gave each other."

That's all he said, but it started me thinking.

99

Two weeks later, Cheyenne and I returned to Idaho to watch Greg and Jen star in their very own commercial. It began with Greg in the middle of a field, his cowboy hat shielding his face, his back to the sun. He quick draws and shoots and then there's a voice-over. "I taught Matt Damon how to quick draw. He learned fast . . . but he's not as fast as me."

And then we see him in the kitchen, at the breakfast table with Jen and the kids.

Another voice-over. "We've got six hundred acres here. We raise Hereford cattle. Nothing is as important to me as my family. I want 'em to grow up healthy and strong. I'm willing to do anything for that to happen."

We see Jen pouring some cereal into a bowl for her youngest child.

And then the clincher: "Great American Cereals . . . for the family in all of us."

It had a great feel to it.

We had the weekend to stay with her family before we would be flying to Tennessee to look for another family.

We had family prayer at ten-thirty, and then I was booted out of the house, back to the barn. The trouble with being in the barn was there was no TV, no Internet access, nothing much to do.

And so, out of boredom, I started reading the Book of Mormon. I breezed through First Nephi, skipped the Isaiah chapters in Second Nephi, went through Mosiah, and then started Alma. Alma was easy to read because of all the battles and wars.

In Third Nephi, I read about the destruction and then what the Savior did and said when he visited the people in the New World.

At five-thirty that morning, I finished the book, then knelt down and prayed to know if it was true.

I received my answer by an overwhelming feeling, which I later learned was from the Holy Ghost.

"So it's true after all," I said, still stunned by what I was feeling.

I was exhausted but too excited to sleep, so I went into the kitchen and waited for Cheyenne's dad. I made myself some toast and peppermint tea. Half an hour later, Cheyenne's dad came into the kitchen and saw me.

"You're up early," he said, going to the refrigerator to get something to eat. "Cheyenne's still asleep."

"I need to talk to you."

"Here?"

"No, not here. Just the two of us. Can I go with you this morning?"

He nodded. "I can always use some help."

"I probably won't be much help."

"That's pretty much a given with you Eastern boys, isn't it?" he grinned.

He made us some sandwiches, filled a thermos with water, left a note to say where we'd be, and turned to me. "Let's go."

We drove around, checking on his cattle and repairing fences where they needed it.

"If I joined the Church, what all would I have to give up?"

"Nothing of any value."

"I know about not smoking and not drinking and no coffee or tea, and I know about tithing. Is that on my gross or my net? I know about chastity. Does that include everything sexual before marriage, or are there some things that are okay?"

"What do you think?"

I nodded my head. "Everything."

"That's right."

"I know about going to church and not shopping on Sundays. I even know about fast Sunday. Cheyenne told me about that. So I know those things, and I guess I could do

101

them, but what I want to know is, is there ever an end to this? Are there a bunch of other things they haven't told me about? Because I need to know. How much more do I need to give up besides what I already know?"

He stared at me like he was seeing me for the first time. "Yeah, there's more."

"How much more?"

"You have to be willing to give up everything."

"That's asking too much."

"Is it? I'm going to give you a little test to see if you're a good candidate to live with Father in Heaven some day." He handed me the keys to his pickup. "I'm giving you my pickup. In fact, I'm giving you everything I own."

"The ranch?"

"Yes."

"Your house?"

"Yes."

"All your equipment?"

"Yes."

"Your cattle?"

"Yes."

I smiled. "Thank you very much. How long will you and your family need to pack up?"

He grabbed the keys out of my hand. "That's it! You failed the test."

"What are you talking about? I said thanks, didn't I?"

"You totally missed the point."

"What was I supposed to say?"

"You were supposed to say back to me, 'All I have is yours.'"

"I'm sure there's some kind of a lesson here, right?"

"Heavenly Father says to us, everything I have is yours. When we say to him, all I have is yours, then we understand what this gospel is all about. It's about sacrifice and consecration. When we're at least willing to give everything up, then he can truly bless us."

"So I take it the ranch isn't mine, right?"

"Of course not. What would an Eastern boy like you do with a ranch?" he asked with a grin.

"Ride around, look at the cattle, go into town, buy some parts. I don't mean to be critical, but what you do around here doesn't look that hard."

He shook his head. "When you look at the cattle, you got to know what you're looking for."

"Hmm, well I could learn. Can I have a sandwich?"

"It's only ten-thirty."

"I'm hungry, though."

"What will you do at noon when I'm eating my sand-wich?"

"I'll try to talk you out of half of yours."

He started laughing. It was the first time I'd heard his laugh. It was almost as contagious as Cheyenne's. "Well, as long as you got a plan." He reached around in back and got his lunch pail and handed it to me, a solid, metal lunch bucket, maybe forty years old.

I grabbed a sandwich, shut the lid, handed the bucket back to him, and removed the plastic bag. I was about to take a big bite when he said, "You going to ask a blessing on that sandwich?"

"You're the one who made it. You think it needs God's intervention?"

"No, but I think you need it."

I bowed my head and started my prayer. It was going to be just a short prayer, but then it kind of got out of control. "Thank you for this sandwich and for . . ." I started to lose it. " . . . what I felt when I asked if the Book of Mormon is true."

I hoped he had his eyes closed because a tear was running down my face. I quickly wiped it away. I couldn't go on

103

because I didn't want him to see me humble. It wasn't my style.

I finished the prayer, then took the sandwich out of the plastic bag like nothing was wrong.

But by then I wasn't hungry. "Who can baptize me? Can you do it? Will you?"

He had his eyes straight ahead and his hands on the steering wheel, like this was a new road neither one of us had ever been on before. He nodded. "I'd be honored to do that."

"Thanks. Oh, one other thing. When it's convenient, could you swing by your place. I was up all night. I need to get some sleep."

I slept until four in the afternoon, then took a shower and got dressed.

Before supper I found Cheyenne. We sat in the swing together and talked.

"What's this about Idaho being the Gem State? What gems come from Idaho?" I asked.

"Lots of 'em."

"Name one."

She was stumped, but she wasn't going to admit it. "Diamonds," she said, like it was common knowledge.

"You're saying there are diamond mines in Idaho?"

"Absolutely. Everybody knows that."

"Let's go see the diamond mines on Monday."

"It's quite a ways."

"It'd be worth it, though. How many times have you been to see the diamond mines in Idaho?"

She started laughing. "So many times I can't even remember."

"I'm sure you can't remember."

"Idaho's the Gem State. I wonder what New York is. The Germ State?"

"Don't rile me, Girl."

"Oh, yeah, like I'm really scared of you."

"I can pump this swing so high the fillings will fall out of your teeth," I warned.

"You have such a rich fantasy life, Beady."

I was going to get her back, so I looked into her eyes, and she looked into mine, and so I quit pumping until we came to a stop.

I was sure she'd have let me kiss her, but I didn't because I knew, if I did, she'd be suspicious about my reasons for joining the Church.

"I think we should pray," I said.

That made her mad. She got out of the swing and headed back into the house.

"What's wrong now?" I asked.

"You can make fun of Idaho if you want, Beady, but don't mock my beliefs."

"I wasn't mocking your beliefs."

"Then why that crack about praying?"

"I was serious."

"You're never serious about anything, except the New York Yankees."

"Come back here. There's something I need to tell you before eight o'clock."

"What's going to happen at eight o'clock?"

"The missionaries are coming to interview me for baptism."

"Yeah, right!" she snapped, slamming the door on her way into the house. I could hear her complaining to her mom and dad. I couldn't hear what her dad said, but a short time later Cheyenne came back outside.

She walked to within ten feet of where I was sitting in the swing, but she wouldn't come any closer. I couldn't tell if she was mad at me or just suspicious of my motives, but one thing for sure, she wasn't overjoyed.

"What's going on here, Beady?"

"I'm going to be baptized."

"Why?"

"Everyone said if I read the Book of Mormon and prayed about it, I'd know it was true. I did and it is."

"There's got to be more to it than just that."

"Why do you say that?"

"Because I know you too well. Are you doing this just to try to impress me?"

"No." I paused. "Although that's a part of it."

"You've got to leave me out of this."

"I'm working on that."

"Because when the summer is over, I'll return to BYU, and you'll stay back East, and we'll probably never see each other again."

"Unless we fall in love," I said.

"I don't see that happening."

"I do. In fact I think it's already happened, and the only reason we haven't talked about it is because you've liked the fact that I'm not a member, so it gives you an excuse to stay away from me."

She shook her head. "I totally disagree."

"I'm going to be baptized. Your dad is going to do it. I'd like you to say a few words."

"You're ruining everything, Beady, just like you always do."

She turned and ran into the house and up the stairs to her room. I could tell because she turned on the light in her room and then pulled the curtains.

A short time later, the elders came and interviewed me. I guess I passed the test because they shook my hand and congratulated me on the decision I had made. Then they left.

I thought Cheyenne would come down after the elders left, but she didn't. At ten-thirty, I had family prayer with her folks, and then they went to bed. I was going to go over to talk with Greg and Jen, but their house was dark, so I just went back to the barn and went to bed.

106

At two in the morning I woke up to a knock on my door. It was Cheyenne, in jeans and a sweatshirt. "We need to talk," she said.

"Not here," I said, partly out of my desire to actually be true to the new life I was about to choose and partly because I knew her dad would rip my head off he knew we'd been alone in a bedroom together.

"Where then?"

"On the swing."

"I don't want to be that close to you," she said.

I nodded. "You can sit in the swing. I'll pull up a chair."

She nodded.

A few minutes later, we were set up to talk, me in a lawn chair in front of where she was sitting in the swing.

"I talked to my dad. He told me he thinks you really do have a testimony and that your reasons for wanting to join the Church are good ones. So I just wanted to say, I apologize for what I said."

"I accept your apology."

She nodded and stood up. "Thank you. I think I'll go back and see if I can get some sleep now."

"Wait a minute. I know you don't like to think there might be something between us, and I know you're waiting for a missionary, and that's fine, but let me just tell you something."

She gulped. "What?"

"I've never had a better friend than you."

She nodded. "You're a good friend to me, too."

I wanted to say more, but I knew it would only upset her. So we left it at that.

On Sunday I went to church with her and her family. That afternoon she drove over to her missionary's family and had dinner with them. When she came home, she seemed a little more reserved.

But we took a walk together just before sunset. It was a glorious sunset, the kind Westerners pride themselves on.

There were some clouds on the horizon, and they were on fire with a red and orange glow. With no buildings to get in the way, it was a spectacular sight.

She taught me a couple of Primary songs, and we laughed together, and she made fun of my singing.

When we got back to the house, it was dark. She said she needed to go write a long letter to her missionary, Justin. And then she added, "Why don't you write your mom and dad and tell them you've taken the missionary lessons and that you're going to be baptized, and tell them how much you've changed, and invite them to learn about the Church, too?"

It was a good idea, but I didn't do it because I wasn't sure how they'd react, and I figured they wouldn't want me to push religion down their throats.

You know what? I should have written.

7

Advantages of joining the Church that are never mentioned by the missionaries: Your parents, recognizing you've joined a church known for its high moral standards, tell you, "It's about time you settled down."

If you are fortunate enough to be friends with someone like Cheyenne, you can sit together in church, and if you lean forward and lower your head, she might put her hand on your back, and, if you're very lucky, she might keep her hand on your back for almost an entire Sunday School lesson.

You have a good excuse when your old high school friends call you up and say they're in town for the weekend and invite you to get drunk with them. And then you have more time to spend with a girl like Cheyenne, who might look at you like she's proud of you.

The girl's father sends you a copy of a church book and asks you to read it. And on the title page, he writes, "Thank you for letting me be a part of your baptismal service. I'm proud of you for the courage it took to be baptized."

The girl begins to treat you like one of her dearest friends.

They should make a pamphlet about these things. It'd probably double the number of baptisms.

◆　　◆　　◆

In the middle of August, Cheyenne and I drove up to my family's cabin on Lake Winnisquam in New Hampshire. It was to be our last week together before Cheyenne headed west for BYU's fall semester. After spending weeks on the road, we were tired of traveling, so we had arranged for my Uncle Eugene and his wife, Marilyn, and their two kids, Caleb and Emma, to be our last featured family for the summer.

On Tuesday Cheyenne and I watched the shooting of the commercial.

Basically, the commercial just relived Caleb and Emma in their swimming suits down on the dock picking out their favorite cereal from the variety pack. And then Marilyn tells an actor standing in place of my mom, "It's economical and nutritious, and that's about as good as you can get with any breakfast cereal." And then, of course, the signature line for the series: "Great American Cereal . . . for the family in all of us."

The commercial was shot in five hours and then the crew left.

On Wednesday, Eugene and Marilyn had to go to the wedding of the daughter of an old friend in Maine, so they left their kids with Cheyenne and me.

After they left, we played canoe wars again until dusk and then ordered pizza and ate it in the living room. We rented five movies and watched two of them until late that night. And then Emma suggested we camp out in the living room together in sleeping bags.

So that's what we did.

By twelve-thirty that night, we were all pretty tired. Cheyenne asked Caleb and Emma if they'd mind if we had a prayer. They may have thought it was a crazy idea, but they agreed because they loved her. And so we did.

The four of us knelt in a circle with just the light from a yard light outside highlighting our profiles.

Cheyenne said the prayer. She asked for blessings of safety for their mom and dad and for everyone in the family.

When the prayer was over, we hugged each other and then slipped into our sleeping bags.

Lying there in the dark, Emma said, "Cheyenne, you're the best."

"No, you are. You know what? I love you guys," Cheyenne said.

"Do you love Ben?" Emma asked.

There was a long, awkward pause, and then Cheyenne said, "As a friend I do. We've had a great summer working together."

"I hope you marry him some day so you'll be in our family," Emma said.

"Well, it's a great family to be in, that's for sure."

"We have so much fun with Ben when you're with him," Caleb said. "He's not much fun when it's just him."

"We do have fun when we're all together, don't we?" Cheyenne said.

"I wish you were my sister," Emma said.

"I'd love to be your sister. And Caleb's sister, too."

"Then marry Ben."

This was getting out of hand. "Let's change the subject, okay?" I growled.

"Ben's right," Cheyenne said. "It's funny how warped your thinking can get when you're tired."

Warped. She actually said warped.

Sleeping on the floor is something you can do when you're twelve but not when you get much older.

I woke up at six-thirty. My first reaction was to look over at Cheyenne. She was gone.

I went to the screen door and spotted her sitting in a lawn chair on the dock. She had her feet pulled up in the chair and was hugging her knees. The morning sun, just popping up over the trees, illuminated her uncombed, morning hair, giving it a golden brilliance. It was a beautiful sight. I was so moved by it that I thought, *This would make a great commercial.*

At first she was staring straight ahead, so all I could see was the back of her head, but then some ducks landed nearby, and when she turned to watch them, I could see her profile.

I thought of a line from *My Fair Lady*, a musical my mom had dragged me to when it played during my freshman year of high school. I, too, had "grown accustomed to her face, it almost makes my day begin."

My appreciation for her was more than just her looks. I know that the phrase "the goodness within her" seems way too cheesy to even be taken seriously. But there's no other way to put it.

There's some things you know you'll never get from Cheyenne: You'll never get her to say mean things about anyone. Not even people the rest of the world hates. You'll never get her to even crack a smile at any inappropriate joke. You'll never get her to make fun of blacks or Hispanics or any other ethnic group. You'll never get her to watch an R-rated movie, even if you tell her you'll fast forward over the bad parts.

On the other hand, here is what you'll always get from her: She'll always try to find something good to say about someone. She'll always look on the bright side. She'll always be willing to talk about her beliefs to anyone who will listen. If you're with her and you're in a hurry, but you happen to walk by a mom with a baby or little kid, you can forget your schedule because she'll always stop and talk to the mom and ask if she can hold the baby. Even in New York, where people grow up being taught not to trust anyone, she'd get mothers to hand their babies over to her.

112

You can also count on her to always be good, not just when she's rested up. It's not something she puts on every morning and takes off at night. It's something that's with her all the time.

I have to admit that when we first met, some of her good qualities really annoyed me. Before Cheyenne, I liked my women sexy, so I'd enjoy being with them, and cynical, so I could talk to them, and uncaring, so I could leave them when it suited me. I liked women driven by ambition so they'd be too busy to settle down—women who just wanted to get together with me once in a while, with no long-term commitments.

But after spending a summer with her, I felt like if I met myself on the street, I wouldn't recognize me because I'd changed so much.

I hadn't joined the Church just because of Cheyenne. It was becoming a part of me, too, but I have to admit I was worried how things would go after she returned to BYU. It was easy for me to be good when we were together every day. If I strayed, even just a little, she'd give me "the look," or talk to me and help me understand what was expected of me as a member of the Church.

It suddenly hit me that she was going to leave, and I didn't want her to go. I wanted us to always be together. With her long-held beliefs and my recent conversion, there was only one way to make that happen. And that way was marriage.

Before she'd come into my life, I'd approved of marriage. Just not for me. It was good for others. I could see how a person might get married if he was tired of going to bars trying to pick up someone as desperate and lonely as himself.

Cheyenne made marriage seem, well, not that bad a deal.

Together, we'd spent the summer searching for husbands and wives who loved each other and loved their kids. You can't do that without it making some kind of an impression on you. Although they were all different in terms of their

113

ethnicity and lifestyle, they all had one thing in common. The marriage partners were a team. They worked together, they stuck together, they were loyal to each other, they enjoyed being in each other's company. They didn't fold when times got tough. They stayed together and worked things out.

So there I was, standing at the screen door looking at Cheyenne as she watched a family of ducks near the dock by some water lilies. I remember thinking the same thing I'd heard my mother say for years: *Benjamin, you need to settle down and get married.*

That was a big step for me. Of course, it's always a big step to admit your mother is right.

But there was more. *If I were going to be married, I'd like to be married to Cheyenne. She'd be good for me and, of course, my family already loves her.*

But there was something else, something new, that I'd never allowed myself to admit. *It's very possible that I'm in love. I mean, I could be. I never think about anyone else. I haven't seen anyone else since I met her, so that could mean I'm in love.*

Am I in love? It sounds so dumb. Falling in love is what you see in chick flicks, and who watches those? Except when Cheyenne insists.

I could be in love. I mean, it's a possibility. That would explain a lot.

Like, why I feel the way I do. What if it's not just that we work well together or that she got me interested in the Church? Why do I always feel like a better person when I'm around her? Maybe it's not just that she looks for the good in others, even me. Maybe I am in love.

I opened the screen door, walked outside, and let the door slam shut. She turned and saw me coming and broke into a big smile. "Hi, sleepyhead, did you sleep well last night?"

"Well, to tell you the truth, I don't think I'll ever be the same again," I said with an embarrassed grin.

"I know what you mean," she said. "Whoever invented mattresses did a great thing for mankind."

I sat down next to her in another lawn chair. "That's not what I meant."

"What did you mean?"

"I'll explain later. Thanks for giving Caleb and Emma a great overnight," I said.

"It was fun for me, too." She stopped talking and looked out at the lake.

"Isn't this a beautiful morning?"

"It is. Aren't we supposed to be drinking Folgers coffee about now?" I asked, referring to a popular commercial of a few years ago.

"I believe you're right," she said with a faint grin.

We sat without speaking for a few moments.

"We've come a long way this summer," I said.

"You have, that's for sure. Taking the lessons, getting baptized. It's been exciting to watch."

I reached out for her hand. She didn't pull away. I thought that was a good sign.

"I decided something this morning," I said.

"You're never going to sleep on a floor again, right?"

I laughed. "Actually, I guess I decided two things this morning."

"What's the second thing?"

"I've decided I care about you a great deal."

"I feel the same way, Ben. Funny, isn't it? When we first met, I didn't know if we'd get along or not, but right now, you're one of my best friends. I'm going to really miss you."

This wasn't going well. She thought we were just good friends. I was hoping we were more than that.

I'd already made her skittish, a word she'd taught me when we were in Idaho. It had something to do with horses. She got up and went to the end of the dock and turned around and looked at the cabin. "I'll miss coming here, too."

115

"Let's go in and see about breakfast, okay?" I asked.

The four of us went swimming in the morning, then ate lunch. Cheyenne went inside to take a nap.

"We want you to come with us in the canoe," Caleb said.

"What for?"

"We need to talk," Emma said.

I got in the canoe as a passenger, and they took me to the same cove where the four of us had played canoe wars.

"Are you going to ask Cheyenne to marry you?" Emma asked.

"Probably not."

"Why not? That makes no sense. You love her, don't you?" Emma asked.

"She's waiting for a friend from high school to get home from his mission. Before he left, they talked about getting married."

"How long ago was that?"

"He's been gone almost two years. He comes home in November."

"Two years is a long time," Caleb said. "I can't remember any girl I liked two years ago."

"You didn't like any girls two years ago," Emma said.

"Well, that's true, but if I had, I wouldn't like them now."

"Are you going to ask Cheyenne to marry you or not?" Emma asked.

"I hadn't planned on it."

"Are you crazy?" Emma shot back. "You think you're going to do better than her?"

"Probably not."

"I'll say not."

Emma, that sweet child, my Barbie girl playmate when she was a kid, now had all the intensity of a forty-year-old New Yorker I'd just cut off in traffic.

"You've got to act now, before she leaves," Caleb said.

I've got to tell you it was more than a little annoying to be getting advice about my love life from mere children, even if they were my cousins.

"Look, I really don't think you understand what's involved here."

"All right, fine, don't ask her to marry you then, see if we care," Emma snapped. "Let's go, Caleb."

Caleb started paddling.

"Stop, I'm not done yet," Emma said. "Are you ever going to get married, Beady?"

I cringed. "Don't call me Beady."

"Cheyenne does."

"That doesn't mean you can."

"Caleb, start paddling, will you?" Emma demanded.

Caleb started paddling.

"You're just going to let her go, aren't you?" Emma asked me. "She's the best thing that's ever happened to you, and you're just going to let her go without even telling her you love her."

"Actually, I haven't actually decided if I do . . ." It was embarrassing to even say it to those two. " . . . love her."

"Don't give me that. You love her. You know you do."

"You're eleven years old, Emma. I hardly think you're qualified to tell me if I'm in love or not."

"I know you're in love with her, so don't try to deny it."

"Look, even if I was in love with Cheyenne, which I'm not saying I am, I sure wouldn't want to confide that information to someone like you who still watches Saturday cartoons."

"You watch Saturday cartoons, too," she shot back.

"Mostly just when I'm with you, though."

"Look me in the eye, and tell me you don't love her," Emma said.

I looked her in the eye for a second and then broke eye contact.

"That's what I thought," Emma said. "You love her."

I shrugged my shoulders. "I love a lot of people."

117

"That's not true, Beady. You hardly love anybody."

"Well, the way you two are harassing me, the list of people I love just got two people shorter."

She put her hand on my knee. "Let us help you," she said.

"How?"

"We have a plan. You want to hear it?" Caleb asked.

The "how" was answered that afternoon. I took Cheyenne to the store to get some milk for breakfast in the morning, but it was just an excuse to give Caleb and Emma time to decorate the dock with Christmas lights and haul the CD player outside so we'd have music to set the tone for the evening. I'd given them some cash so they could order Chinese food and have it delivered.

It was the longest go-to-the-store-for-milk run in history because I'd made arrangements with Caleb and Emma not to show up at the house until six-thirty.

"You know, since you probably won't be getting back here for a while, I'd like to show you some of the historic landmarks around this area," I said on the way to the store.

"Sure, that'd be great."

We visited the easy landmarks first and then the less obvious ones.

Like a parking lot. "On this site in history, a group of Indians pitched their tents and had a two-week encampment in 1713."

"How does anyone know that?"

"There's a historical marker around here somewhere."

She looked around. "I don't see any historical marker."

"That takes us to the second important date that happened here."

"Which is?"

"On this site, a group of vandals tore down the landmark that told about the first historical landmark."

As you can see, I was getting desperate. We visited the

118

cheese factory and got a free sample of cheese. I know it made my day.

"This is real interesting and everything, but I think we should go back so we can be with Caleb and Emma. This is my last night here with them before I go west. I want to spend as much time with them as I can."

"Sure, let's drive once around the lake, and then we'll go back."

I turned into the driveway to our cabin at six-fifteen. At first there was no indication they'd done anything. Except they were nowhere in sight.

"I wonder where they are," I said.

The moment we stepped on the dock, Christmas lights running along both sides of the dock turned on. "Oh, whoa," Cheyenne said softly.

At the end of the dock was a picnic table covered with a white table cloth with a single white candle in the middle.

And then, on cue, soft romantic music from the CD player filled the air.

"What's this all about?" Cheyenne asked.

"It was Caleb and Emma's idea for our last night here." I reached out and took her arm and escorted her to the end of the dock and seated her at the table.

Caleb, wearing a white shirt and carrying a towel on his arm, approached our table. "Good evening," he said in a formal manner. "My name is Caleb and I will be your waiter this evening. Would you care to have a drink before you order?"

"Yes, what do you have?" I asked.

"We have sparkling apple juice mixed with ginger ale, or you can have water."

"The sparkling apple juice sounds wonderful," Cheyenne said, getting immediately into the act.

"Two sparkling apple juices, please," I said.

"Yes, of course."

A minute later as we sipped our drink, Emma, in a vintage

119

1930 elegant creamy-white dress she must have found in some trunk in the attic, struggled to make it onto the dock in high heels.

She was singing "I'm in the Mood for Love," trying with all her heart to bring a romantic mood to the occasion. It was a little embarrassing to see my little Emma in the role of a torch singer.

When she finished, we applauded with great enthusiasm.

Next, she tried to do her version of the lounge entertainer. She approached us. "Where are you two from?" she asked us.

"New York City."

"The Big Apple, right? And how about you?" She thrust an imaginary microphone in Cheyenne's direction.

"Idaho."

"Home of Idaho potatoes, right? In honor of your being here, I'd like to sing you, "Home, Home on the Range."

She sang it as if it were a love song. It seemed awkward and corny to me, but Cheyenne acted like it was the best thing she'd ever heard.

As we applauded, Emma took a couple of bows and then walked toward the house. It was slow-going in high heels. Finally, she took them off and went the rest of the way barefoot.

"Why did Caleb and Emma want to do this?" Cheyenne asked.

"Because they love you."

"I love them, too. They're both amazing."

"They are, aren't they? I never realized they were anything special until I saw them through your eyes." I reached out and took her hand in mine. "That's true of a lot of things."

"It's been a good summer for both of us, hasn't it?" she said.

"It has."

"I'll miss being here."

"Me, too," I said.

"You can come here anytime," she said.

"I won't though. I never did before you came and I won't after you leave."

"How come?"

"I guess it's because . . . it won't be the same without you."

"You have a wonderful family, Ben. I do love them . . . very much."

"They love you, too." This was getting too weird. "You know," I chuckled, "the reason Emma and Caleb went to all this work was to set the mood so I'd ask you to marry me."

Her jaw dropped. "Really? And how do you feel about that?"

I could tell right away that this was not going to go well. "I don't know. I haven't thought about it much. But one thing for sure, I could never do better than you."

"So, for you, deciding who to marry is more like going shopping and trying to get the best deal you can."

"Emma is the one who said I could never do better. So if you have a problem with that, talk to her."

"I don't have a problem with Emma. I love her like she was my sister. And I have the same kind of love for Caleb."

"How do you feel about me?" I asked.

She didn't answer immediately.

"It's like the stock market, Beady."

"In what way?"

"Some days you close higher, some days lower."

"I haven't always liked you, especially in the beginning," I said.

"We have something in common then, don't we?"

I knew then that this whole thing was a waste of time.

She squeezed my hand. "But, you know what, on the whole, there has been a bull market in regard to your stock."

"Let's drop this whole discussion about marriage and just relax and enjoy ourselves," I said. "For Emma and Caleb's sake. They want to see us having a good time."

121

"Good idea."

A short time later, Caleb approached our table, carefully carrying a tray of food, the best available from our local Chinese restaurant.

We ate slowly and watched the sun set. For dessert we had cherry cheesecake.

And then Caleb and Emma approached the table.

"We are going to leave you two alone now," Emma said.

"We're not even going to hide in the bushes and watch," Caleb said.

Emma glared at him. "We're going to walk into town and see a movie. We'll be back about ten-thirty."

"So you'll be all alone," Caleb said with a wink.

As they walked away from us, Emma unloaded on Caleb. "What were you thinking?"

"What?"

"You didn't have to go, 'So you'll be all alone.'"

"What's wrong with that? They will be all alone, won't they?"

"You didn't have to say it, though."

They changed clothes and then left.

"Well, looks like we're all alone," Cheyenne said with an amused grin.

"But we've been alone before, so I think we'll be able to handle it, don't you?"

"I do. We'll be okay."

"What would you think about being married to me?" I asked.

"I don't know. I've never thought about it before."

"Never?"

She ducked her head. "Well, almost never."

"Would it help if I get down on my knees and ask you to marry me? Because I am fully prepared to do that."

"Who'd be the most surprised if that happened, me or you?"

122

I paused. "Will you?"

"Will I what?"

"Marry me?"

"Beady, that's really not something to joke about."

"I'm serious."

She looked directly at me. "You're serious?"

"Yes."

"I can't see me making any kind of a decision like that until after Justin comes back from his mission."

"When's that?"

"November."

"If things don't work out between you, would I have a chance?"

"Maybe. We'll see. Even after Justin gets home, it might take him and me a while to decide if we want to get married. So you might have a long wait."

"It's okay, I can wait."

"Also, whatever happens, I'm going to be married in the temple. It's something I've dreamt about all my life."

"That's fine with me."

"You can't go to the temple until a year after your baptismal date."

More delays. I remember thinking *It's a miracle anybody in the Church gets married*—missions, waiting, education.

"Have I ever told you I love you?" I asked.

"No."

"Well, I do."

"When did you decide that?"

I looked at my watch.

She gave me a sympathetic smile. "When you have to look at your watch for the answer to a question like that, then don't you think that talking about marriage might be a bit premature?"

"Maybe if we kissed. Sometimes that helps. And, you know, we've never done that," I said.

"That's true."

"I think we should."

She ran her hand over her forehead which was now beaded in perspiration from stress. "Why do you think we should kiss?"

"It's what people in love do."

"We're not sure we're in love."

"It's what people who possibly might be in love do."

She stiffened and turned her back to me. I felt ashamed to have put her in the awkward position of having to make a choice.

She gulped. "All right, go ahead. One kiss is all, though."

We stood up. For some dumb reason I moved the chairs away from us.

She watched in amazement as I cleared the area. "What kind of a kiss are we talking about?"

"You ever seen Sumo wrestlers?" I put my hands on my hips, squatted, and ceremoniously transferred my weight from one foot to another in the manner of Sumo wrestlers.

"Best two out of three, right?" she asked.

"Right."

That got us in a silly mood. I went to put my arm around her, but she started to laugh. "I'm sorry, Beady, but this is way too weird. Busting a gut laughing and kissing don't go together."

The mood was lost, so we went inside and watched a movie, not even sitting very close to each other.

When Emma and Caleb returned, they kept looking at me for some sign that I'd proposed and that Cheyenne had said yes. While I was brushing my teeth, getting ready for bed, with the door partially open, Emma barged into the bathroom. "Well, did you ask her?"

"You can't just burst in when I'm in here."

"I could hear you brushing your teeth, so what's the problem? You afraid I'm going to see toothpaste dribble on your chin?" She closed the door behind her and asked confidentially, "What did she say when you asked her?"

"She said she had to wait for her friend from high school to get home from his mission."

"Did you tell her you love her?"

"Yes."

"What'd she say?"

"She asked me how long I've known that."

"What did you say?"

"Nothing. I looked at my watch, though."

Emma threw up her hands. "What is wrong with you, Beady?"

"She's not ready to think about getting married. And I'm not, either."

"And you never will be. You'll be one of those old men who never gets married."

After Emma left, I locked the door. While I finished up in the bathroom, Emma went to Cheyenne to plead my case. By the time I left the bathroom, I overheard Emma tell Cheyenne how, the night before, I'd moved my sleeping bag next to Cheyenne's and watched her as she slept.

That must have freaked Cheyenne out because when we gathered in the living room for bed, Cheyenne said that she and Emma would sleep outside on the deck under the stars.

That's what happened.

The next morning for breakfast we had a pancake-animal contest. The rule was you had to come up with a recognizable animal shape, like a bear or a bunny, with each pancake you cooked.

It was great fun. My pancakes never looked as good as the ones done by Emma or Cheyenne, or even Caleb, so in order to save face, I had to invent animals to go with my misshapen pancakes.

I slid a weird blob of a pancake out of the pan.

"You lose, Beady!" Cheyenne rubbed it in.

125

"What? You don't recognize that?"

"Recognize what? It's not even a circle. It's a weird shape. There is no animal that looks like that."

"This is the shape of a camel's hump."

"Oh, right!" Cheyenne said sarcastically. "I should've seen that right away."

"Yes, you should have."

"You lose, Beady. No question about it."

"Let's take a vote. All in favor that this looks like a camel's hump, say aye." Caleb, of course, voted with me. "All those misguided individuals who lack the sensitivity to see that this is an artistic rendition of a camel's hump, please say nay."

Two nays.

"It's a tie then. Ties get counted as a win."

"What?" Cheyenne complained. "Where do you get these rules anyway?"

"They're in a book for the IAPA."

"And what is the IAPA?" Emma asked.

"International Association of Pancake Animals."

"Don't believe a word of what he says," Cheyenne said to Emma.

"I never do," Emma said, sticking her tongue out at me.

"Well, I've never been so insulted in my life," I said.

"Me, either," Caleb said.

After breakfast we went swimming. We had a great time together.

At eleven Eugene and Marilyn showed up. We talked them into going swimming with us. Marilyn wasn't much of a swimmer, but she did like to take pictures. And Emma and Caleb wanted lots of pictures with Cheyenne and me, so they'd have something to look at after Cheyenne was gone.

At one point, Eugene and I were each floating on inner tubes, watching as Emma and Caleb dived or jumped from the floating platform a hundred feet from the dock. Cheyenne was lying on the dock talking to Marilyn.

126

Eugene and I were a great audience for Emma and Caleb. One of them would say, "Watch this," and then they'd do a dive or some other trick, and Eugene and I would shout out, "Great dive!"

Emma and Caleb never tired of showing off in front of their dad, so it gave him and me a chance to talk.

"This is the life, right?" Eugene asked. "Just floating here, not a care in the world. Watching my kids."

"They're good kids."

"They are. They're the best. I don't see them enough, though. Being in my business, I'm always gone nights. You're in advertising. See if you can get more people to have their wedding receptions in the morning."

I smiled. "I'll get right on it."

"You do that, Ben."

"Dad, watch! Caleb is going to do a cannonball," Emma called out.

"No, no, don't do it, son, it'll drain the lake!" Eugene teased.

Caleb broke into a big grin and jumped from the diving board making a big splash.

When he broke the surface of the water, he looked over at his dad to catch his reaction. "How was that?" he asked.

"That was the best cannonball I've ever seen," Eugene called out. "If there was Olympic competition in cannonball, you'd get a gold medal."

Caleb grinned. "I can do even better."

"These kids ask so little of me," Eugene said to me. "All they want is for me to pay attention to them once in a while." He got a pained look on his face and shook his head.

"What?"

"I was just thinking of all their school activities I've missed. Band concerts, choir concerts, plays Emma has been in. I've missed a lot. Never go into the catering business. If you do, you'll never get to see your kids perform."

127

"I'm sure Caleb and Emma understand."

"I should have made arrangements to get time off when I needed to. That's what I should have done." He sighed. "But I didn't. That's my one regret." He shook his head. "And now look at them. They're growing up so fast. Before I know it, they'll be gone to college. I need to set aside more time to be with them. That's what I need to do."

"Okay, everybody, now we're going to do a double cannonball!" Emma shouted.

"Oh, man, look out! We're in trouble now!" Eugene called out.

They perched on the diving board for a long time, trying to coordinate their jump. And when they jumped, they made two big splashes, although Caleb, being the heaviest, made the biggest.

We made such a fuss over the double cannonball, that Emma and Caleb called for Cheyenne to come so they could do three at a time. She had been talking to Marilyn, but she could never turn Emma and Caleb down, so she dived into the water and stroked out toward us.

"How ya doin'?" I asked her.

"How ya doin'?" she answered. You do things like that when you're in advertising and watch a lot of commercials. She turned to Eugene. "How ya doin'?"

Eugene didn't watch a lot of TV. "What's that all about?"

"It's from a beer commercial."

"Can Mormons watch beer commercials?" he asked me.

"As long as they don't put their mouth on the set," I said.

Cheyenne swam past us and joined Caleb and Emma. It took them forever to figure out how they were going to do the three-at-a-time jump.

"That one's a keeper," Eugene said, referring to Cheyenne.

"I know."

"Any chance you two will get married some day?"

"Maybe. We'll see."

"Caleb and Emma love her."

"Cheyenne feels the same way. If she ever married me, it would be just so she could be part of the family."

"We'll take her any way we can get her."

"She has some unfinished business with a guy she knew in high school. He's been away for two years, so she's going to wait until he gets back to see how it is between them."

"Has he been on a mission?"

"Yeah."

"I know all about that. When I was in the army, one of my best buddies was a Mormon. He'd served a mission, too. You know what? I had a missionary lesson once. But then we got split up. I got transferred to another base, and for some reason I just never got back to taking the other lessons. So I could've been a Mormon like you are now."

"I never knew that."

"I haven't thought about it for years, not until Cheyenne entered our lives."

"So what did you think about what you learned about the Church?"

"It was good. It made sense. I could see myself being a Mormon."

"Maybe sometime I'll send the missionaries over again."

"Well, Marilyn might have other ideas. She's fairly involved in her Catholic women's group."

Finally, Caleb, Emma, and Cheyenne jumped together and did a cannonball. Eugene and I, of course, did our part, exaggerating how big the splash was.

"That was the splash of the century!" Eugene roared. "I think it got Flight 480 from Boston wet! There may even be a lawsuit."

"Oh, Daddy!" Emma called out, grinning as she treaded water.

Cheyenne started swimming to me, humming the music to *Jaws*. Just before she got to me, she submerged. A moment later I felt her arms around my legs, and then she popped up inside the tube, so we were nose to nose. "Did I scare you?" she asked.

"Absolutely! I was scared to death. I was sure it was a shark."

"It was just me," she said.

It wasn't that big of an inner tube and so, since we were both inside it, we were much closer than we had ever been. I was a little surprised she didn't move away from me. I suppose both of us realized that if we could pretend it was just two friends sharing an inner tube, it was safe territory.

Marilyn called for Caleb and Emma to help with lunch. Eugene decided he'd had enough, too.

I'm not sure why we didn't go in, too. I think it was because we both realized our summer together was almost over.

It was a little too intimate for Cheyenne, so she ducked down and ended up outside the inner tube, her arms locked over the tube facing me.

"Have you ever kissed a guy underwater?" I asked.

"You mean this week?" she teased.

"No, ever."

"Uhm, not really. Why do you ask? Are you conducting a survey?"

"I think we should."

"Why?"

"Maybe it would be very nice."

"Well, if it's underwater it's not going to be a long kiss."

"That's not necessarily true. I can hold my breath for a minute."

"No, you can't. Nobody can do that."

"I can."

"You go underwater and I'll time you."

I took a deep breath and let myself sink underwater. I could hear her counting.

When I couldn't stand it any longer, I surfaced.

"Thirty- five seconds," Cheyenne said.

"Is that all? I used to be able to go a minute."

"Try it again."

I got all ready to go again and then I stopped. "Hey, wait a minute. What's going on here? I ask you to kiss me and you sidetrack me into seeing how long I can hold my breath underwater."

She started laughing. "C'mon, Beady, go for it. You can do it! I bet if you try really hard you can go forty-five seconds this time."

I splashed her with water. "You are evil!"

"What are you talking about?"

"I want to kiss you."

"I know. Me, too. But it might give you the wrong idea about us . . . you know, that there is some kind of a future together for us. And the thing is I can't decide something like that now."

That pretty much killed the mood. "Sorry I asked. Well, I think I'm through swimming." I swam back to the dock, went inside, and took a shower.

When I was done with my shower, Cheyenne took a shower.

We ate lunch with Eugene and his family, gave everybody hugs, and headed home.

◆　　◆　　◆

The last meeting that Cheyenne and I had with Saddlemier before she left for BYU was very relaxed. And why not? The commercials featuring Great American Families were being well received by the public. Sales were up dramatically, and Saddlemier was ecstatic.

"You two are magic together, you know that?"

That night Saddlemier gave us a night to remember. We

ate at a fancy restaurant and then he took us to the Broadway production of *The Lion King*.

In the morning Cheyenne packed up and got ready for her long trip out west. She would leave the next day. My parents invited her to spend her last night with us.

Our hours together were dwindling down to a precious few.

8

Everybody in my family wanted one last visit with Cheyenne before she headed west, but Emma and Caleb seemed to take top priority with her. After some wrangling, we agreed that Cheyenne and I would have supper with my parents and my grandfather, then around eight-thirty we'd drive to Eugene and Marilyn's home, where Cheyenne and I would stay the night. The next morning she'd begin her three-day drive west.

Cheyenne followed me in her pickup from her apartment in the City. I grew up in Manhassat on Long Island, in a three-story house. When we walked in, my dad gave Cheyenne a big hug, showing more affection to her than I ever remember him showing me. "Thanks for coming."

"Thank you for inviting me."

"Our pleasure. Has Ben been treating you right?"

"Oh, yes. We had a great time today. We took a boat tour all the way around Manhattan."

"Oh, yes, well, good for you."

We sat in the living room and had cheese and crackers and tomato juice.

"You have a lovely home," Cheyenne said. I was suspicious of her using the word lovely. Was she trying to sound like an Easterner? In Idaho it would have been, "Nice place you got here."

"Thank you. We've added on to it four or five times. I can't remember which," my mother said. "Do you recall how many times we've remodeled the house?" she asked my dad.

"I'm sure Cheyenne doesn't care about that," my dad said.

"You're right," my mom said. "But now I'm curious. Let's see, there was the screened-in back porch . . . And after that we redid the upstairs bathroom . . . And then . . ."

I waited for my dad to blow up and leave the room or tell her nobody cared and couldn't we talk about something else, but he didn't. He was on his best behavior. I knew it was because of Cheyenne.

And what was I doing for the sake of honesty? Very little. I sat and smiled and listened to the conversation and ate my cheese and nibbled on my crackers and drank my tomato juice. I also really wanted Cheyenne to like us.

I tried to imagine what life was going to be like with her gone, but it was a blank, almost as if I didn't exist without her. It was a jolt for me to realize that. I'd never had that feeling about anyone else.

"Would it be possible for me to learn more about your catering business?" Cheyenne asked.

"Well, yes, of course," Dad said. "Would you like to see our shop?"

"Yes, I would. Very much."

The office of Morelli and Sons Catering is located on Northern Boulevard, just five minutes from my parents' home and only fifteen minutes from where Eugene and Marilyn live. My father and Cheyenne and I piled into my car and drove over there. The place isn't all that impressive—just a box-like structure with an idea room in the front end where those wishing to have an event catered could leaf through several large bound volumes and choose everything from plastic dinnerware and utensils to elegant table settings and floral arrangements.

The place was closed for the day, and since there was no event to be catered that night, Hazel Yeager had gone home. Hazel is an all-purpose secretary who runs the inside operation. She is a large woman with a hoarse, deep laugh, and she rules the roost. When I was young, she always gave me candy, so no matter how gruff my dad might be about things not going right, she was always my friend. She'd worked there long enough and had proven herself so valuable in answering the phone and managing the books and charming the customers, that I think sometimes she thought my dad worked for her. At any rate, he was always respectful of her because if he wasn't, she'd come after him. More than once I'd heard her say, "Who do you think you're talking to?" He always backed down when she said that.

The rear of Morelli and Sons is where the food is cooked and prepared. It's a large, open space, with a bank of sinks and stoves and ovens and a large walk-in refrigerated room where food is kept after it's been prepared.

I'd spent so many hours and days in there while I was growing up that to me it was nothing special, but as we walked past the long stainless steel tables, and as my dad explained the assembly line manner in which food and desserts were prepared, Cheyenne seemed completely intrigued.

"This is absolutely amazing!" Cheyenne said.

"We didn't start this way, of course. But over the years, it's all come together."

"What's the most people you've ever fed at one time?"

"Six hundred. And we got them through in ten minutes."

"That is so amazing!"

135

My father was beaming. I wondered when was the last time anyone had been that impressed with what he did for a living. Or, more precisely, when was the last time I'd been impressed with anything he did.

He went to the walk-in cooler and brought out a pastry that was his specialty, one that I had tasted only a few times in my life.

"Here, try this," he said.

Cheyenne took a taste. "Oh, my gosh! This is so good!" Cheyenne practically shouted.

"We are the only ones who make this. It's been imitated but never duplicated."

"I wish my mom were here. I know she'd want the recipe."

"We don't give out recipes for this. It's like a trade secret," I said.

"Oh, I might be able to give you the recipe," my dad said.

I was shocked. I'd heard of people offering a thousand dollars for the recipe and being turned down.

We went into the office and sat down while my father wrote down a scaled-down recipe and handed it to Cheyenne. "Try to keep this within your own family," he said.

"I will. I promise."

A short time later, we locked up and headed back to my parents' house. "Thank you so much for showing me around. And thank you for the recipe. I can hardly wait to get home to show this to my mom."

"Glad to be of service," my dad said.

Back at the house, Cheyenne looked through my high school yearbooks, enjoying every bad photo of me from ninth grade through my senior year.

My grandfather came for supper. He lives ten minutes away in a house that had been converted into two apartments. He lived upstairs. Sometimes, when his arthritis was acting up, it was hard for him to get up and down the stairs.

"Ah, wonderful, the medicine woman is here," he said,

going to Cheyenne and giving her a hug. "What potions and herbs do you have for me today?"

"I'm fresh out, but how have you been anyway? Any more headaches?"

"You know what? I've been using feverfew every day like you suggested, and it's really made a difference."

"I'm glad to hear it."

He kissed her on the cheek. "Such a lovely girl," he said, glancing at me so I'd get the message.

Cheyenne and I sat in the living room with my dad and grandfather while my mother worked in the kitchen. My mother wouldn't let them in the kitchen when she was cooking because they made too many suggestions and were too critical.

"So, how was your summer?" my dad asked.

"Working with Ben has been just great," she said.

My grandfather winked at her. "Well, you know, it doesn't have to end with the job."

I'd had enough. "Would you like to see my tree house in the back?" I asked.

"You have a tree house? I've got to see it!"

We had a very small backyard, but we did have a large tree. My dad had built the tree house when I was six years old.

"Are you expecting to go inside?" I asked.

"Is that a problem?"

"Girls aren't allowed," I said, trying to sound serious.

"I'll be on my best behavior."

"Sorry."

"How about if I'm on my worst behavior then? I can belch like a boy."

"I'll make an exception then."

We climbed up the makeshift ladder and into the tree house. "Funny, I remember this being much bigger when I was a kid," I said. The trunk of the tree went right up through

137

the middle of the room, so there was barely enough room for us to sit cross-legged on the floor, facing each other.

"So what do boys do in a tree house?"

"They make plans for what they'll do if a girl tries to come in."

"Did any girls ever try to come up here?"

"No, but we were ready if they did. We had buckets of water to throw down on them."

"So, no girls, right? How boring."

"It would be now."

"Did you work for your dad when you were growing up?"

"I'd worked for him starting in ninth grade. Off and on. Mostly off. I doubt if they made any money from my efforts. At first I was too slow to earn my keep, but then in high school I could almost keep up." I sighed. "But then something happened."

"What happened?"

"There was a retirement party. I was in my junior year of high school. The man who was retiring was the grandfather of a girl in my class, who I liked.

"She saw me filling water glasses, and I made the mistake of smiling at her. Everyone was eating at a large table in a luxurious dining room. When I filled her glass, I leaned down and smiled at her and touched her arm and said hello. Her grandfather saw me and called for my dad, and in a voice that everyone could hear he told my dad to 'tell your help to keep their dirty hands off my granddaughter.'"

"My dad took me into the kitchen and yelled at me for ruining his reputation and told me to go home.

"The girl never spoke to me again. Which was no great loss, but at that time, the whole thing was devastating to me. I never worked for my dad after that." I paused. "He probably figured I thought I was too good to work for a living. He doesn't respect what I do now. So, I guess you could say we're not real close."

"I like your dad."

"He's on his best behavior around you. You've never seen him blow up like I have."

"Why is he on his best behavior around me?"

"Because he's hoping you and I will get married. Everyone in my family feels the same way."

"I like your family very much."

"I know you do."

A few minutes later, my mother opened the back door and called out, "Ben, supper is ready!"

We went inside for what I feared the most, eating supper with my family.

Mealtime in our home is sometimes a tricky business. My dad was usually so sick of preparing food he didn't help out, but he couldn't help being critical of the food he was served, so I was a little worried how it would turn out.

He never ate much. I suppose there were so few times when he felt he could relax and eat, but this was one of those times.

My grandfather looked for every little opportunity to praise my mom's cooking, even though he was usually more critical about food than my dad was.

"The celery is so crisp, isn't it? Sometimes the celery in the stores is not so crisp."

"I'd say the quality of food in general has gone down in the past ten years," my dad said.

"Maybe it's your taste buds and not the food," I said.

Cheyenne gently kicked me in the shin. "This salmon is so good!" she said to my mom.

"Thank you, dear. I'm glad you like it."

Later on my dad actually said he liked the dessert. It had been a long time since he'd complimented Mom about her cooking.

Over supper my dad and grandfather started talking about their investments in the stock market. "I used to be more conservative than I am now," my grandfather said. "And what did it get me? Four percent a year. Now I'm favoring energy stocks. Oil, natural gas, hydroelectricity, that's always going to be good. We're never going to use less energy than we are now, that's for sure."

We talked for another half hour, and then I announced that Cheyenne and I had to go.

"I need to go, too," my grandfather said. "I hate to walk much after dark these days."

"Let us give you a ride home," Cheyenne suggested.

"It's not that far," he said.

"Oh, but it's no trouble for us."

"Well, in that case, I'd appreciate a ride."

My grandfather rode with me, and Cheyenne followed in her pickup.

When I let him off, we walked back to Cheyenne's pickup, and he asked, "Would you two like to come in for a cup of coffee?"

"Well, actually . . ." I began.

"Of course we would. For Ben and me, though, could it be something else?"

The three of us followed the sidewalk around to the back of the house and began climbing the stairs.

"This is quite a climb," Cheyenne said as we stood on the second floor landing while my grandfather unlocked the door.

"It can be sometimes. But the way I look at it, it keeps me young."

It had been years since I'd been there. In fact, the last time was when he moved in, just after my grandmother had died. I helped carry up some of his boxes.

He kept it spotless, which in a way surprised me because nobody ever saw it except him. Well, maybe my parents, too. But nobody else.

He seemed pleased to show Cheyenne around the place.

The kitchen had hardwood floors, and a large round oak dining table that overlooked the backyard.

In contrast to the kitchen, which was well organized, the living room was cluttered with junk my grandfather had brought with him from the house when he'd moved into the apartment after my grandmother died. It was like going back in time. Not only were the couch and easy chairs from another era, but the walls were covered with framed photographs of his family. In addition, he had two large albums full of family photos, which, unfortunately, Cheyenne asked to go through with him.

I didn't have much use for any of it, but Cheyenne sat eagerly next to him on the green sofa as he turned each page and then explained in detail every photo.

I went into the kitchen and made him a cup of instant coffee and us some peppermint tea. I found a package of cookies and put them on a plate and took them into the living room.

"I made us something to eat."

My grandfather looked at what I'd done and said, almost automatically, "You forgot the napkins."

And they wonder why I wouldn't go to work for them after college, I thought.

"Thanks, Ben," Cheyenne said with a big smile.

We stayed there until eight-forty-five, then said our good-byes to my grandfather and drove to Eugene and Marilyn's place.

Eugene and Marilyn and their kids lived in a cul-de-sac just off of Northern Boulevard.

Emma and Caleb were waiting for us when we drove up. They both ran out and let Cheyenne give them a big hug. "I'm so glad to see you guys again!"

We sat and talked until ten, and then Emma and Caleb begged Cheyenne to sleep in the TV room with them.

"She has to get some sleep," I said. "She's got a long day of driving tomorrow."

"We'll go right to sleep," Emma said.

"We want it to be like we were up in the cabin," Caleb added.

Cheyenne couldn't say no to them. And so, the four of us ended up in their TV room on the second floor in sleeping bags, or blankets, on the floor. They crowded next to her on either side, leaving me by myself.

They were too excited to watch a movie, so we turned off the light and sang songs until they fell asleep. By the time they were asleep, I was asleep, too, so we didn't really even say goodnight.

The next morning at nine, Cheyenne drove away. Emma and Caleb and Marilyn and I stood in the driveway and waved until she was out of sight.

"Such a girl," Marilyn sighed.

I didn't get mad this time. "She is that, all right."

I drove to my apartment in Jersey. The traffic wasn't that bad because it was midmorning and because it was Saturday.

I sat on the side of my bed and tried to decide how to spend the day, but without Cheyenne I couldn't think of anything. If she'd been around, maybe we'd have taken Caleb and Emma to a museum or a Broadway play, or maybe we'd have been at the lake with them.

It was like I was suddenly a stranger to myself. I didn't know who I was anymore. Even my joining the Church seemed a consequence of being with Cheyenne for the summer.

The reason I'd gone into my bedroom was to change clothes, but the only problem was I couldn't decide what to change into because I had no idea what I was going to do for the rest of the day.

I don't know how long I sat there. It was like I was trying

to decide, "Who am I? Am I what Cheyenne wants me to be or am I what I used to be?"

I couldn't decide.

And then, around one in the afternoon, the phone rang. It was the bishop of the singles ward Cheyenne and I had attended when we were in town during the summer. He asked if he could meet with me after church the next day.

Up to then, I hadn't made a decision if I was going to church the next day, but I said yes, and then I asked, "What's this about?"

"We'd like to put you to work in the ward. Is that okay with you?"

"I guess so."

"Good, well, I'll see you tomorrow, then, right after church."

Suddenly, I knew where I was going. With or without Cheyenne in my life, I was going to be, as they say, *active* in the Church.

To tell you the truth, that was news to me.

9

Cheyenne and I stayed in contact by email twice each day and with hour-and-a-half phone calls every other night. I'm not sure about her, but it kept me going.

I was a member of the Manhattan Sixth Ward, a single adult ward. It meets on Columbus Avenue across from Lincoln Center and is definitely not your Idaho ward meeting-house with its traditional red brick exterior and satellite dish. Oh, no. This is a six-story building with a Family History Center on one floor and chapels and classrooms on the other floors. It is home to eight wards and so, on Sunday, it's the busiest place in the City.

What a ward! We had nannies from the West, Broadway actors, Wall Street traders, artists, students, and musicians. Not only was there diversity in professions but also in ethnicity, with blacks, Hispanics, and Europeans represented. It was like what artists envision heaven to be like. I loved that about the ward.

My first calling was to be the president of a Sunday School class. I had to phone Cheyenne to tell her about it.

"Way to go, Ben! I'm proud of you."

"Not only that. When I was interviewed, the bishop told me that in a couple of months, I might be ready to receive the Melchizedek Priesthood and be made an elder."

"That is terrific, Ben!"

"Thanks. I just had to tell you. You know, I'm doing all this for you."

I knew by her long pause that I'd messed up. "I don't want you to do it for me," she said. "I want you to do it because you know it's the right thing to do."

"That's what I meant. Of course I'm not doing it just for you. I'm doing it for me."

"And for Father in Heaven," she added.

"Yes, of course. For him, too. I was just about to say that."

I'm not sure she believed me. And, the truth is, sometimes it was difficult for me to separate my feelings for Cheyenne from my faith in the teachings of the Church.

For example: I wanted to marry Cheyenne. Since she would accept nothing less than a temple wedding, that became my goal, too. But how could I be expected to value a temple wedding when I'd just heard about it? I wasn't like her. I didn't have any older brothers or sisters who'd been married in the temple and who could tell me from experience that it was the best way to go.

I didn't agonize much about it because I guess I thought that with a little luck things would be easy for me and that I wouldn't have to put my new faith to the test.

It almost happened that way, too.

◆　　◆　　◆

September 10, 2001

I spent the night in a Holiday Inn in Syracuse. The day before, I'd visited with Dirk and Shannon Rice again. They'd

145

done our first Great American Cereal commercial, and we wanted to do a follow-up, thirty-second spot with them.

That night in my motel room I phoned Cheyenne, but one of her roommates told me she was out with a guy from her ward.

I hadn't thought about her dating anyone else, and I felt as though I'd been kicked in the head. Then I became desperate. I kept calling until one in the morning, Eastern Time (eleven o'clock her time), before giving up and going to bed.

The next morning, I slept until eight. Since it would be six her time, I decided to wait a couple of hours before I telephoned.

I didn't talk to anyone, didn't stop for breakfast, didn't get gas, didn't turn on the radio. I just got in my car and started driving. I was on my way to Albany to meet with a prospective client.

At eleven-fifteen, Eastern Time, I called Cheyenne on my cell phone, hoping she wouldn't have left for classes yet.

She picked up on the first ring.

"So tell me what's going on with this guy you were out with last night," I said.

There was a long pause. My first thought was that she'd fallen in love and didn't know how to break the news to me.

"Ben, have you heard the news?" she asked.

"What news?"

"Where are you now?"

"I'm in my car heading east on I-90."

"Pull over and stop."

"Why?"

"Do what I say, Ben. Pull over and stop."

I had a sinking feeling in my stomach that this was going to be bad. But I didn't pull over and stop because people don't pull over and stop unless there's an emergency. And this was no emergency. Okay, she went out with a guy, and maybe she liked being with him, but I could handle that. I'd just fly out and talk to her.

"Are you stopped yet, Ben?"

I saw a sign for a rest stop a mile ahead. "I'm going to pull into a rest stop. It'll take me a minute, okay?"

"Okay."

She didn't say anything until I told her I'd pulled over and stopped. "So, what's so awful you have to have me pull over? Did you get engaged last night?"

"Ben, this morning, two large passenger planes crashed into the Twin Towers of the World Trade Center. They say it was the act of terrorists." She started crying. "Both towers . . . collapsed. They say there could be ten to twenty thousand people dead."

I shook my head. "There must be some mistake. That could never happen."

"I've seen it on TV. It happened. You'd better call your mom and let her know you're okay."

"When did it happen?"

"It was around quarter to nine your time. Call your mom, Ben. Let her hear your voice."

"I'll do that."

"Call me back as soon as you've talked to her. They've canceled classes, so I'll be here all day."

I called my mom. The line was busy.

I wasn't worried about my family. Morelli and Sons catering business is located in Great Neck, Long Island, miles away from the World Trade Center. I used the rest room at the rest stop and then called my mom again. This time she answered.

"Mom, I just heard what happened. Are you okay?"

"I haven't heard from your father, but they say all the phone lines are tied up."

"Is he at the office? Just drive down and talk to him."

She paused. "I don't keep up with the details of the business, but I think he told me they were catering a brunch for a

147

company at the World Trade Center. But I can't remember if it was today or tomorrow."

"I bet it was tomorrow."

"You're probably right."

"Or else it was for later in the day. I'm sure everyone is okay. Have you talked to Marilyn?"

"No. All the lines are busy."

"Let me see if I can get through. I'll call you back as soon as I've talked to her."

It took me two hours, but I finally got through to Marilyn. She told me that my dad and Eugene and my grandfather were indeed scheduled to cater a brunch at the World Trade Center at ten o'clock.

"Why would anyone ask a caterer from Long Island to do a brunch in Manhattan?"

"It's for one of their customers who lives out here. Your dad and Eugene catered their daughter's wedding. They loved the chocolate-strawberry mousse . . ." She fought to stay in control. ". . . and insisted on having it at the brunch."

Because I'd worked for my dad and Eugene in high school, I knew their routine. They always made sure everything was set up an hour before any event was scheduled to begin. If it was a small event, they'd be able to set it up in an hour. That would have them carrying food, tablecloths, and serving utensils up a freight elevator around eight in the morning. So they might have been in the building at eight-thirty, or, if it was a very small event, they might have still been on their way at eight-thirty.

It would be close. It just depended if they were going to feed twenty people or two hundred.

I still felt confident they were safe, but a nagging thought kept coming into my consciousness, and that was, if it were only for twenty people, my grandfather wouldn't have been asked to help. He'd retired from the business years ago, and he only helped out when there was too much work for my dad and Eugene and their regular staff.

The fact that my grandfather was working that day meant it was a large event. And if it was a large event, they'd be in the building at seven or seven- thirty at the latest, if indeed the brunch were scheduled for ten in the morning. Of course, Marilyn might have been wrong. Brunches are usually scheduled for eleven. If you're serving at ten, you might as well call it breakfast. Typically, a brunch will take place somewhere from ten-thirty to eleven. If it started at eleven, then if my dad and Eugene and my grandfather planned to show up at nine, that'd be plenty of time, especially since most people would be to work by then, so they wouldn't have to worry about traffic as much.

So whether my dad and uncle and grandfather were safe rested on when the brunch was scheduled and for how many people.

I realized I could find out by calling my dad's secretary, Hazel Yeager.

I called, but nobody answered.

I called Marilyn again. "I'm in the car heading back to the City. I'm about three hours away. Call me if you find out anything. I'm sure everything is fine and that they're safe but just haven't been able to get through to tell you."

"Yes, I'm sure that's true."

"How are Caleb and Emma handling this?"

"They're having a tough time. Do you want to talk to them?"

"Yes, of course."

Emma came on the line first. "Ben, where are you?"

"I'm in my car. I'm about three hours north of the City. I'm going to stop by and see you guys, and then I'm going into the City and make sure your dad and my dad and Granddaddy are okay."

"They're not letting anyone in or out of the City," she said.

149

"As soon as they do, I'll go in, but, look, I'm sure they're okay, Emma. I bet they're trying to get through, too, but all the lines are tied up. They'd have come home by now, but they can't. But they're okay. We just have to have faith, that's all."

"Okay," she said in a little girl voice I hadn't heard for years.

Caleb was next. I said the same thing to him I'd told Emma, then added, "Caleb, you have to be strong now and be positive and be a big support to your mom and Emma. That's what your dad would want you to do. Don't worry. Your dad will be home as soon as he can. As soon as he can call or get out of the City, you'll see that I'm right."

I think I made him feel better. That's what I wanted to do.

I stopped for gas. When I went in to pay for it, there was a crowd of people inside the gas station watching a small black-and-white TV. They were showing a video of a second plane flying into the World Trade Center. I couldn't believe what I was seeing. It didn't seem possible. *If they can do this, what can I count on to always stay the same?*

In the gas station, we were ten to fifteen strangers riveted to a small TV set, and yet, in that one moment, we were family. Other drivers came and went, but I couldn't pry myself away from the news coverage. I noticed a Holiday Inn nearby. I drove there and went inside to the desk. The desk clerk was watching TV, too. "Can I watch in one of your rooms? I'll pay for it."

He shook his head and gave me a key. "Room 131. The room isn't made up yet."

I went to the room and closed the door and turned on the TV and sat down on the bed, which wasn't made up from the previous guests.

I didn't even bother to turn on the lights. The curtains had been drawn shut the night before, so the only light coming in from outside was from the sides of the window.

It was surreal. It wasn't just the Twin Towers. It was

the Pentagon, too. And another plane had crashed in Pennsylvania. By now the towers had collapsed in a tremendous cloud of dust that rolled through the streets. People were running for their lives, panic-stricken, desperate, in shock.

A reporter stopped one of the women who was fleeing. She was covered with dust and her hair was wild and her clothing dirty and disheveled. She said she had been in one of the towers but had made her way down the stairs.

"What was it like in there?" the reporter asked.

"Total chaos," she replied. "As we were coming down, fire fighters were going up the stairs." She began to cry, then blurted, "They were all young, good-looking guys . . ." She couldn't go on.

I tried to remember how many times I'd visited the Twin Towers. Maybe a hundred times. Anytime we had out-of-town guests, we took them to the Statue of Liberty and to the Twin Towers. Once, after taking Caleb and Emma to the musical *Annie,* I took them there, too.

I stayed in the motel room for over an hour. I knew I should get on the road, but I couldn't seem to break away. I kept hoping I'd see my dad and Eugene and my grandfather on TV, telling how they had narrowly escaped when the towers had collapsed.

A cleaning lady opened the door. She was a large black woman, in her late-thirties. She was accompanied by a girl in her early twenties. "We're sorry. We'll come back later."

"I was just watching the news," I said, standing up to leave.

"Are you okay?" the older of the two asked.

"I'm worried about my dad . . . and my uncle . . . and my grandfather . . ." I didn't finish the sentence.

She set a stack of clean towels on the bed and reached to give me a hug.

The girl looked puzzled. The first woman said something

to her in Spanish, and then this girl, a total stranger, joined us and made it a group hug.

I lost it. I could hear myself sobbing. The woman patted me on the back. "There, there."

I was ashamed of breaking down in front of strangers, so I pulled away. "I need to go now."

"Let me get you a glass of water."

I nodded. She went to the bathroom and brought me back a glass of water.

I drank it and handed the empty glass back to her.

"Jesus is the lover of your soul," she said.

I nodded, patted her on the arm, and walked away, wiping my eyes in the hall so the desk clerk wouldn't notice.

A short time later, I was on the road again. As I drove, listening to the radio, I kept waiting for a phone call from my mom or from Marilyn, telling me that everything was all right, that my dad and Eugene and my grandfather had called and said they were okay, or else that they'd walked into the house and told their story of where they'd been when it'd happened.

But nobody called.

I called Cheyenne and told her where things stood.

"I'm sure they're okay," I said. "We just haven't heard from them."

"Do you want me to come out?" she asked.

"What would you do?"

"Whatever I can. I'm worrying about Caleb and Emma. Are they okay?"

"I don't know. Look, don't worry. I'm sure my dad and Eugene and my grandfather are okay. The phone lines are tied up, so they can't call and let us know. And the police have stopped all travel into the City. I'm sure that any minute my dad will call my mom and tell her where they are. Or else they'll just walk through the door. When that happens, I'll call you. Until then, all we can do is wait. Besides, they've shut

152

down all commercial flights. There's no way you could even get here now."

As I got closer to the City, I tried to figure out what my route would be. They were still blocking any traffic into or out of the City. Instead of trying to go in and see if I could find my dad and Eugene and my grandfather, I decided to go to my folks' place and wait until they opened up traffic into the City.

By calling around, I found out my mom was at Eugene and Marilyn's house, so I headed there. I talked to Marilyn on the phone and told her everything was going to be all right.

I took the Throgs Neck Bridge, then headed east on the Long Island Expressway. Traffic was light. Everyone was home watching TV.

When I got to Marilyn and Eugene's place, I was afraid that a knock at the door would panic Marilyn, that she'd think it was a police officer come to tell her that Eugene had died. So I just opened the door and called out, "Anybody home?"

Caleb and Emma and Marilyn ran to greet me. Maybe they thought I'd come with Eugene and my dad and grand-father.

"Have you heard anything?" I asked Marilyn.

"Not yet."

"I'm not worried. They'll be home soon. I did think maybe if you could give me a set of keys, I'd drop by the office and look around."

Emma and Caleb looked lost to the world.

"Everything's going to be all right. I'm sure of it," I said.

Emma and I held each other, unable to express our fears. I kissed her on the forehead and told her everything was going to be all right, even though I wasn't sure of it. With tears in her eyes, she nodded her head.

I was sure that Caleb wanted me to hold him, too, but he held back because he was at the age where any kind of physical contact was difficult to accept. I hugged him anyway.

My mother was sitting on the sofa staring at the TV. She hadn't gotten up when I came in. I went over to her and knelt down beside her. "Mom, I'm home. I'm going to go to the office and check the records, and then, as soon as I can, I'll go into the City and see if I can find Dad and Eugene and Grand-daddy."

"I'm afraid of what may have happened," she said, her voice flat and lifeless.

"We don't know that. Everything's going to be all right," I assured her.

She nodded, her gaze fixed on the TV. They were showing once again the hideous video of the plane flying into one of the towers.

At Morelli and Sons, I unlocked the door and went inside. The lights were still on in the food preparation room in back. I checked the walk-in cooler. There was no food there. If they hadn't left for the World Trade Center, there would have been food in there. I went to the garage adjoining the preparation room. The Morelli and Sons Catering van wasn't there.

I went into the office and checked the calendar. There on the date of September 11 was written the words: "Brunch, WTC, North Tower, 10:00 A.M., 200."

I sat down and went through the files in the in-box on Hazel's desk until I found a copy of the complete order form for the event at the World Trade Center. It was at an investment firm on the thirtieth floor of the North Tower, the first of the twin towers that had been hit by a plane. The brunch was for two hundred people. So that meant that by 8:30 my dad and Eugene and my grandfather would have already transported everything up to that floor, by the time the first plane had hit the building.

The news reports had said the first plane struck the North Tower at 8:47 AM; the second plane struck the South Tower at 9:03 AM.

But there was time for them to get out. They had time to

walk down the stairs. So they probably got out okay. That's probably what happened. They're probably helping in the rescue effort. That's why they haven't called. I'll just go find them, and then I'll call and tell my mom and Marilyn that everything is all right. That's what I'll do.

I hadn't eaten anything all day, so I went to the walk-in cooler. Not much. A little cheese. I also found a box of crackers in the stash Hazel kept in her bottom drawer in the office. She had first told me about her stash when I was five or six years old. It was the one thing I could always look forward to when I visited.

I knew from the radio that all traffic into the City had been closed, but, I felt so useless, I decided to try it anyway—for Emma and Caleb's sake.

Until then I hadn't realized how much I loved Emma and Caleb. I'd just taken them for granted. I didn't want to admit it, but if it was true that their dad and my dad and our grandfather had all been killed, then I had a responsibility to do what I could for them.

I took the Long Island Expressway. An electronic sign read, "All Crossings to New York Closed." I ignored the sign, got on 278, hoping to take the Williamsburg Bridge into Manhattan. At the bridge, two police cars blocked the way. I pulled to a stop. I noticed three National Guard soldiers armed with machine guns behind the cars.

"You'll have to turn around. We're not letting anyone into the City," a state policeman said. People in the cars behind me were honking their horns.

"My dad and my uncle and my grandfather were in the World Trade Center. I need to find them," I shouted.

"I'm sorry, but I can't let you through."

"Is there any way I can get in?"

"Not that I know of. Take the emergency turnaround and head back."

I turned around and drove to Marilyn's house. I told her

155

what I'd found out, told Caleb and Emma that I'd tried to go into the City, and then, like every other family in America, I sat down and watched CNN.

Marilyn was on the phone in the kitchen. After many tries, she finally got hold of the New York City police and reported Eugene and my dad and grandfather missing. She then started calling hospitals.

I sat down next to her and listened as she talked on the phone. I couldn't think of anything else to do, so I made up some coffee for Marilyn and fixed some sandwiches and heated up some tomato soup. Marilyn refused the food but did take a cup of coffee. At first Caleb and Emma and my mom said they weren't hungry, but I left the sandwiches on the coffee table in the living room, and fifteen minutes later they were all gone.

I felt like I should be at the World Trade Center, digging through the rubble, trying to find my family. Or doing something that would answer our questions, but there wasn't anything that could be done, except for what Marilyn was doing.

I went out on the porch and called Cheyenne on my cell phone. I told her where we stood and then confessed, "I don't know what to do."

"Have you talked to Caleb and Emma?"

"I did. I told them not to worry, that everything is going to be all right."

"Can I talk to them?"

"Okay, hold on." I went into the house. "Emma, Cheyenne wants to talk to you. Then you, Caleb."

Emma shrugged her shoulders and came outside with me. We sat down on the porch swing. I gave her my cell phone. I tried to put my arms around her, but she shook me off.

At first Emma answered Cheyenne's questions with a yes or a no. But then she started to open up—so much so that she started crying over the phone.

"And my birthday is coming up!" she blurted out.

156

"Don't worry. I'll get you a good present," I said.

Emma ignored me.

I sat and listened. Emma talked about how she didn't think she could go on if her dad wasn't around anymore to help and encourage her. A few minutes later she said she was afraid they'd lose the house and have to move into an apartment and that she'd have to change schools. She said she was afraid there wouldn't be any money for her to go to college.

"Your dad has plenty of money in the stock market, so don't worry about that," I said.

The conversation went on for another half an hour. I couldn't see what it was accomplishing. As far as I could tell, Cheyenne had not given a single solution that would solve the concerns Emma was bringing up. She was just letting Emma unload.

Next, Cheyenne talked to Caleb. She didn't get him to open up as much as Emma had, but he did admit he thought that his dad had died because if he was all right, he would have contacted them by now.

When Cheyenne finished with Caleb, I got back on the phone.

"Ben, could I be of any help to your family if I came out?" she asked.

"I'm okay. You might be able to help Caleb and Emma, though, but how could you even get out here? They've stopped all air travel in the country."

"I could drive."

"It's too dangerous for you to drive out here all alone."

"I did it before. I could do it again."

"But what about school? You'd miss classes if you came out here."

"This is more important."

"You'd better talk to your folks about it."

"I will. I'll call you back after I talk to them."

While I waited for her to call back, I went out to the car

157

and got my suitcase and took it inside. Marilyn was still on the phone, frantically calling around, trying to find out anything she could, leaving names with hospitals and morgues.

"Where do you want me to stay?" I asked.

"The corner bedroom upstairs, next to Emma's room."

"Cheyenne might drive out here to help out," I said.

"That would be wonderful if she could."

I went back into the living room and watched the news coverage. When Cheyenne called, I went in the backyard because I didn't want Emma and Caleb to think Cheyenne was coming, only to be disappointed that her parents wouldn't let her.

"I talked to my folks," she said.

"What did they say?"

"They wanted me to tell you they feel very bad for your family, but they don't think I should go out there. They said that, even though I love you guys like my own family, you're not my family. They're afraid if I go there, I won't come back. So my dad isn't going to let me use his truck to drive out, like he did last time."

"Well, you tried, that's the important thing."

"I *am* coming, Ben."

"How will you get out here?"

"I've decided to drop out of school, take the money I get back from tuition, buy a used car, and then drive out. If all goes well, I'll be on the road by noon tomorrow."

"But why would you do that?"

"Emma and Caleb need me."

"Yes, of course. They do need you." I felt bad she wasn't coming out for me, but then I decided that as long as she came here, it didn't matter what her reasons were.

"You're going to do this against your mom and dad's wishes?" I asked.

She sighed. "Yes. I feel bad about it, but I just can't sit

158

around knowing what Caleb and Emma are going through and not try to do something to help them get through this."

She paused, then added, "My dad accused me of wanting to be there just to be with you. I told him I couldn't believe he would say that."

I tried to hide my disappointment. "Of course. You'd never come out for me."

"Ben, I do love you. You know that, don't you? I'm not sure I want to marry you, but I do love you. And I want to be there for you, too."

"I'm doing okay. You're right. Emma and Caleb are the ones who will need you the most."

Marilyn quit phoning at eleven-thirty. By that time, she had a severe headache. She took some pills and went to bed. My mother went to bed a short time later.

Emma and Caleb and I sat on the couch and watched TV until we fell asleep. I woke up at two-fifteen to use the bathroom. When I returned to the living room, I turned off the TV and draped a blanket around Caleb and Emma and went downstairs.

I went into the kitchen and turned on the light, opened the fridge, but decided there wasn't anything I wanted to eat. I closed the fridge and went to a bulletin board. There on a 3 x 5 card were some phone numbers. One of them was Eugene's cell phone number. I couldn't remember if we'd even tried it. I hadn't since I'd been there.

I punched in the numbers and soon heard that it was ringing.

I pictured Eugene and my dad and my grandfather somewhere in the World Trade Center, physically okay, but trapped in the rubble.

Pick up, will you?

My mind raced. If they picked up, then they'd be able to trace where the signal was coming from, and they could dig there, and find them, and everything would be all right. All they had to do was pick up.

In my mind a picture of their circumstances became more clear. They were in an open area, buried under the rubble, but protected by heavy beams that had wedged together as they fell. Those beams had protected them from being crushed. And not only that, a vending machine from an upper floor had fallen and landed not far from where they were now. And the vending machine had food and water and everything they would need until they were rescued.

It was all so clear in my mind, and it made me very happy to think they were all right.

Maybe this is like a message from God, so I'll know that everything is going to be all right, I thought. *I can hardly wait to tell Emma and Caleb. They'll be so excited.*

I called several times over the next five minutes, but they didn't pick up.

I was a little discouraged at first, but then I reasoned that if they were under tons of rubble, it might be difficult for the signal to get to them, so I went outside and stood in the middle of the front yard and hit redial.

Still, no answer.

Well, maybe they've turned the cell phone off because it's late at night and they'd know we'd be asleep. But in the morning they'll turn it back on and I'll talk to them and then I'll contact the authorities and they'll do some kind of a trace on the call and they'll pinpoint exactly where they are and they'll go in and very carefully go down through the rubble. It might take a day or two, but they'll get them out. I'm sure of it.

I was so excited. I wanted to wake up the whole house and tell everybody not to worry, that they were all right. It was all so clear to me.

I decided to call Cheyenne first and tell her she didn't need to leave school and drive out because they were all right.

I woke her up and told her my good news. "So you won't

need to come out here, after all. Now I'm going to wake up the family and tell everyone."

"Ben, please, don't wake anyone up."

"Why not?"

"Ben, you don't know for sure what you just told me is true."

"How can you say that? You're the one who taught me that a person can be inspired to know something is true."

"Ben, please listen to me. Don't tell anyone about this— especially not Emma and Caleb."

"Why wouldn't I tell them?"

She paused. "Because it isn't true, Ben. It's just something you made up. It's your mind's way of dealing with what happened."

"No, it's true. I'm sure of it. And in the morning, Eugene will wake up and turn on his cell phone, and I'll call him, and then we'll know they're okay. I'd say by noon tomorrow they'll be with us again. You'll see."

"Oh, Ben, I really hope that happens, but please don't tell Emma and Caleb. If what you're saying is true, then it's only a short time before they'll be rescued. But, if it's not true, then you'll have given them false hope, and that's not what they need right now."

"You're wrong about this. You'll see. But, okay, I'll wait."

We ended the conversation. I got in my car and drove as close as I could get to the World Trade Center and be still on Long Island. I pulled over and got out of my car and held my cell phone over my head and pushed redial.

Again and again.

Then moved to a new location and did it.

Again and again.

Then moved to a new location and did it.

Again and again.

It's no use, I thought. *Eugene has turned his cell phone off for the night.*

161

I drove back to Marilyn's and grabbed some blankets and went into the TV room where Caleb and Emma were asleep on the floor and plopped down beside them. I fell asleep thinking, *In the morning I'll get through.*

♦ ♦ ♦

The next morning when I woke up, the first thing I did was go outside and try Eugene again. No answer.

He's sleeping late, I thought. I decided to follow Cheyenne's advice and not say anything to my family until after they'd been rescued.

I found Marilyn in the kitchen. She was going through family photo albums.

"What are you doing?"

"This morning on the news they showed how some families are putting up pictures of their loved ones around the City, in case someone sees them walking the streets in shock."

"Can I help?"

"Yes, of course." She handed me a photo album. "I found this picture of Eugene. It was taken last year, by a girl at a wedding reception. They gave all the children disposable cameras and told them to take pictures of anything they wanted. One girl took this picture. After they got all the pictures developed, the mother of the bride sent it to us. I actually liked it. All the pictures we have of him are from holidays and family vacations."

The picture showed Eugene in his crisp, white caterer's jacket, standing over a huge prime rib roast with his carving tools in hand. He had a big smile on his face, no doubt posing for the girl with the camera.

"To me, this is Eugene," Marilyn said.

"You're right. I liked working with him. He never yelled at me like my dad did."

"Your dad is always uptight when he's working. He wants

everything to be perfect. Eugene is always more relaxed. I think customers respect your father, but they love Eugene."

"So, you think you'll use this picture?"

"Yes, I think so. Now all we have to do is find a picture of your dad and your grandfather."

"We probably have some at home."

"Yes, I'm sure you do. I just thought I'd go through our pictures first, just to see what we had. I'm not sure we have many pictures of your grandfather. I think we quit taking pictures of him."

We continued looking through the albums, some going back to before they were married.

"Is it hard for you to do this?" I asked.

"Actually, it's better for me to keep busy . . . and not think about what might happen to us."

"I'm sure they'll come home today."

"You don't have to keep saying that."

"I'm sure of it, though. You'll see I'm right. Maybe even today."

Marilyn placed her hand on my arm. Her voice was forceful. "If Eugene were alive, he'd have contacted me by now."

"Unless he's buried under the rubble and can't get out. That's probably what's happened. I'm going to call his cell phone all day, and when he picks up they'll be able to pinpoint where they are in the rubble, and they'll go down and get them."

Marilyn patted my arm. "Ben . . ."

"What?"

"If it happens that way, then we'll all be very grateful to God, but we have to accept the idea that they might not come back."

"They could be in a hospital unconscious."

"I called all the hospitals."

"He could be wandering the streets. Like maybe he has amnesia."

163

"Yes, of course. That's why we'll get pictures made and put them up all over once they let people back into the City." She paused. "They're asking people to get dental records of those they've lost. They could be used for identification. So I could use your help today for that. I'll call our dentist and ask him to copy the records, if you can pick them up. Can you go to your mom and dad's home and Granddaddy's place and look for pictures?"

I nodded. "It will give me something to do."

"Yes, it's better to keep busy."

I drove home. On the front porch was that morning's *New York Times,* filled with pictures and articles about the disaster of the day before. I let myself in and went to the kitchen and put the newspaper on the kitchen table. My dad liked to read the paper in the morning before he went to work. Since he often worked late at night, when I was in high school, I'd often get up before him, and on my way out the door sometimes I'd get the paper and put it on the kitchen table.

I realized I was doing that again, just out of habit.

On days when he got up before me, when I went into the kitchen, he'd be at the table reading the paper and enjoying a cup of coffee. All he ever had for breakfast was coffee. I think sometimes when he woke up, after working so hard catering a party the night before, he was sick of food.

Without even thinking about what I was doing, I made coffee. It was just automatic with me. It was a part of our family routine. Coffee in the morning.

I love the smell of coffee, especially in the morning. To me it's the promise of a new day. I know that sounds like I've watched too many Folgers commercials, but it's the way it was for my family when I was growing up.

I knew I wasn't supposed to drink it now because of having been baptized, but I was hurting so much, and it reminded me of the few good memories I had of my dad, that after I got our photo album, I sat down at the kitchen table and drank my coffee while going through the albums.

We didn't have as many family pictures as Marilyn and Eugene had. For one reason, we didn't go on vacations like they did. My dad was always too busy for that—always working, always complaining that Eugene wasn't pulling his weight. In fact, as far as my dad was concerned, nobody who worked for him was worth the money they were getting. Not Eugene, not me certainly. He was the least critical of Hazel, because she'd have quit if he'd given her any grief.

I could find practically no pictures of me with my dad. I knew why. I'd grown up feeling my dad was ashamed of me, or, if not ashamed, at least terribly disappointed I wasn't more like him.

I was okay for a while, and then I opened the newspaper and took a sip of coffee and realized I was doing the same thing I'd seen my dad do hundreds of times before. It hit me that I'd probably never see him again at that table, drinking coffee and reading the newspaper.

I couldn't help it. I started to sob. I could hear myself crying, and it sounded like it had when I was a little boy, except the voice was lower.

My cell phone rang, and I immediately answered it, hoping it was Eugene or my dad. It was Cheyenne. So she wouldn't know I had been crying, I took a deep breath. And I pushed the cup of coffee away from me, knowing what she'd think if she knew I'd been drinking it.

"I'm at the Ford dealership here in Provo. Any suggestions on what I should get?"

"They'll probably be rescued today. Just as soon as Eugene picks up."

"Ben, I'm going to move ahead on this. If I get part way and you call and tell me they've been rescued, then I'll turn around and go back. Okay?"

165

"Okay. I talked to Marilyn. She says it'd be great to have you here, especially for Emma and Caleb."

"Then I'll come. I checked out of school already and got some money back from tuition. I've sold back my books, too. So I've got about fifteen hundred dollars cash, but that's not going to buy much."

"You'll just be buying somebody else's car problems if you buy a car that cheap. Let me help you. I could kick in some money for a loan."

"I didn't call to ask you for money. I just wanted to know what kind of a car would be best. In my family, we buy pick-ups, not cars."

"Why don't you ask your dad for advice?"

"He's too mad at me to give much in the way of advice. I just got off the phone with my folks. My dad told me this is a big mistake and that I'll regret it some day."

"So why are you coming if he's against it?"

"I can't see how wanting to help Emma and Caleb could ever be a mistake."

"Your mom and dad are worried about you and me, aren't they?"

"Yes, actually, they are."

"Tell them they don't have anything to worry about. You're coming out here for Emma and Caleb."

"I'm coming for you, too, Ben."

"You are?"

"Yes, of course. Because we're friends. And friends help friends when there's trouble."

"Yes, we are friends," I said, almost as if I was trying to convince myself that's all we were. "Just friends."

"We're more than just friends."

"I'm glad you think so, too. It's hard to know where this is going, isn't it?"

"It is that, all right."

I asked to speak to a car salesman. When he came on the

line, I told him I'd kick in five thousand dollars. I asked him to find her a very reliable, late model car.

"I've got just the car for her."

I gave him my credit card number and my fax number at work and told him that when I got into work I'd sign it and send it back, but that he should go ahead with the purchase without my signature, since it might be days before I could get back to work.

When Cheyenne came on the line again, I told her what I'd done.

"I can't let you do that."

"Just think of it as a loan. Once things settle down here, Saddlemier will want us to keep doing Great American Family series, so you can pay me back then."

"Well, okay, I guess it's all right then."

I'm not sure why it made me feel so good to be doing this for her. Maybe I liked the idea of her being in debt to me. Maybe I thought that if I was very generous with her, she'd decide to marry me.

After I returned with the pictures, Marilyn and I worked up a flier, using her and Eugene's scanner and computer. Then Marilyn went to a print shop to get some copies made.

By two o'clock, our time, Cheyenne was on I-80 heading east. We promised to keep in touch by cell phone as she drove out.

I went to the catering office to see if Hazel was there. She wasn't. The place was empty.

There were several phone messages, people canceling events that had been scheduled that week.

It was quiet. The only sound was the compressor of a refrigerator going on for a few minutes once in a while. I sat there alone in the office, where a day earlier my father and my Uncle Eugene and my grandfather had worked. I wondered when they had first entered the building the morning before and if they had needed to prepare any of the food they would be serving at the brunch or if they'd prepared it ahead of time. For two hundred people, they would have brought in their part-time staff, people who worked somewhere between five and fifty hours a week. And they would have set up a kind of assembly line. I wondered what it would be. Maybe a tossed salad with burnt almonds fried in brown sugar. I liked that, too. That's what I'd taken from that place: great food and bad memories.

I called Hazel's cell phone. She answered.

"This is Ben. I was just calling to see if you'd heard anything from my dad or Eugene or my grandfather."

"I'm sorry for not calling. I just walked out of the office when I heard what happened. My nephew worked at the South Tower. I'm at my sister's trying to help out. I should have called."

"It's okay. I'm sorry about your nephew. Is it true that my dad and Eugene and my grandfather were doing a brunch yesterday morning at the North Tower?"

"Yes. They'd left before I showed up for work at eight. Have you heard from them?"

"No, we haven't heard anything. Have you heard from your nephew?"

"No."

"I hope he turns up."

"Thanks. I hope the same thing for you."

There was nothing more to say in terms of trying to give comfort.

Hazel had me check what was on the calendar and, if necessary, call and let customers know we weren't prepared to cater that day. I did check, but the only event scheduled was a retirement party, and those folks had already left a message saying they'd canceled it.

I closed up the place and spent the next couple of hours visiting dentists, getting dental records. At the first office, it was a new girl, and she just shrugged and gave me the dental records of Eugene and my grandfather. At the second office, the office manager knew my dad and said she was sorry about what had happened.

"We still have hope they're okay," I said.

"Yes, of course," she said, but I could tell she didn't have any hope.

All through the day, I kept trying to get through to Eugene, but he didn't answer.

I returned to Marilyn's place. We made plans to go into the City the next day. We'd visit all the hospitals and put up fliers everywhere we could.

After supper I told Emma and Caleb that Cheyenne was coming to stay with them for a while. They were very excited, and I had them call her. They talked for a couple of hours, until eleven-thirty, and then Marilyn made them get off the phone and get ready for bed.

Caleb and Emma and I decided to sleep on the floor in front of the TV and watch a movie. After the movie, we got into sleeping bags. I turned off the lights.

"Remember when Cheyenne was at our family reunion?" Emma asked.

"Yes, of course."

"And we played canoe wars?" Emma continued.

"Yes, that was a great day, wasn't it?"

"That's one of my happiest memories," she said.

"We'll do it again next summer."

"Promise?"

"I promise."

"She said I was one of the smartest boys my age she's ever known," Caleb said.

"Hmmm. She said that about you?" I teased. "I wonder why she didn't say that about me?"

"Maybe it's because you're not very smart," Emma teased back.

"You're probably right."

Emma seemed disappointed. "Ben? You gave up too soon."

"This isn't over, my sweet. Oh, no, this is just the beginning. Don't think I won't remember you called me stupid."

"Don't worry, Emma," Caleb said. "If he's as dumb as we think he is, he'll probably forget."

I thought about wrestling with them like we used to do, but it was like there was a slow leak in my usual playful manner with them, and I couldn't do it because the thought came to me that they might already have lost their dad, and how can you horse around on the floor with two kids who are trying to deal with the fact that their father is probably dead.

So I didn't do anything.

And they didn't do anything, either.

That night I dreamed that my dad and Eugene and my grandfather were alive and well. They'd gone deep-sea fishing instead of working that day, and they brought home a tuna, and we cooked it, and it tasted wonderful. My dad told me he was sorry for yelling at me when I worked for him, and he told me that he was going to sell the business and that he and my mom would travel around the world and that everything would be good between us from now on.

It was a wonderful dream. The best I'd ever had. I still remember the way it made me feel.

I still wish it had been true.

10

The next morning, at nine, I woke up on the floor of the TV room with Caleb and Emma draped over me like two extra blankets. I slowly worked to pry myself away without waking them up and finally freed myself so I could go use the bathroom.

A few minutes later, I tiptoed down the stairs and into the kitchen. Marilyn was up and dressed, waiting for me so we could go into the City. She looked haggard and worn, as though she hadn't slept.

I went upstairs and shaved and took a quick shower, then changed into the same clothes I'd been wearing the day before. When I came down, Marilyn suggested I go into their bedroom and see if there were some things of Eugene's I could get into. At first I didn't want to but she said she didn't want to go with me in what I was wearing, so I took her advice.

I stood at their closet looking at Eugene's clothes and wondered what would become of his clothes if he had died.

I don't want any of them, I thought, but then felt guilty because if Marilyn wanted me to have them, then I should take them because otherwise she'd just give them to the Salvation Army, and whoever wore them wouldn't care anything about the person they'd belonged to.

Eugene mostly wore white shirts and conservative ties. I found a white shirt made out of an oxford cloth. I liked the texture of the shirt. If you're going to wear a white shirt, you almost have to wear a tie. I chose a brown silk tie, probably very expensive.

Marilyn smiled when she saw me. "You look nice."

"Thanks," I said with little enthusiasm. I had no interest in dressing like a younger version of my uncle.

We took the Long Island Railroad (LIRR) into the City. After all my warnings to Cheyenne, I noticed that there was now more eye contact and small talk between strangers, people being polite, even thoughtful. Somehow we were all brothers and sisters because of what had happened.

On the way in, I called Cheyenne. She'd spent the night in Grand Island, Nebraska, and was now just passing Omaha.

Marilyn talked to her as well. She thanked her for being willing to come out and spend time with Caleb and Emma.

And then Cheyenne and I talked. With Marilyn listening in to my part of the conversation, I kept having the feeling this was the way Cheyenne and I would talk if we'd been married for a while and had been separated for a short time. We were pleasant to each other, we asked about how we were doing, we gave news about our families. I didn't ask, though, what her dad's reaction had been when he found out she'd dropped out of school and bought a car and was driving out to stay with us.

I did have some bright news, though. I'd heard on the radio that morning that they were holding out some hope that there could be people still alive in the rubble. So I told that to Cheyenne. "So I'm not crazy after all."

172

"As I understand it, there are fires raging underneath. Is that right?" Cheyenne asked.

"Well, yes, but, don't you see, that totally supports the idea that there could be survivors, because if there's fire, then there's oxygen, and if there's oxygen, then that means people could still be alive under the rubble. Of course, they'd have to be in a place away from the fires, but it's still possible."

"Ben?"

"Yes?"

"What are the chances of that happening?"

"Not very good, but you know what, as long as there's still hope, we need to think positively."

"All right, if you say so."

The first place we went to in the City was Bellevue Hospital. People were milling about everywhere, looking for any news about missing loved ones. There, on a wall, were fliers about others who were missing. "We should put up ours, too," Marilyn said.

"I'll do it."

There wasn't much room left, but I could put them in spaces between fliers.

"I think we should put all three together," Marilyn said. "Over there."

What she was suggesting would require me to move two of the fliers a few inches.

I read the one I would need to move. It told about a man, not much older than me, who had two children. One of the children had written, "We love you, Daddy. Please come home."

"I can't move it," I said softly.

"I'll do it then." Marilyn knelt down beside me and put her arm around me. "It's just a few inches. It will be okay. People will still be able to see the ones we move. We just have to make room, that's all. I'll do it." She moved the two fliers for me.

"Would you like to put ours up?" she asked.

I nodded my head and carefully placed our three fliers on the wall.

We stayed there for over an hour, reading the others, crying together, holding each other. The saddest were the ones drawn in crayon by children, and the poems and sweet messages written by husbands and wives and older sons and daughters.

We went inside to check if they had admitted my dad or Eugene or my grandfather.

The woman at the desk checked her records. "No, I'm sorry, they're not here. Are you aware that The Greater New York Hospital Association has a website you can use?" She handed us a card with the name of the website and instructions on how to use it. "Once you get into the site, click on Patient Locator System. That way you don't have to visit every hospital individually. It will save you time."

"I don't have much left these days except time," Marilyn said in a dull monotone.

"Yes, of course, I'm sorry. I just wanted to help, that's all. You can use the computer over there if you'd like."

We walked away.

Marilyn shook her head. "Eugene hated websites. He used to say the Internet is making us a nation of robots."

"Do you want me to check for you?" I asked. "She's right, it will save us time."

"I would crawl on my hands and knees to every hospital if it'd make any difference. What do I do if we check the Internet site? If we can learn everything from this website, then what's left for me to do? What can I do to fill up my days then?"

She broke down crying. I held her in my arms. And then she said, "I'd better sit down. I feel a little faint."

We sat down. For a while we just sat there and watched others coming to see if their loved ones were there.

I decided we human beings come in a variety of sizes,

shapes, and ethnicity, but it's our common grief that makes us brothers and sisters.

Finally, after about an hour, Marilyn turned to me and said, "You'd better check the website. If they are in a hospital, it will speed up the time when we'll be with them."

I went to the computer and found no record of our family members on the Patient Locator. I returned to Marilyn and shook my head. "There's nothing."

She nodded. "Let's go then."

"Where?"

"I don't know. Some place. We have to go some place."

We went outside and started walking.

"Where are we going?" I asked.

She sighed. "Let's go to Union Square. There's a memorial there to the victims. I saw it on TV."

"Do you want to take a taxi?"

"No. I want to walk."

We were walking more slowly than anyone else, so we were passed by others in a hurry. I wondered where they were all going.

"Before Eugene and I were married, he took me to a Broadway play. We saw *Cats.*"

"Did you like it?"

"I did, but he didn't. He said it was too much money to see a bunch of neurotic dancers prancing around the stage in their underwear pretending to be cats."

"What did he expect from a play called *Cats*?" I asked.

"I never asked." She sighed. "I never asked."

At Union Square, we stood for a long time and looked at the posters and photographs, the tiny American flags, the flowers, the teddy bears, the notes, the written prayers. Others came and looked and cried and then went on.

We added our fliers to the wall and then stepped back. "There are so many," Marilyn said.

"Yes."

"How could this have happened?"

"I don't know."

We must have stood there for an hour, and then Marilyn said, "We have to go to where the World Trade Center was . . . or at least as close as we can get."

"That will be difficult to do."

"How do you mean difficult? That they won't let us or that it will be very sad?"

"Both."

"I have to go. I have to be there. I have to see for myself. It's the closest I'll get to Eugene and the closest you'll get to your father and your grandfather."

Once again we started walking. But we were stopped less than a block from where we'd started. Yellow police tape and a police car blocked all traffic.

We tried to go past but were intercepted by a policeman. "All traffic south of Fourteenth Street is closed."

"My husband was in the World Trade Center."

"I'm sorry, lady. But I still can't let you through."

"We won't get in the way."

He shook his head. "There's too much going on down there. You'll get a chance to come to the site later, but not today."

A man standing nearby said to us. "I heard they found someone in the rubble today. A woman. She's alive. They took her to the hospital. They say she's going to survive."

"That's good they found someone," I said to Marilyn. "Maybe they'll find others, too."

"Well, I guess we'll just have to see what happens," the policeman said.

Marilyn turned and started walking back the way we'd come.

"Maybe they'll find Eugene and my dad and Granddaddy today," I said.

"Yes, maybe so," Marilyn said without much conviction.

"We can only hope and pray," I said.

176

She looked at me with a puzzled expression. "How can I believe in a God who doesn't care enough about us to protect us from men who would do such a terrible thing to innocent men, women, and children?"

I had no answer to that question, either.

We spent the next few hours walking around, putting up fliers where others had done so before us.

We passed a group of singers on one of the streets. They were singing gospel songs. It was like everyone was stunned. Strangers talked to each other, and people were more polite than usual, as though they felt a kinship in the face of the overwhelming tragedy. Some were handing out fliers with their missing loved one's picture on it. Large trucks rumbled by, hauling away debris from the site of the disaster. Firemen were cheered as they went to take a break before returning to work, digging through the debris, searching for any survivors.

As we walked, I searched the crowds hoping to catch a glimpse of my dad or Eugene or my grandfather.

We stopped at a café and watched the news on TV. The attack and its awful aftermath had consumed the nation.

Marilyn said she wasn't hungry but agreed to split a BLT on rye, and we both had coffee. I thought about having orange juice, but I couldn't do it. Coffee is what I wanted.

Around two in the afternoon, we went home.

That night I checked my voice mail. I had a message from Saddlemier. I called him. He wasn't in, which was just as well. I left him a voice mail, telling him about my family and about Cheyenne coming out to stay with us. I told him we'd contact him. I also called Ross, my boss, and talked to him, telling him essentially the same thing.

Nothing to hope for except for the arrival of Cheyenne. She was my one hope for the future.

I could hardly wait until she arrived.

11

Cheyenne spent the night just outside Toledo, Ohio. When she called from her motel, she said she thought she'd be able to make it to us the next day.

The next morning Marilyn approached me, somewhat apologetically. "Ben, I don't mean to intrude into your private life, but I need to work out sleeping arrangements. Will you and Cheyenne be staying in the same bedroom?"

"No. We'll be in separate rooms."

Marilyn nodded. "I had to ask. One never knows these days."

"Cheyenne has always been a good girl."

For the last fifty miles, Cheyenne and I stayed in contact on our cell phones so I could guide her in.

At nine-forty-five that night, when she pulled into the driveway, I ran out to welcome her. When she got out of the car, she stumbled with her first couple of steps, from sitting in the same position for so long.

We threw our arms around each other and just held on. "Thank you for coming," I whispered in her ear.

"I had to come."

We started inside. "You must be exhausted," I said.

"Just tired of driving. I need some exercise in the worst way, and then I'll be okay."

I carried her bags into the house. I was surprised she'd brought so much, then realized it was everything she'd taken to school for the semester.

Once inside, Marilyn came, and they hugged. "Thank you so much for coming."

"Thank you for having me."

My mom was in front of the TV, much as she'd been for the past four days, not saying much, just watching. Cheyenne knelt beside her and kissed her on the cheek. My mother looked over at her as though she were a stranger.

"It's Cheyenne, Mom," I said. "She's come to be with us."

"They're dead. They're all dead."

"Isn't it terrible that such a thing could happen?" Cheyenne said and began to cry.

My mom nodded. "Yes, it is. It's terrible."

Cheyenne took my mom's hand.

"They're dead. They're all dead," my mom repeated.

I couldn't take it. It was bad enough what had happened, but I couldn't deal with my mom not being able to cope with our loss. She'd always been able to help me when I was in trouble. Her being confused and depressed made everything worse.

With Cheyenne talking to my mom, I went in the kitchen to make myself a cup of coffee. It suddenly hit me that Cheyenne might find out I was drinking coffee again. But I was going through a tough time, and I craved the things that had always brought me comfort—like a cup of coffee.

It wasn't just me as I found out later. One of the ways the entire nation reacted to 9/11 was to seek comfort foods, those things from the past that people associate with happier times.

179

Things like Campbell's Tomato Soup, and turkey with all the trimmings.

For me it was coffee. I'd always associated a cup of coffee with a gathering of friends. I'd grown up around people who loved to get together for a cup of coffee.

Cheyenne was still in the living room with my mother, so she didn't know what was going on with me over the issue of coffee.

Poor Marilyn, working at the kitchen table, going over Eugene's life insurance policy and a record of his investments, must have wondered what was going on. First, I made myself a cup of instant coffee in the microwave, then poured it into the sink. And then I made myself a cup of hot chocolate, took a sip, swore, and then poured that out, too. Then I mumbled something about "being a man" and made myself a pot of coffee in the coffeemaker. But I was afraid Cheyenne would be able to smell it in the living room, and she'd come out and bust me, so I threw it out and turned on the fan above the stove.

Marilyn didn't even look up from her work. "Ben, will you please make up your mind?"

"She thinks she can run my life, doesn't she?"

"Who are you talking about?"

"Cheyenne."

"Cheyenne doesn't care if you drink coffee or not."

"No, that's where you're wrong. She cares. She won't marry me if I'm drinking coffee."

Marilyn shrugged. "Then quit drinking coffee."

"Why should I?"

"If you want to marry her, then quit drinking coffee. It seems a perfectly reasonable, although somewhat quirky, conclusion."

"But, don't you see, it won't end with coffee. Oh, no, it will just keep going on and on and on. She won't settle for anything less than a temple marriage. And then it'll get worse.

Home teaching, family prayer morning and night, storing wheat, grinding wheat, having a garden, writing in a journal, it just never ends. You know what? Mormons teach that a marriage can last forever. Well, maybe it's not that the marriage lasts forever. Maybe it just seems like forever."

She turned to face me and with a surprising intensity asked, "Are you telling me that Mormons believe a marriage can last forever?"

"Yeah, so?"

"Why haven't you told me about this before?"

"Why would you want to know?"

Her lower lip quivered. "If you think about it hard enough, you'll probably be able to answer that question yourself."

Once again I felt like an idiot. "I'm sorry. If you want to know more, ask Cheyenne."

I opened the fridge, poured myself a glass of orange juice, and went outside and sat on the porch.

A short time later, Cheyenne left my mom and went upstairs to talk to Caleb and Emma.

She came down an hour later. I could tell by how red her eyes were that she'd been crying. "I'm ready for that walk now," she said.

At first we walked fast but didn't say much. "It feels so good to finally get some exercise," she said.

"That's a long way to drive in three days."

"Especially knowing my mom and dad were against the idea. This is the first time in my life I've gone against their wishes."

"Eventually, they'll see that you were right to come out here."

"I hope you're right." She took my arm and let out a troubled sigh. "I did have a good talk with Caleb and Emma, though, so that's good."

"They love you."

"I love them, too. Very much."

We ended up at a park. I tried to kiss her, but she turned away. "Ben, I don't think we should kiss while we're living in the same house."

"Why's that?"

"My dad warned me that if I came out here to stay that eventually you and I would end up sleeping together."

"He's never liked me."

"It's not that."

"Yes, it is , and you know it. Well, we'll just have to prove him wrong then, won't we?"

"Yes, let's do that. And we can still give each other hugs, which I could use right now."

She came into my arms, and we held each other tight. "This feels very good," she said.

"Hugs are good."

"Let's head back," she said.

When we got back, Emma was mad at us for not taking her. "I need some exercise, too."

"It's too late to go on a walk," I said.

As usual Cheyenne had a solution. "I know. You guys want me to lead you through an aerobics routine?"

"Oh, yeah, that'd be great!" Emma said.

It took us fifteen minutes to get it all arranged. Marilyn loaned me a jogging outfit she'd given to Eugene for Christmas, which he'd never used. We decided to do it in their garage where we'd be far enough away from the house not to disturb my mother and also have some privacy and not disturb the neighbors.

I had no worries about not being able to keep up. After all, I was a guy.

The shorts Cheyenne was wearing were baggy and went down past her knees. She was also wearing an extra large BYU T-shirt.

When we first started, I felt so superior. We were just marching in step.

"Caleb, after this is done, we men may still need some exercise, so maybe we can play a little one-on-one basketball, okay?"

"Right," he said.

After ten minutes I was so bushed I could hardly keep up. Cheyenne didn't look tired and, in fact, seemed to be as enthusiastic as ever. "One . . . two . . . three . . . four . . . Lookin' good . . . except for Ben . . . Pick up the pace, Ben, okay?"

Caleb wasn't doing much better. "I thought you said this was going to be easy," he puffed.

"This is girls' exercise, Caleb. We're not expected to be good at it."

Caleb and I dropped out.

Emma kept in step with Cheyenne for the entire twenty-minute workout.

"Okay, Emma! You go, girl!" Cheyenne cheered her on.

When they finished, Cheyenne told Emma how proud she was of her, and for a brief second, Emma was happy, and then her lips turned, and she became very sad and then began sobbing.

Cheyenne held her in her arms. "What's wrong?"

"I started to think that if my dad were here, he'd be proud of me and tell me how good I'd done . . . and . . . he's not here."

Emma cried in Cheyenne's arms. And then Caleb fought back tears and ran outside.

I ran after Caleb and caught up with him half a block later.

He stood there, under a streetlight, all alone.

"This is tough, isn't it?" I said.

He nodded, and the tears rolled down his cheeks. I stood

there awkwardly for minute, then went to him and held him and let him cry.

I had nothing to say to him. Certainly nothing about his father being still alive in the rubble.

The four of us ended up in the TV room on the second floor. Emma suggested we all sleep there on the floor. And because we couldn't sleep, we watched a movie.

Caleb was the first one to fall asleep, and then Emma, leaving Cheyenne and me still awake.

"How come you're still awake?" I asked.

"I'm on Mountain Time. It's two hours earlier for me. You'd better get some sleep."

We kept the movie running because if it stopped, then it was no longer a party. And we had to have it be a party or the reality of the situation would fill the room with sorrow.

The next morning when I woke up, I looked at the clock. It was nine-forty-five. Caleb and Emma were asleep next to Cheyenne. Emma's arm was resting on Cheyenne, and Caleb's leg was draped across the bottom of Cheyenne's sleeping bag.

When Cheyenne first woke up, she saw me lying beside her and panicked, then realized where she was and relaxed once again. "We're the sleepyheads, aren't we?"

"We are."

"Will Caleb and Emma be returning to school on Monday?" she asked.

"Yes, at least that's what Marilyn wants them to do."

"I think it will be good for them to get back into a familiar routine."

"I probably need to go back to work on Monday. I'm sure Saddlemier would love to see us working together again."

"I'd like to be here when Caleb and Emma get home from school in the afternoons."

"I'm sure that can be arranged."

"Do you know if Caleb and Emma were in the habit of attending church services?"

"I'm not sure. If they did, it was because Marilyn took them."

"I hope they can go to their church on Sunday."

"Yes, it might help them deal with this."

Cheyenne worked loose from Emma's arm and sat up. "Well, I guess I'll be the first one to take a shower." She smiled. "So at least I'll have plenty of hot water."

"In our family, we have a very strict two-minute shower limit," I said sternly.

"Nice try, Beady, nice try."

While she was taking a shower, I went downstairs.

Marilyn was at the kitchen table, on the phone, calling around to see if anyone had any news for us.

"I see. Well, thank you. Good-bye." She hung up the phone, made a small check by the name on the list, and then looked at me.

"Find out anything?" I asked.

"No. It's the same as yesterday. No news."

"It's just a matter of time," I said.

"Is it? I'm not sure. They say that the heat of the jet fuel burning may have vaporized many of the bodies, so they may never find any trace of them."

"I still think they're alive."

"I don't. Not anymore."

"Then why do you keep checking back?"

She shrugged. "I have to do something. How do you handle this?"

"It's not as great a loss for me as it is for you."

"Why's that?"

"My dad and I weren't that close. I wasn't his fair-haired son anymore. He had no respect for me. He felt like I'd betrayed the family by not going into the catering business, so, you see, it's no great loss for me."

She shook her head. "It will be even worse for you, then. Maybe not now, but someday."

"Why do you say that?"

"Because there will be greater regrets."

I shook my head. "I don't think so."

"And what about the loss of all the men in your family? You're going to have to step up. You have a responsibility to Caleb now—to teach him what it means to be a Morelli."

"It means making your son feel like he's a complete failure. That's what it means."

"Oh, grow up, Ben! Forget about it. That was a long time ago. Get over what happened in the past and be a man for once in your life."

Marilyn had never spoken to me like that before, and it made me so mad at her I swore and went outside. She followed me outside. "Don't you talk to me like that!" she yelled. "May I remind you that you're a guest in my house. I don't appreciate you talking like that around Caleb and Emma."

"They didn't hear what I said. They're still asleep."

I wanted to get in a shouting match with Marilyn. I think we would have both enjoyed it, but then I realized that if I did, I would probably get myself thrown out, and then I would have no access to Cheyenne. So, for that reason alone, I backed off. "I'm sorry. I shouldn't have lost my temper like that."

"You're just like your dad sometimes."

She might as well have slapped my face as tell me that. Being like my dad was the last thing in the world I wanted. I needed to talk to Cheyenne.

She was out of the bathroom. I knocked on her bedroom door.

"Yes, what is it?"

"Can I come in?"

"No. I'll be out in a couple of minutes."

I talked to her through the door. "I just wanted to inform you that you took an extra eight minutes in the shower."

"What does that mean, Beady?"

"No showers for you for three days."

"Really? You people are very strict."

"Yes, it's true, things are different here. We're not like you people in Idaho. We don't have the Snake River running through our state."

She opened the door and came out. She was wearing jeans and a sweatshirt, and her hair was combed down but still damp.

Just looking at her made me feel better. I loved her face. Like the ranch she came from, her beauty was simple and natural.

"Whatever you do today, can I be with you?" I asked.

"I'll just be with the kids. You're welcome to join us."

We had a contest to see who could make the most noise as we clomped down the stairs, then went into the living room. My mother was there, watching CNN as she had done constantly for the past few days.

I had mostly ignored my mother. Maybe it was because all she did was watch the news. She had gone into a deep depression, and nothing anyone could do seemed to do any good. So I left her alone. I know that sounds cruel, but I didn't know what else to do.

Whatever I did in life, I wanted it to count, to be measurable, to show progress, to make a difference. I didn't do well with things that didn't change no matter how hard I tried. Like waiting to hear word they had found the bodies of my father, my uncle, and my grandfather.

Cheyenne didn't seem to have that kind of high expectation.

"Good morning!" she said to my mom with a kindly smile, kneeling down so she could have more direct eye contact.

"They're dead. They're all dead."

Cheyenne took her hand. "Mom, can I do your hair today?

I think it needs it. If you want, we can wash it in the sink. I could even give you a perm. My mom does that all the time to her hair. She showed me, so I know how to do it."

Mom's voice sounded hollow. "It would be nice to have a perm."

"Okay, let's get you going. Would you like to have a bath, too? A warm bath can be nice. I wish we had bubbles. I always liked a bubble bath when I was a kid. Did you?"

"Yes, I did as a matter of fact."

Cheyenne helped my mom into the bathroom and closed the door.

Half an hour later, she opened the bathroom door and asked me if I could go home and get some of my mother's clothes.

"I wouldn't know what to bring."

"Bring everything then," she said, then closed the door.

I drove home, went to the garage where we kept our suitcases, and then proceeded into my parents' bedroom. The room seemed empty and cold and desolate. More like a morgue really than a bedroom. I felt a cold chill as I gazed into my parents' closet. On the right were my father's clothes: three black tux pants, three starched white shirts, and three black vests. To the right of that was a bow tie holder containing half a dozen bow ties. All of this, of course, was used in his role as a caterer. Not much else in his closet. One pair of slacks for when he worked around the house, two sports shirts, long-sleeved. On the closet floor were four pairs of black shoes, each shined to his high standards.

There was a sense of formality even in his closet and, once again, I felt bad for offenses committed long ago, offenses for which I might never be forgiven as long as I lived. Like putting the napkin on the right side under the knife instead of on the left side under the fork. Or having one of the guests see me sneak one of the cream puffs the host had paid for and eat it when I thought nobody was watching. Or, of course, the incident when I put my hand on a classmate's shoulder while serving food. That was the most painful to me. Being humiliated in public by the girl's grandfather, and then receiving a tongue-lashing in private in the kitchen, and then having the girl never speak to me again because I was, from then on, just one of the help.

For years I had never talked to my father about how that one event had put up a barrier between him and me. If I'd said something, he might have said, "I can't even remember that, but if I made you feel bad, I'm sorry." And I would have said, "All I wanted was to make you proud of me. I tried so hard to do everything you told me to do. The only reason I put my hand on the girl's shoulder is because we were friends from high school, and I wanted her to know it was me because she never looked at the help much, because she'd been taught that they were not like her, they were underlings, inferior, not to be given the same treatment as friends. I'm sorry I embarrassed you."

And what would he have said?

I don't know.

Now that he's gone, I'll never know. There's so much we should have said to each other. We should have talked until we were no longer distant and remote, until we could throw our arms around each other and say how much we loved each other.

He can't be dead, not now, when I can see so clearly how we could be reconciled and that we could be father and son again, the way it was when I was very young, before I started to work for him, when he spent mornings with me, and we went to the park, and he swung me higher than my mother would, or when he even went down the slide with me, the only father who did. But even in going down the slide, his back was upright, he had good posture, and when he got off the slide, he pulled out a white handkerchief and wiped his hands and checked his clothes to make sure they were still clean, without dust.

He can't be dead. Not now. Now when I need him so badly. Not when I can see how we can fix our relationship.

Maybe he's still alive, though. Maybe if I try Eugene's cell phone this time, he'll pick up.

I did try his cell phone. No answer.

Maybe the battery in his cell phone has gone dead. I bet that's it. He tried until the batteries went dead. So they'll just have to dig through the rubble until they find Eugene and my dad and Granddaddy.

They pulled that woman out, and everyone thought she was dead, so maybe they'll pull my father out and maybe Eugene and maybe Granddaddy. Maybe we'll be together again tonight. Or tomorrow. Or the day after.

I felt good again, hopeful that my thoughts were in some way inspiration to me not to worry, that everything was going to be all right.

If my dad is coming back today, there's really no need for me to empty out my mom's things and take them to Marilyn's. I'll just have to haul them back later today.

I'll call and tell Cheyenne my good news.

I went into the kitchen and picked up the phone and started to dial.

And then I stopped.

Anticipating Cheyenne's response.

Recalling the pictures of the World Trade Center from CNN.

Knowing that very few more would be found alive.

Who am I kidding? They're gone. There comes a time when you have to face reality. They're dead. They're all dead.

I had to force myself to go back into my parents' bedroom.

I had to pull everything out of my mother's closet, but I was haunted by the black tuxedo pants and vests neatly hung, crisp, clean, and impenetrable.

I quickly grabbed my mother's things from the closet and threw them on the bed and went back for what I'd missed, then bent down and gathered up my mother's shoes and tossed them behind me, and then I closed the closet.

I dumped everything from my mother's dresser into one suitcase, tossed the shoes into another suitcase, then went into the bathroom and opened the medicine cabinet and, holding a suitcase over the sink, shoveled my mother's things off the shelf into the suitcase, ran into the bedroom, grabbed as many of the clothes on hangers as I could carry, then ran them out to the car. In all, I made four trips before I'd cleared out my mother's things.

On my way back to Marilyn's, I drove too fast because I was being chased by my memories of the past.

When I got home, Marilyn's car was gone. I went in and asked Cheyenne where Marilyn was. She told me Marilyn had taken Emma and Caleb out to lunch.

I dutifully carried my mother's things to the room she was staying in, hung them up as best I could, put her shoes in the closet, and piled neatly on the bed the things that had come from the drawers.

Cheyenne picked out a dress for my mother, then fussed with her in the bathroom, and then brought her out.

"Well, here's your mom, Ben!"

I turned and looked. My mother, looking happy but fragile at the same time, as if her smile might at any moment turn into tears, walked timidly from the bathroom, her hair looking better than it had for a long time.

"Mom, you look great!"

"Cheyenne did it."

"Well, she did a fantastic job!"

She smiled at me, then walked to her place in the living room, turned on the TV, and began watching CNN again. Her smile, frightened at the terror of the hour, withdrew once more.

"They're dead. They're all dead," she muttered, back again in the place she'd been before Cheyenne had tried to rescue her.

"Mom, would you like to have lunch in the kitchen?" Cheyenne asked. "Or outside in the backyard. It's such a beautiful day."

"I'm not hungry, thank you."

Cheyenne and I retreated into the kitchen.

"Thank you for trying to help my mother," I said.

"For a while, she was like her old self."

I checked by voice mail and found I had a message from Harold Saddlemeier. "The nation has gone through a terrible ordeal. We need hope now, Ben. The nation needs comfort foods. Call me please."

I had Cheyenne listen to the message, then let her know what I thought of it. "Comfort food! He thinks the country needs comfort food? I lost my father and my uncle and my grandfather! And he thinks a bowl of corn flakes is going to make it all better?"

Cheyenne tried to calm me down. We held each other tightly.

"This is too much for me to handle," I confessed.

"I know, Ben. It's just awful."

We heard the sound of car doors closing. Just before Caleb and Emma and Marilyn came into the house, we separated and acted like nothing had happened.

Acting like nothing has happened is one thing I'm very good at.

12

We fell into a predictable pattern in the next week. In the evening, Cheyenne and I played games or watched videos with Caleb and Emma. When it was time for bed, we crawled into our sleeping bags and slept together in the TV room—Cheyenne in between Caleb and Emma on the floor, and me on the couch. It wasn't the best arrangement, but even though they weren't little kids anymore, in the aftermath of the Twin Towers attack, they were reluctant to sleep alone in their rooms.

On Monday, September 17, school started up again. Cheyenne and I drove Emma and Caleb to school that morning and told them we'd pick them up after it was over. It seemed too soon for them to go back to school, but Marilyn felt that if we waited much longer they wouldn't want to ever go back. They seemed reluctant to be in large crowds.

I called Ross and Saddlemier and told them I wasn't ready to go back to work. They said they understood.

I also checked the Patient Locator for the New York

hospitals. Marilyn made a few phone calls and found that nothing had changed.

That morning Marilyn went through their long-term investments and Eugene's life insurance in detail. Managing their financial affairs was something Eugene had always insisted on doing, although he tended to go along with whatever stock tips or investment strategies my father came up with.

"What company has ticker symbol ENRNQ?" she asked.

"I'm not sure. Why do you ask?"

"Eugene has invested in them quite heavily. I wonder why."

"Must be a good investment. I bet my dad gave him a good stock tip."

"Is it possible to find out about it on the Internet?" she asked.

"Sure, I can do that."

I went to nytimes.com and in a short time I had a graph showing the price per share over the past year. The company was called Enron, and it had gone from eighty dollars a share in September 2000, down to a little over thirty dollars a share, but then, of course, the entire stock market was down. I decided not to worry Marilyn, thinking that in a short time it would go back up to where it had been.

"It's down a little, but I'm sure it will go back up. No matter what happens, we're always going to need more energy."

"Thanks for checking, Ben."

After lunch Marilyn decided to work in the backyard. I was helping Cheyenne with the dishes. Well, to be more exact, I was standing around talking to her while she did the dishes.

"How come I'm doing all the work?" Cheyenne asked with a grin.

"What, you think I'm either not willing or incapable of washing a few dishes?"

"That's what I'm thinking, all right."

"Stand aside, woman, and I'll take over."

She stepped aside and grabbed a towel to dry her hands. "Be my guest."

I began washing the dishes.

"I've got to get my camera to record this."

"For our kids to see?"

She started to blush. "Anything's possible I suppose."

The phone rang.

Cheyenne answered. "Hello . . . Just a minute." She held the phone out to me. "It's for you."

"Put it on speaker phone."

"Hello?"

"I hate to bother you at home, but I haven't been able to make contact with anyone in the office. My daughter Morgan is getting married on Friday and, with all that's happened the past week, I just wanted to confirm that you're still planning on providing the catering."

"Well, the truth is . . ."

Cheyenne put her index finger on my mouth and shook her head.

"Excuse me," I said. "I have another call coming in. Can I put you on hold?"

"Yes, of course."

Cheyenne put the phone on mute.

"What?"

"This is the biggest day of any girl's life . . . and the biggest day for her mother, too. A bride deserves to have her dreams come true on her wedding day."

"She can get someone else."

"Do you have any idea how much stress that would put on the mother of the bride?"

"So?"

"We could do it, Beady."

"Are you crazy?"

195

"Look, back in my campus ward I'm a cochairman of the activities committee. I plan ward parties all the time. You did weddings before with your dad, didn't you?"

"Yes, but I just showed up and did what my dad told me to do."

"C'mon, we can't abandon this mother. Let's tell her we'll do it."

"I don't like doing this kind of work."

"It's just for one time. It won't kill you, and, besides, we'll be working on it together."

I dried my hands, switched the phone back to speaker, and said, "Sorry, for the delay."

Cheyenne got a pad of paper to write down information.

"I'm not at my office right now, so let me just get, once again, the details for your reception."

Ten minutes later, we were off the phone. The first thing I did was phone Hazel, my dad's secretary. She answered on the first ring. I knew why. She was waiting to hear about her nephew.

I asked her if she could help us.

"I need to be home in case they call."

"I understand. I'm sorry about your nephew."

"I'm sorry about your loss also. I wish I could help you, but I can't. All I do is watch the news, hoping they'll have some word about survivors."

"I know."

"I wish I could help," she said again. "Someday I'll come back."

"You're fine, really. Maybe if you could just get me going. I need to get hold of some of the people who worked part-time for my dad and Eugene."

"Get a piece of paper and I'll give you some names. You can find their phone numbers in the office in a black book in the center drawer of my desk."

Cheyenne wrote down the names as Hazel gave them to

196

us. And then we drove to Morelli and Sons, found the phone numbers, and started calling. An hour later, we had five people lined up who agreed to work the wedding reception.

On the way home, Cheyenne said, "Ben, I have an idea."

"What?"

"What would you think about asking Caleb and Emma to help us?"

"That's a dumb idea."

"Why? Because you had such a bad experience when you were growing up working for your dad? That doesn't matter now. I know you'd never yell at them like your dad did at you."

"What would be the point?"

"It would be a way they could honor their father."

"Their dad is probably still alive. In fact, he and my dad and my grandfather will probably show up in time to cater the wedding. They'll dig their way out of whatever open area they're in, take a shower, and be ready to go to work."

Cheyenne put her hand on my arm. "I know you wish that were true."

"Go ahead and say it. I mean you know everything, right? You're the world's expert on every topic. Catering? 'Hey, no problem. I do that all the time.' Right? I mean isn't that how it is with you? Do you ever pity me because I'm so weak, so incapable of doing anything without your help? Or do you just consider it your life's work to bail me out of every crisis and answer every question and fix every problem?"

We pulled into the driveway. I got out of the car and went inside.

Cheyenne came in, went to her room, and came out a few minutes later in sweats and running shoes. "I'm going to get some exercise. I'll be back in an hour."

We glanced at each other and then looked away.

"Good riddance," I said softly as the front door closed.

197

I felt miserable that she'd left me, even to go jogging, but even worse for the things I'd said.

I walked into the kitchen to talk to Marilyn.

She glanced up from what she was doing on the kitchen table. "You okay?"

"Why shouldn't I be?"

"Where's Cheyenne?"

"Running. Maybe she'll find a marathon she can win and bring us back a trophy. Or maybe it'll be a down day for her, and she'll just rescue a child from a burning building."

"You're mad at her because she's strong and capable?"

"No," I said, but in my heart I knew Marilyn was right.

"Look, she's knocking herself out to make things better for us. Why is that such a terrible thing to do?"

I let out a large sigh. "It isn't. It's just that . . ."

"What?"

"I have nothing to give back in return."

"That would be paying for her services, Ben. That's not the way it works with love."

I went to the cupboard. "I'm going to make up some coffee. Would you like some?"

"No. You don't want any, either, Ben."

"I don't?"

"Are you in love with Cheyenne or not?"

"I'm not sure. I just know that I can't live without her."

Marilyn smiled. "Some would interpret that as love."

"I suppose."

"Do you tell her you love her every day?"

"No. I did once, though."

"Once is not enough. You need to do it every day. Eugene did."

"My dad never did. At least, if he did, I never heard it."

"Your father was not as affectionate as Eugene. I would suggest you tell Cheyenne you love her every day."

"This is so weird. Everyone gives me advice about how to

win Cheyenne over. Emma has. Caleb has. You have. Eugene did. It's like a TV dating game show where the audience gives advice."

"Is it a crime to want Cheyenne to be a permanent part of our family?" she asked.

"I guess not."

I wandered out of the kitchen and sat on the porch and waited for Cheyenne to return.

I could see her coming a block away, moving in long, even strides, her hair tied up so it wouldn't flop around.

She stopped in front of the house and then walked up the sidewalk. Half the distance between the curb and the porch, she saw me and stopped, wary of how I'd be, no doubt wondering if I would continue to harass her.

"Uh . . . I . . . need to apologize to you for blowing up. I said some things I shouldn't have said. I'm sorry."

"It's okay, don't worry about it," she said, coming toward me on her way inside. "I'm sweaty. I'm going to take a shower."

"I love you," I said just after she passed me on the steps of the porch.

She turned and, with a smile, said, "I say I'm sweaty and you say you love me. Is there some connection between those two statements?"

"Probably not, but it's true."

"Which one is true? That I'm sweaty or that you love me?"

I looked at her face. It was beaded with sweat. "Actually, both statements are true."

"You have the worst sense of timing of anyone I've ever met. I'll talk to you after my shower." With that she started inside and then stopped and came back.

"Beady?"

"Yes."

"I love you, too," she said.

"You do?"

"I do."

"I'm glad."

While Cheyenne was taking a shower, I went into the living room and sat on the sofa next to my mom. I grabbed the remote and turned off CNN.

"Mom, I'm not sure it's such a good idea to watch this all the time."

"I have to watch."

"Why, Mom?"

"I have to know exactly what happened."

"We may never know that. Mom, as terrible as it was, we have to move on. That's one thing Cheyenne is trying to teach me. At some time, we have to move on and live our own lives. In fact, that's how we honor our loved ones, by moving on, by trying to live the way they'd want us to live."

My mom reached for the remote, took it from my hand, and turned the TV back on.

"You look very nice today, Mom. Do you remember Cheyenne helping you with a bath and giving you a perm?"

I'm not sure she even heard the question.

I went to the bathroom door. "Are you done with your shower?"

"Yes."

"Can I come in then?"

"Go away and quit being such a pest."

"I could dry your back for you."

"Are you crazy? Listen to me, you'd better be away from this door by the time I count to ten. One . . ."

"Okay, I'm going. But don't blame me if you get a rash because your back isn't completely dry."

"Get out of town!" It was a New York expression used badly, but at least she tried.

"I'll be on the porch."

"Thanks for the warning. I'll avoid the porch."

"Very funny."

While I waited for her, I made us both a cup of peppermint tea and put some chocolate chip cookies on a plate. And because I'm the son of a caterer, I remembered napkins.

She came out a few minutes later, looking radiantly alive and relaxed.

"I thought we could have a peppermint tea party."

"Okay. Actually, milk is my favorite drink with cookies."

"And I'm sure that's great if you're from a big dairy state like Idaho."

She sat down closer to me than was necessary, given how big the porch swing was.

"What was that all about back there, you asking if you could come in and dry my back?"

"I don't know where that came from."

"You suppose the fact that we're living in the same house might have something to do with it?" she asked.

"Could be."

"We need to be careful, Ben."

"I know. We will be."

"You think we should keep on sleeping in the same room, even though Emma and Caleb are always there with us?"

"Nothing will happen."

"I know, but still. I am always aware that you're only a few feet away," she said.

"I also have that awareness," I said.

"I just don't want anything to happen."

"Nothing will happen. I guarantee it."

She let out of sigh of relief. "Thanks. You want to know a secret? When you asked if you could come in and dry my back, my first reaction was, sure, why not? Isn't it strange that I would think that? I mean it was like, for a moment, I thought we were actually married, and it'd be okay for you to come in."

"That is very interesting," I said, trying to control my raging hormones.

She cuddled next to me and rested her head on my shoulder, and we just stayed there, enjoying the closeness we felt.

Just before we fell asleep, I whispered in her ear, "I love you."

"I love you, too, Ben."

I was impressed. She only called me Ben when she was serious or wanted a big favor.

Later that afternoon, I decided Cheyenne was right about having the kids help us. That night we told Emma and Caleb that their father and uncle had agreed to cater a wedding reception. We asked them if they would like to help us and explained that it would be a way of honoring the men in our family. We'd do it up in style, in the tradition of Morelli and Sons. They were excited to help.

On Friday, at twelve-thirty in the afternoon, we drove a rented van to the large hall where the reception would be held and spent most of the afternoon setting up.

The reception didn't start until seven o'clock, but we wanted to make sure everything would go smoothly.

We couldn't afford to pay the five servers for more than five hours, so we set it up as best we could until they came at five-thirty. They told us all the things we'd done wrong. We all worked together, and we were ready by six-fifteen. And then we changed clothes.

Caleb and I changed together in the men's rest room. Caleb was very excited to be following in his dad's footsteps, and he wanted to know all the things that most boys his age don't know: how to put cuff links on a starched shirt, how to put on a cummerbund.

And then, in the main hall, we went over each detail of what he'd be doing, which was to clear up and take used plates and glasses to the kitchen.

"How you do this will make a big difference in how the guests feel about the kind of job we're doing," I said. "If there are plates with half-eaten food and dirty glasses all around, they'll think we're not doing a very good job."

"What if I drop something?" he asked.

"Well, in the first place, it's better to take more trips and not try to carry as much, but if you do drop something, don't make a big deal of it. Just get down and clean it up, then go on about your business."

At the same time I was coaching Caleb, Cheyenne was training Emma in her job, which was to approach the guests as they sat down in her designated area at the round tables in the reception hall and provide them with a plate of food, then serve cake and either coffee or punch.

The wedding reception was a big success. At least for us anyway. The father of the bride probably thought it was too expensive. The bride probably thought it wasn't exactly what she'd wanted. The groom was probably glad it didn't take any more time.

To most people, it was just what they'd expect for a catered reception, but that was good because it was our first attempt.

I made sure, as the guests were leaving, to put my arms around Caleb and Emma. "You both did great. Your dad would be so proud."

In my heart, I wished my own father had put his arm around me and told me I'd done a good job. But just because he hadn't done that didn't mean I couldn't do it for Emma and Caleb.

The reception ended just after ten. It took us an hour to clean up, pack up, and haul everything back to the shop. The people we had hired helped us carry things inside, and then we told them they could go.

Cheyenne and I took Caleb and Emma home, then returned to the shop. We put the leftovers in the cooler, then rinsed the plates, glasses, and silverware. We'd come in the next day to finish up.

We ended up exhausted, sitting in the office, eating wedding cake with our fingers because we didn't want to dirty another dish or fork.

"We did it," Cheyenne said with a tired but enthusiastic grin.

"We did." I paused. "Thanks."

"No problem."

"I can't seem to get along without you," I said.

"That's what I'm here for," she said.

"Cheyenne, let me ask you a question. How long will you be staying?"

"For as long as you need me."

"That might be a very long time."

She shrugged. "It doesn't matter."

I was sitting at the desk in Hazel's swivel chair with my feet on the desk. Cheyenne came over and wedged next to me in my chair and put her feet on the desk, too.

"What are you doing?" I asked.

"It looked comfortable, so I thought I'd try it."

I put my arm around her shoulder. It was almost comfortable.

"There's just one problem with this," she said.

"What's that?"

"I have no idea how we get out."

"Well, we just push back with our feet," I said. "Like this."

I pushed with my feet, but instead of rolling, the chair started to teeter backward. Cheyenne squealed, and we were barely able to keep from tipping over.

Cheyenne started giggling. "We're stuck here forever, aren't we?"

"How about this?" I said. "You lift your feet up, then put them on the floor and get off."

The trouble was my leg was over one of hers.

"We have to lift both our feet together," she said.

We did, and the chair threatened to topple over again.

204

That broke us up.

"This is some kind of a trap, isn't it?" she asked.

"No, no. I've got it now. We just scrunch down in our seat, then we'll be able to get out."

We scrunched down, so we were practically lying in the chair.

"Now what?" she asked.

"Now one of us lifts her legs up off the desk and stands up."

She tried and then started laughing again.

"Your leg is still on top of mine," she said.

"Do I have to do all the work around here?"

"Well, I just know I can't lift my left leg when your leg is on top of it."

It must have been because we were so tired, but by then we were laughing so hard tears were rolling down our face.

"I've got an idea," I said. "You turn on your side."

She turned on her side, and our faces were practically touching. "Now what?" she asked.

"I don't know." I made a kissy face. "Actually, this isn't that bad."

She punched me in the stomach.

"Okay, okay, just kidding. The first thing we need to do is get our feet untangled."

"I can't even see my feet," she said.

Three more changes and we ended up sliding off the chair, with our backs on the floor and our feet still up on the desk.

But at least we were free from the killer chair.

We sat cross-legged on the floor facing each other. "This place is very dangerous," she said.

I stood up. "Well, we'd better go home and get some sleep."

"The kids will probably be asleep."

"We'll give them a goodnight kiss."

205

"We're beginning to sound like an old married couple," she said.

"We are, and that's a fact." I wasn't sure if I should even say it. "I wouldn't mind it . . . if we were married, that is . . . it might be . . . okay . . . maybe even fun."

"I suppose it could be fun." She started to laugh. "With the right person, of course."

"Excuse me? Did you say with the right person?"

"Oh, I'm sorry! Were you talking about you and me being married to each other? I didn't realize that. I guess I must have misunderstood."

We were both exhausted. I reached for her hand. "I'm going to get you for this."

"How will you get me?"

"I don't know yet. But I'll think of something."

She yawned. "I'm so tired."

"Me, too."

Holding hands we walked to the door, turned off all the lights, and made our way home.

◆　◆　◆

The most frustrating thing for me during the time we waited for news about my dad, Uncle Eugene, and Granddaddy was that there was nothing we could do. When someone dies, you have to arrange for the funeral and all the details that go with that. But with this, we didn't even have any proof that they were dead. So we were left in limbo, unable to bring anything to a conclusion.

We needed some way to pay tribute to them, to get some closure. Their deaths were swallowed up in the tragedy of so many more who had died. I started to wonder if anyone would remember they'd ever even lived.

Fearing they would be forgotten, I decided to keep the catering business running. I guess I figured that if it continued on with the same name, at least that would stand as a tribute to them.

The one success we'd had with the wedding reception made me think we could do it. The *we* being Cheyenne and me. I asked her if she'd stay on until I could find someone to replace her.

"If that's what you want, I'll stay," she said.

And so she stayed.

13

Cheyenne and I continued to camp out in the TV room each night with Caleb and Emma, but now instead of just watching popular movies, Cheyenne would occasionally throw in a Church movie like *Together Forever,* and she'd talk about where we were before we were born, and the purpose of our earth life, and where we go after we die. It seemed to help Caleb and Emma. Also, she made sure they did their homework. And we began insisting they turn the TV off at ten and try to go to sleep.

Oftentimes, I would wake up in the middle of the night and from my place on the couch see both Emma and Caleb crowded close to Cheyenne. All of us were shaken, numbed by the events of 9/11. But following the terror of the attack on the Twin Towers and the loss of the men in our family, Emma and Caleb were especially traumatized and seemed to need the comfort of some kind of physical contact to help them get through the night. So, no matter how they had arranged their sleeping bags when they went to sleep, by night's end Caleb and Emma were cuddling next to Cheyenne.

Although money was being raised for families who had lost loved ones, none was coming our way. And yet my mom and aunt still had to pay the mortgage on their houses and other bills.

We traveled to Ground Zero twice, but then we didn't want to go back. It was too painful to be there and, besides, what had once been a rescue operation had more and more become a salvage project. As the days passed, workers digging into the rubble had pretty much given up any hope of finding someone alive. Now, they were recovering only the remains of those who had been trapped.

Cheyenne and I went each day to my dad's office. Much to our relief, Hazel returned to work. She knew everything about the business and soon made up for our sloppy bookkeeping. Business was slow, though, and we barely made enough to stay open. But at least it was something to do.

People were still reeling from the effects of 9/11, and parties or events that weren't canceled were done much more simply. Many people who lived near the City had a fear of large crowds—what might have been large, extravagant banquets became small receptions with finger foods and crackers being served.

Cheyenne worked alongside me in the office each day until after school, and then she went home to be with Emma and Caleb.

Hazel was the one who trained us, which, in effect, meant she became our boss. She was not always the most diplomatic person in the world. Like what she said when she found out we'd bought paper products at a store: "What, are you crazy, throwing good money away when you could get this wholesale?"

Although she made us feel bad at times, she did teach us a great deal.

Hazel didn't work full time, either. She had lost her

nephew in 9/11, and she had a family to look after also. She was usually gone by two in the afternoon.

With lots of time on our hands and not much business, Cheyenne and I worked out an advertising campaign for Morelli and Sons. It gave us something to do, and we were good at it. Even with very little money to work on, we did a few things. Fliers and a few radio ads. It brought in some new business, so we were happy about that.

Several times a day I checked the value of Enron stock and other stocks my dad and Eugene had invested in. It made a recovery in October, so I was hopeful. I knew Marilyn was counting on me to advise her what to do with the investments Eugene and my dad had made.

When you own a stock that's gone down in value, you have a choice—either wait until it increases in value to what it had been when you bought it, or else sell it and cut your losses.

I decided to hold on to the stock. I couldn't see how energy stocks could stay depressed for very long. The U.S. uses a lot of oil from Saudi Arabia and Iraq. Since September 11, those sources were less reliable. I felt certain that the price of those stocks would come back up as soon as the stock market rebounded.

Even though their bodies hadn't been recovered, the last week in October, we filled out the paperwork that would result in death certificates being issued for my father, Eugene, and my grandfather.

A week later, with Marilyn and my mother's approval, we had a memorial service at a reception center on Northern Boulevard not far from Morelli and Sons. Isaac Feldman, an old friend of the family, gave us the use of the building for nothing. We could have held the service at a mortuary, but we weren't having a funeral because we had no bodies, and the people at the mortuary wouldn't come down in price. Besides, Marilyn thought Eugene and my dad would prefer a hall where they'd worked for weddings and other neighborhood events for years.

The memorial service was sad but also really good for all of us. Father Macmillan had grown up with Eugene and my dad, and he had some stories I'd never heard about them when they were younger. Like the time they'd borrowed an old junker car, taken it apart, moved it piece by piece into their high school in the middle of the night, and reassembled it in the principal's office. What was even more impressive was the fact they'd never been caught.

Eugene liked music and so, at Marilyn's request, Cheyenne sang some of Eugene's favorite songs. Hazel told some hilarious stories about what it was like working for Eugene and my dad and my grandfather.

And then Marilyn read from some remarks she had prepared for the occasion: "None of us could ever dream September eleventh would be such an awful day in so many lives. It is, of course, true that our family will never be the same. That is true of nearly two thousand families just like ours. But it is also true of the entire country. We will never be the same again. But we have to move on. And some good has come from this. Ben is now an important part of our family. He has been so good to spend time with us. Before, he had no interest in going into the catering business, but now he has taken over, I think, because of his love for the men in our family who preceded him. And Cheyenne has come and held us together. I love her with all my heart for what she has done for my children. Of course we miss our loved ones, but, looking out at all of you who have come, I sense your love and your support, and that will see us through this. Heartfelt thanks to all of you."

After a prayer by Father Macmillan, we adjourned into the hall. We formed a line and people filed by and told us how much they loved our family. At first Cheyenne had not wanted

211

to be in the line, but Marilyn and my mother and Emma and Caleb insisted she stand with us, and so she did.

The reason I love New York is because of its diversity, and that was evident in the people who came through the line:

A Jewish rabbi with an accent so thick I have no idea what he said, but there was no mistaking the bear hug he gave me and the tears he shed as he spoke to my mother and Marilyn.

A black poet, nearly seven feet tall, with his head shaved bald, wearing a white Nehru suit, and with a voice as low as I'd ever heard, gave us a poem he'd written for our family.

And friends of Caleb and Emma who came through and mumbled something to us but hugged Caleb and Emma and cried with them.

Neighbors, people I'd grown up around, people who'd yelled at me when I ran through their yards or threw rocks at their dogs, they also greeted us, but they'd already been at the house many times before, with casseroles and desserts so fancy they made them for their own families maybe only once every two years.

Many people assumed Cheyenne and I were married. For the first few people through the line, we tried to explain we weren't, but after a while we just smiled and let them go on their way.

It was good. It was all good, even though we cried more than we ever had and even though we had officially surrendered all hope. My fantasy about them living in a cavern under all that rubble, eating from a vending machine, was now gone.

We had faced death, and we had experienced its pain, but now we no longer avoided it. We had looked it in the eye and faced it down. And when we did that, it lost some of its sting. And that was good.

♦　♦　♦

Two weeks later, on a Wednesday morning, after a night before when Cheyenne and I had stayed up late, working a bar mitzvah, Cheyenne and I were the only ones in the TV room when I woke up. Emma and Caleb had already gotten up and gone to school.

"Good morning," she said. She was barefoot, wearing her sweats, sitting on the couch, with her scriptures in her lap.

"Looks like we lost our chaperons," I said.

"Looks that way."

"Been awake long?" I asked.

"A little while. I have a confession to make. I was watching you sleep."

"I didn't do anything disgusting, like drool, did I?"

"No, you were fine. You know what? Sometimes I forget this isn't my real family."

"It *is* your family. If you don't believe me, ask Emma or Caleb or Marilyn or my mom. All the neighbors think we're married anyway, so that means you're a part of the family."

"I just read something in the Bible," she said. "Can I read to you?"

"Sure, why not?"

"It's in the Old Testament, in the Book of Ruth."

She began reading, "'Intreat me not to leave thee, or to return from following after thee: for whither thou goest, I will go; and where thou lodgest, I will lodge: thy people shall be my people, and thy God my God.'"

She closed the book, gazed out the window, then looked down at me and said, "That's how I feel."

"Let me say how pleased we all are that you feel that way about us." The reason I said it in such a formal manner was because, even though she might feel close to my family, I wasn't sure she had strong feelings for *me*.

213

She picked up on my choice of words. "It's not just your family. It's you, too, Ben."

"I see. Well, that is good news, isn't it?" I said, very much aware we were in the house alone. I stood up and stretched. "Wow, what a great way to start the day, right? Let's do this more often, okay? You know what could make this day even better?"

"What?"

"If I'm the first one to take a shower!" I ran for the bathroom.

"Don't forget the two-minute rule!" she shouted after me.

"Yeah, right," I scoffed.

"I'll be timing you!"

She did time me. I could hear her calling out the numbers outside the bathroom. I went fifteen minutes and then turned off the water.

"You are in such serious trouble!" she called out from the hallway.

"Did you say something?" I said, turning on the ceiling fan to drown out her voice.

While she took her shower, I went downstairs, picked up the newspaper from the porch, then made my way to the kitchen to fix some bacon and pancakes for Cheyenne and me.

She came down a few minutes later, wearing a winter jacket of Marilyn's she'd found in the closet.

"What's with the coat?" I asked.

"The shower was so cold I'm still freezing," she complained.

"It's good for you. Builds character."

She came over and put her hand on my back and peeked into what I was cooking. "What's in the pan?"

"That's a pancake."

"Really? It looks like some growth that's threatening to take over the world."

"Oh, really? Well, Missy, it might surprise you to know that you're going to have that growth for breakfast."

She laughed. "Not without a lab test."

"Oh, you are, and, not only that, you'll beg me for more. Because this is my special recipe. I mixed chocolate chips in with the pancake batter."

She looked in the frying pan. "I don't see any chocolate chips."

"Well, no, not in yours, of course."

She thrust her chin toward me in an almost menacing way. "Are we going to have to duke it out right here in the kitchen?"

"It might end up that way. You insult my pancakes, you insult me."

We had a great breakfast, laughing through most of it.

Marilyn and my mother came back while we were cleaning up. They'd been grocery shopping.

"You two behaving yourselves?" Marilyn asked.

"I have, but she's been awful," I said. "She made fun of my cooking." I faked a tearful sniffle. "Sometimes I don't know why I care so much."

That night around nine-thirty, while Cheyenne, Emma, Caleb, and I were putting a huge jigsaw puzzle together in the TV room, the phone rang. Marilyn called up the stairs, "Cheyenne, it's for you."

"Who is it?"

"He didn't tell me his name."

"I'll take it downstairs."

I wanted to go downstairs with her to find out who it was, but I didn't.

She came upstairs an hour later. By that time, Caleb and Emma were asleep on the floor.

Cheyenne came in and sat down on the couch. I was in my sleeping bag, with Caleb on one side and Emma on the other. I sat up.

"Who called?"

"Justin. He just got off his mission."

215

"I see."

"He wants me to come home this weekend. He's giving a talk in church about his mission."

I sighed. "Well, we both knew he was going to come home sometime, didn't we?"

"I told him I wouldn't be able to make it."

"You did?"

"Yes."

"Why did you tell him that?"

"Because this is where my life is. I'm needed here. Besides, I don't feel the same way about him now."

"Two years is a long time. Maybe if you two spent some time together, it would bring back that loving feeling."

"Do you want him and me to get together again?" she asked.

"No, not at all."

"I know something now that I didn't know before I talked to Justin."

"What?"

"I want to be your wife."

"Really?"

"Are you still in the market?"

"I am, actually."

"Do you have any objections to me?" she asked.

"Not a single one."

"There is just one hitch, though. I want to be married in the temple."

"Yes, of course. I'll be a member for a year in, let's see, just nine months."

"That's a long time," she said.

"It is for two people living in the same house. Can I be perfectly honest? I'm not sure, with our present housing situation, we'll make it for nine more months."

"So what do we do?" she asked.

"You go back home. I'll fly out in nine months, and we'll

drive to the temple and get married. There would be very little temptation with you in Idaho and me here."

"I don't want to wait that long. Besides, I feel like Emma and Caleb still need me."

"Okay, how about this? I fly to Idaho and live with your folks for nine months. It will give your dad and me a chance to bond. Then you fly out and get me."

She smiled. "I'd love to see the look on my dad's face when we told him about that plan."

"So what do we do?" I asked.

"I can't leave Emma and Caleb. And you can't leave because Marilyn and your mother need you, and you need to keep Morelli and Sons going."

It seemed odd to me then, and still does, that we were talking about marriage, and yet, we were so separated physically. I was on the floor, sitting up with the sleeping bag up to my waist, and with Caleb and Emma sleeping beside me on the floor. Cheyenne was on the couch, avoiding eye contact with me, wrestling with a decision that she had never thought she'd have to make.

She looked up. She had a sad look on her face. "Ben, if we were to get married outside of the temple, would you promise to take me to the temple as soon as we can after we get married, so we can be sealed together as husband and wife so that our marriage will last forever?"

"Of course I'd do that. You know I would."

She closed her eyes and tears rolled down her cheeks. I knew she was giving up on a dream she'd had all her life, to be married in the temple.

"You have to promise me," she said.

"I absolutely promise you."

She nodded, but it wasn't enough. "This is so hard."

"I know."

Five minutes passed, then ten.

217

"Would it help if I came and sat next to you and held you in my arms?" I asked.

She stood up. "No, I need to go to my room and pray about this. Oh, also, I probably won't come back. I'd like to sleep in my own room tonight."

"Sure, whatever you'd like."

An hour later, the phone rang. I had been sleeping, but the phone woke me up. I heard Marilyn climb upstairs and knock on Cheyenne's door. "It's your father," she said.

"I'll take it downstairs," Cheyenne said.

I waited a few minutes and then walked barefoot down the stairs. I paused in the dining room, not sure if I should be listening in or not.

"I can't leave now, Daddy. I have to stay here. They need me."

A pause and then Cheyenne continued. "Don't you understand? Emma and Caleb lost their father, their uncle, and their grandfather all on the same day. They need me. I can do some good here. Instead of just talking about helping people, I can actually do it."

Another long pause, and then Cheyenne said, "Yes, I know he's home. He called me tonight . . . Well, because I don't feel the same way about him anymore. I have to stay here. Don't you understand? Do you ever watch the news? Do you have any idea what happened on September eleventh?"

I was in the process of sitting down when I jarred the table and a plastic apple fell off an arrangement and hit the floor. Cheyenne heard it, came into the living room, turned on the light, and motioned me to come into the kitchen with her.

"Dad, I'm going to put you on speaker phone. It'll be easier for me to talk to you that way."

I could now hear both ends of the conversation.

"How long do you plan on staying back there?" her dad asked. He was clearly frustrated and sounded angry.

"I'm not sure."

218

"I want you to give me a date when you will return. If you want to stay a couple more weeks, okay, that's fine. Or even a month. Just give me a deadline, and then I won't worry about you so much."

"I can't do that."

"Why not?"

"I just can't, that's all."

"It's because of Ben, isn't it? What's going on between you two?"

She didn't answer for a moment, then said, "I'm in love with him. We're starting to talk about getting married."

"Are you pregnant?"

"How can you even say that?"

"I want the truth, Cheyenne, and I want it now."

"I'm not pregnant!"

"Have you been sleeping with him?"

We'd talked about that before, joking about what Cheyenne would say if her folks asked her that question. The truth was we did sleep in the same room, but always with Emma and Caleb next to her.

It was the pause before answering her dad's question that did her in.

"Cheyenne, what have you done?" her dad said.

"It's not like that. We sleep in the same room with Caleb and Emma. They're always with us."

"You expect me to believe that you and this Ben fella are sleeping in the same room night after night and that nothing is going on? You come home and tell me nothing's happened, and then I'll believe you."

"I'm not coming home, at least not now."

"He's no good for you. I could see that the first time I met him."

"I'm sorry you feel that way because Ben and I are planning on getting married."

"In the temple?"

"No."

"That's what I thought. Why don't you just tell me the truth?"

"I am telling you the truth! We haven't done anything wrong!"

"Then I want you to come home right now, before it's too late."

"No! I won't do it!"

We could hear Cheyenne's mom in the background. "Let me talk to her."

"You can talk to her as soon as I talk some sense into her head," her dad shot back. "Cheyenne, is Ben there? I want to talk to him!"

"He's right here."

"Hello, sir," I said.

"What in blazes is going on back there?" he roared. "What have you done to my daughter to turn her against her family?"

"Nothing."

"Nothing? You call the way she's talking back to me nothing? I can't get the truth out of her. Maybe I can from you. Have you gone and got her pregnant?"

"No sir."

Cheyenne spoke up. "Daddy, I want you and Mom to come to the wedding. It will be here, in Ben's aunt's house."

"You are pregnant, aren't you? When did this start? Last summer in some cheap motel? I thought we'd raised you better than that. The first lowlife who comes along and you throw away everything we taught you. Well, fine, get married outside the temple if that's what you want! But don't expect your mother and me to show up and act like we approve of this! You hear me? Don't expect us to be there!"

"Daddy, you don't know anything!" Cheyenne slammed the phone down and ran into my arms. We made our way into the living room. We sat down on a couch. I held her in my arms as she sobbed.

The phone rang again.

"I'm not talking to him again," she said bitterly.

I went into the kitchen and disconnected the phone. Later, we found out it was her mother trying to undo the damage her father had done.

I came back to the couch and held her.

After a few minutes, she quit crying. "Ben," she said softly.

"Yes."

"Let's get married as soon as we can."

"All right."

"What does our schedule look like as far as receptions?"

"I think we're free Thanksgiving week, after Tuesday night."

"Let's get married on Wednesday of that week then," she said.

"Do you want a big wedding? Because if you do, I can recommend a very good caterer. Besides, I need the business."

She smiled. "I don't think we can afford us."

"Yes, of course. We are very expensive."

"Let's just have it be family." She paused. "I mean, your family . . . not mine."

We stayed up until two o'clock working out the details. We would get married on the Wednesday before Thanksgiving, then drive up to Lake Winnisquam, where we'd stay in the family cabin. We'd stay there through Sunday and then drive home. We had to be home on Monday because we had a wedding reception to cater.

"We need to get some sleep," she said.

"That'd be good."

"Now that we're engaged, we can't sleep in the same room," she said.

"How come?"

"I don't want anything to happen."

"Sure."

"One of us should stay with Caleb and Emma."

"Why don't you do that? Sleeping on the couch is killing me. Besides, Caleb and Emma like you better."

"All right." She blew me a kiss, and we separated for the night.

I slept in until Hazel called at nine and reminded me we had a luncheon to cater.

I woke Cheyenne, and we hurried to get ready.

When I went downstairs, Marilyn was at the kitchen table.

"Cheyenne's mother has called three times. She wants Cheyenne to call her back as soon as she wakes up."

"We don't have time for that now. I'll tell Cheyenne she called, though."

"Her sister called, too. What's going on?"

"She told her dad we're getting married."

"You're getting married? When?"

"The Wednesday before Thanksgiving. Can we do it here? It will be just family."

"Is her family coming out?"

"No. It will be just us. Is it okay if we have it here?"

"Yes, of course." Marilyn paused. "I take it her family does not approve."

"Her dad holds me responsible for corrupting his daughter."

Marilyn pursed her lips. I knew she wanted to say something but wasn't sure if she should or not.

"What?"

"Maybe you two should wait until they can get more used to the idea. I'm not sure it's such a good idea to make her choose between her family and you."

"If it doesn't bother Cheyenne, why should it bother me?"

"Go out and talk to her parents. Work out some kind of a compromise."

"Why should I do anything for her family? No, we'll get married on our schedule, not theirs. If they want to come out for it, then that's fine. But if not, that's fine, too."

222

Marilyn nodded. "At least let me call and talk to Cheyenne's mother."

"You can do what you want, but it won't do any good."

While we were at work, Marilyn did call and talk to Cheyenne's mother. She tried to assure her as to what kind of a person I was, and she invited anyone from their family to stay at her home.

Even though Cheyenne's mother had never flown and was terrified to fly, especially because of 9/11, Marilyn was able to put her mind at ease and talk her into coming out for the wedding. She asked if Cheyenne's father would be coming but was told probably not. She told Marilyn that he was against the marriage and felt that attending the wedding would be showing approval.

By the time we came home from work, Marilyn had good news, that Cheyenne's mother had purchased a ticket to fly out for the wedding.

That seemed to remove a great burden from Cheyenne. "I'm so glad she's coming," she said several times during the evening.

On Sunday we talked to Bishop Gaglione. We explained why we were getting married outside the temple and asked him to perform the wedding at my aunt's house. He agreed to do it but then spent another fifteen minutes talking to us about the importance of being sealed in the temple one year after our marriage date.

"Ben has promised to take me to the temple on our first anniversary," Cheyenne said. "So it's going to turn out okay, after all."

"Is that right, Ben?" the bishop asked. "Will you take Cheyenne to the temple on your first anniversary?"

I wasn't comfortable with the intensity of his gaze.

"Yes, of course, that'll be no problem."

He seemed to relax. "Very well."

I really meant it, too.

At the time.

14

Emma was in her glory as the director of her one-act play called *Cheyenne and Ben's Wedding.* "We need more flowers!" she called out the morning before the day of our wedding, waving a clipboard in her hand. Yes, the little twerp actually had a clipboard.

"It's just family, Emma," I said. "I mean, it's not the coronation of the queen, okay?"

"I know, but it's you guys's wedding, and it's the only one you're going to have."

"Maybe, maybe not," I teased, looking for Cheyenne's reaction. "There could be others if this one doesn't work out."

"Really? You think you can get married if you're dead?" Cheyenne teased.

"Whoa, tough girl."

She laughed. "You have no idea."

"I'll help her do it, too," Emma chimed in.

For Cheyenne it was not all blissful anticipation. Shortly after breakfast, a dark cloud of remorse passed over her. She excused herself and went to her room. When she came out, I could tell she'd been crying.

I decided we needed to talk about it. "You wish we were getting married in the temple, don't you?"

"It's just that all my life . . ." She fought to hold back her tears. "I always thought . . ."

She covered her eyes with her hand so I wouldn't see her tears.

"Let's wait until we can go through the temple then," I said.

"Emma is having such a hard time getting through this. She's even thought about committing suicide. She comes to me almost every day and we talk and that makes it so she can get through the day. She doesn't go to her mom because she doesn't want to add to her burdens. Don't you see? I have to be here for Emma and for Caleb. So I can't leave, and you and I are together all the time, and . . . well, it's difficult. So I don't know what else to do except for us to get married." She wiped her eyes. "I think once my mom comes and sees how it is here, she'll understand why I'm doing this."

Her mother's flight was scheduled to leave Salt Lake City at eleven o'clock Mountain Time, or one o'clock Eastern Time.

True to his promise, her father refused to have any part of the day. And, in fact, Cheyenne's sister Jen was driving their mother to the Salt Lake Airport.

A little after one o'clock, Jen called.

"Did the plane leave on time?" Cheyenne asked.

"I think so."

"Great."

Long pause. "Cheyenne, let me put Mom on the phone."

Cheyenne turned to me. "Oh, my gosh!"

"What?"

"Mom and Jen are both coming! I wonder if my dad is coming, too." Anticipating great news, she put the phone on conference call.

"Cheyenne?" her mother said.

"Hi, Mom. So you have Jen with you? Who else is there with you?"

"We're not on the plane."

"Is there a delay in your flight? Do you know when you'll be taking off?"

Her mother began crying.

"Mom, what's wrong?"

"I couldn't make myself get on the plane," her mother said, then broke down completely.

"Don't cry, Mom. It's all right."

Her mother was sobbing.

"Mom, could you put Jen on the phone for a minute?" Cheyenne asked.

"Yes?" Jen said.

"What happened?" Cheyenne asked.

"When we got into the terminal, there were all these National Guard soldiers with automatic rifles. And then there was the security check, and it seemed to take forever, and they escorted one man away, and we don't know why. Mom was sure it was because he was a terrorist, and she started to picture everyone as a terrorist. She started crying and didn't even make it through the security check. She wants me to tell you how awful she feels about it."

Tears were blurring Cheyenne's vision. "Could you put Mom back on?"

"Mom, it's okay. You tried. I know it's hard to fly now. It's okay. Don't worry about it. Ben and I will come visit you real soon."

"I'm so sorry," her mother wailed.

"I know, Mom. Really, it's okay. We'll be fine here. You know what? When Ben and I get sealed in the temple, we'll do it in Boise. How would that be? That's the ceremony that counts the most."

A short time later, Cheyenne got off the phone. "Nobody

from my family will be to the wedding," she said in a dull voice.

"I'm sorry."

"We'll survive."

Hours later Cheyenne's dad called. "Your mother and Jen just came home from the airport. They told me what happened. Cheyenne, you've got to postpone this so-called wedding of yours until your mother and I can be there for it."

"How long would you like us to postpone it for?" she asked.

"At least a year."

"It doesn't actually take a year to drive from Idaho to New York, Daddy. So, how about we give it a week? Then you and Mom can drive out here."

"If you'll come back and postpone the marriage for even three months, then if you still want to marry him, we'll support you in your decision."

"This isn't about travel time then, is it? It's about you trying to live my life for me, isn't it?"

"Cheyenne, for the last time . . . why are you even thinking about marrying this . . . this . . ."

She cut him off. "Careful, Daddy, Ben's right here listening in."

"Let me talk to Ben."

She handed me the phone.

"What?" I asked.

"If you really love Cheyenne, don't marry her. She'll never be happy with you."

"Look, if you'd been at the airport with your wife, she'd have boarded that plane with you. Your bullheaded refusal to be with Cheyenne on her wedding day is the cruelest thing you could have done to her."

"Listen to me . . ."

"With all due respect, sir, do you ever worry that when we have children, you may never see them? Does that ever worry you? It's a long way to Idaho. You two obviously don't want to take the time to be with us on our wedding day. Well, when we have kids, maybe we'll never come to visit you. In fact, I think I can guarantee it!" With that, I slammed the phone down.

Cheyenne ran to her room and closed the door. She stayed in her room for the rest of the night. And when I knocked on the door, she told me to go away.

So I did.

◆　◆　◆

I didn't see Cheyenne until the next morning. She was at the kitchen table, her elbows on the table, her head supported by her two hands, as she stared at an untouched bowl of shredded wheat.

"Whoever invented that must have grown up feeding cows bales of hay," I said, sitting down beside her.

She looked up at me, frowned, and then lowered her gaze to the two mounds of shredded wheat.

"It's not that bad with ice cream," I said.

She looked up at me. "I'm such a mess this morning."

"Let me guess. You didn't get much sleep, right?"

She nodded, then brushed away a clump of hair from in front of her face.

"Me, either, actually."

She took a spoonful of shredded wheat, put it in her mouth, and frowned.

"Moo!"

She nearly smiled.

I decided I would have to face the real issue. So I was very serious when I said, "We don't have to get married today, if you're having second thoughts."

"I'm having second thoughts, but not about you."

"About what then?"

"I'm wondering if my mom and dad have ever loved me. I used to think they did, but now I'm not so sure."

"Of course, they love you."

"What if what I interpreted as their love was only that I always did what they wanted me to do?"

"They love you, Cheyenne. They're just disappointed . . . that of all the guys you could have married, you picked me."

She reached for my hand. "And I still pick you."

"Really?"

"Really."

She kissed me on the cheek. "Let's go get married, okay?"

"All right, but I'm not marrying somebody who has shredded wheat in her digestive tract." I grabbed her bowl and dumped its contents in the sink. "Whataya say we have ice cream for breakfast?"

"Ice cream?"

"Sure, why not? It's our wedding day, right?"

She broke into a smile. "You're right. It is our wedding day! We can do anything we want. Let's break out some butter brickle and a spoon and go for it!"

"Now, right there, you see? That's the reason I'm marrying you!"

Since nobody outside my family would be at the wedding, we moved it to four-thirty so we could get an earlier start on our way to the family cabin in New Hampshire.

The ceremony itself only took five minutes.

And then we all had a piece of cake. Cheyenne and I thanked the bishop for performing the wedding, kissed my mom and Marilyn and Caleb and Emma, and went out to the car and drove away.

It took us until a little after eleven that night to make it to the cabin. There was snow on the ground, and inside it was very cold, so we started a fire. The cabin had not been built for winter use, but once the place warmed up, it wasn't too bad, at least not right next to the wood burning stove.

229

"Which bedroom do we want to use?" Cheyenne asked.

We went upstairs to look around. My grandfather still had clothes in his closet and that brought back memories, so we went downstairs to the room where Cheyenne had stayed when she first came to the cabin.

There were old clothes in the closet there, too. Maybe my grandmother's or possibly someone else's in the family.

The place smelled of my grandparents, though, or at least the smell I associated with them, a cross between cinnamon and tea.

I thought we had agreed on a room, so I brought in a space heater and turned it on to try to warm things up. Cheyenne left the room. I thought she'd gone into the bathroom to brush her teeth and get ready for bed, but when I went in the hall, the light was off in the bathroom.

I found her outside, standing on the porch in the cold, looking out at the dock, which was now covered with snow. The lake appeared to be frozen.

I put my arm around her. "You're going to freeze out here."

She wouldn't look at me. "I don't think I can stay here tonight," she whispered.

"How come?"

"Everything around here reminds me of Eugene and your dad and your grandfather."

"What do you want to do?"

"Let's go to a motel."

We drove into town and stopped at the first motel we came to. I paid cash and drove around to the room we'd been given.

A party was going on in the room next door. They were some snowmobilers from Boston on a Thanksgiving weekend outing. From what we could tell from the noises next door, they were watching porn videos and drinking beer.

The room was freezing. I turned on the space heater but nothing happened.

The video in the next room was so loud we could hear every line of dialogue and the resulting hoots and hollers.

Cheyenne sat on the bed, her shoulders slumped, her hands hanging at her sides, her eyes closed, as she tried not to listen in on the sounds from the movie next door.

I called up the manager and complained about him giving us a room with no heat and informed him there was a party going on next door. He said that's all he had. I told him the whole place was empty except for the two rooms at the end. He said they were doing some remodeling and that's all he had.

"Listen to me! I want another room! And I want it now!"

"Give me a few minutes, and I'll see what I can do."

I turned up our TV loud enough so we couldn't hear what was being said or done next door.

Ten minutes later, the manager knocked on our door. "Well, I've found something else. It's not completely remodeled, but it's better than nothing."

We walked through the snow to a room halfway between the office and the party. He opened the door without a key and let us in.

He'd already swept up some of the construction mess before he came to us, but there were still bits of Sheetrock on the carpet.

I tried the heater. It worked. I went in the bathroom and turned on the hot water. After a few seconds, it was warm. "I guess this will do," I said.

The manager nodded and left.

I went over and sat on the bed and looked into Cheyenne's eyes. I'd never seen her more depressed.

"You okay?" I asked.

"This isn't the way I pictured my wedding day."

231

"We're both tired, so . . . maybe we'd just better get some sleep."

"I think that would be for the best."

We slept in separate beds and didn't even share a good-night kiss.

At seven the next morning she crawled into my bed. "What's going on?" I asked.

"Don't talk, Ben."

I didn't talk.

We slept until nine, and then a carpenter, who was working the holiday, walked into our room to finish up the remodeling. At first he didn't see us.

"We're in here," I said.

"Oh, my gosh," he said, backing out of the door.

"We'll be out of here in ten minutes," I called after him.

Cheyenne made me stand guard at the outside door until she was dressed and ready to go and then I got dressed and we made a hasty retreat.

We bought some groceries and then drove back to the cabin.

The feeling of sorrow for losing our loved ones on September eleventh was not as strong in the light of day. And, in fact, it was beautiful with the sun lighting up the snow and the lake, making each snowflake seem like a tiny diamond.

We got a fire going and fried some bacon and eggs and made pancakes. Later, we made our way carefully to the dock. Each step we made was the first for that winter.

We stood there and took in the beauty of the day. And then we got into my grandfather's winter clothes and walked along the shore. The thick forest of trees rimming the lake had lost their leaves and thrust their bare limbs into the cloudless sky. The snow sparkled in the sunlight, and as long as we kept walking we weren't cold. The whole place seemed like a magical new world, and we felt a part of it.

By the time we returned, we were starving, so we opened some cans of hash and fried them with a couple of potatoes.

In the afternoon, we played Scrabble. Cheyenne won but that was because she cheated by using the word *Zed,* which I challenged. We didn't have a dictionary, so we tried to call the local library and ask, but they were closed because it was Thanksgiving Day.

We decided we'd sleep that night in the room where Cheyenne had stayed her first night, but because it had so many memories from the family, we moved some of the clothes and pictures upstairs to my grandparents' bedroom.

For supper we drove into town and found a café that was open. We had their "Thanksgiving Special." We were the only ones there, but the waitress said more would be coming later on. "The truckers come around nine-thirty at night," she said.

I bought a copy of *The New York Times* to read later.

On the drive back to the cabin, I asked, "Are you happy?"

"Oh, yes, very happy," she said with a slightly forced smile.

While Cheyenne took a shower, I sat down at the table and started to read the newspaper. The headlines read: "Enron's Growing Financial Crisis Raises Doubts about Merger."

I began to read. "Shares of Enron plunged 23 percent yesterday . . ."

I closed my eyes.

I could hear Cheyenne singing in the shower. I put on a coat, grabbed my cell phone, went outside, and called Marilyn.

She was surprised to hear from me. "Is anything wrong?" she asked.

"I just read about Enron. I'm so sorry."

"It's not your fault. You did the best you could do."

"What are you going to do?" I asked.

"I don't know. If I sell, I'll only get pennies on the dollar of what Eugene put in. I'm so afraid I'll end up with nothing, and with Emma and Caleb approaching the time when they'll be wanting to go to college, well, I'd feel better if you could help me."

"I'm so sorry. I should have told you to sell when you asked me."

"Who knew?"

After I hung up, I felt awful. I just wanted to be by myself for a while, so I took a walk. The ice on the lake was thick enough for me to walk on.

Standing out there on the ice, in the cold, and thinking about all we had lost since 9/11, it seemed more than I could take. My father, Uncle Eugene, and Granddaddy gone. My career in advertising over. Our family finances in the toilet. And now, Cheyenne's parents hating me, not only for what I was but for marrying her outside the temple. Life seemed hopeless, and all I wanted was to run and get away from it all.

Cheyenne, wearing a robe, opened the door and called my name.

"I"m out here on the ice," I said.

"Are you going to be coming in anytime soon?"

"Not for a while."

In my mind it was like I was wrestling with a demon. I'm not sure how long I would have stayed out there, but after maybe half an hour Cheyenne, dressed in winter clothes, gingerly walked toward me.

"You okay?" she asked.

I nodded. "I just need to be by myself, that's all."

"Is anything wrong?"

"No, nothing's wrong."

"Is it me?" Her voice quavered as she said it.

"No."

"Are you sure?"

"Yes."

"What is it, then?"

"I can't tell you."

"Why not?"

"Look, can't you just leave me alone? I really don't want to talk right now."

I thought she'd go back to the cabin, but she didn't. She just stood there. We were about twenty feet apart.

Five minutes passed, and then she said, "Ben, can we at least go back to the cabin? I'm freezing out here."

"Go back then."

She didn't say anything for a while and then, in clear, even tones, quoted what was becoming her favorite scripture: "'Intreat me not to leave thee, or to return from following after thee: for whither thou goest, I will go: and where thou lodgest I will lodge.'"

"Your folks were right, you never should have married me."

"I did, though, didn't I?"

"Yes."

"Ben, please, let's go back. I really am freezing out here."

I nodded, and we walked back to the cabin. She slipped her arm through mine as we made our way back.

In the cabin it was warm and cozy.

"Do you want some hot chocolate?" she asked.

"No."

"Do you want something to eat?"

"No."

"Fine. Let's just sit here and scowl at each other then, if that's what you prefer."

We sat across from each other at the kitchen table but didn't say anything.

And then, in a tiny whisper, I said, "I've done a very bad thing."

"What have you done, Ben?"

I pulled out the *New York Times* article and let her read it.

235

"I don't understand," she said.

"My dad and Uncle Eugene and my grandfather were very heavily invested in Enron. A while back Marilyn asked me what to do. I told her not to sell. So now my mom and Marilyn have lost nearly everything, and it's all my fault."

"You couldn't know what it was going to do, so it can't be your fault."

"It is, though. It's all my fault."

She was about to hug me when I stopped her from coming any closer. "It's not too late for you to have the marriage annulled."

"You silly boy, I'm not about to do that. I'm yours, for better or worse."

I sighed and nodded, and she came to me and sat on my lap and threw her arms around me.

And so we stayed. And the next day we drove back.

That was our honeymoon.

15

One week later, on Thursday, November 29, 2001, Enron collapsed. The day before, its shares were selling at sixty cents a share. Our family alone lost over two hundred thousand dollars.

Marilyn knew how horrible I felt about not telling her to sell the stock, and she went out of her way to tell me over and over again it wasn't my fault.

Marilyn and my mother and I met to go over our finances.

Marilyn said, "The rent on your grandfather's apartment is due on the tenth of December. Let's give notice and move his things out." She turned to my mother. "Maybe you should think about selling your place and moving in with us."

"It doesn't matter where I live," my mother said.

"Well, you think about it."

Two days later, Marilyn, my mother, Cheyenne, and I showed up at my grandfather's apartment after Emma and Caleb had gone to school. We took two cars to haul everything we decided to keep.

I was determined to be hard-hearted and throw away most everything. Marilyn and my mom started in the kitchen.

Cheyenne was with me as we went through the clothes in his closet.

There were none of my grandfather's clothes that I wanted. And I didn't think Caleb would want them, either. And so I went to his closet and began stuffing everything into a large black trash bag.

I could tell Cheyenne didn't approve of what I was doing. "What?" I asked.

"Maybe you should wait and ask your aunt and your mom if there's anything they want to keep."

"Why should they want to keep anything? They can't wear any of this, either."

"I just think you should ask them, that's all I'm saying."

"If I ask them, they'll take forever. I'd like to get this done sometime in this century."

"Ben?"

"What?"

"He was your grandfather."

"True, but now he's dead, along with three thousand others. So what's your point?"

"I'm not your enemy, Ben."

"Did I say you were?"

"No, but sometimes you treat me like I am."

"You care more about Caleb and Emma than you care about me."

This was fast becoming an issue with us. The previous three nights Cheyenne had ended up sleeping in the TV room with Caleb and Emma. I didn't like waking up alone after only a few days of marriage.

"They're hurting, Ben."

"Who did you marry? Them or me?"

"I married you."

238

"Would you have married me if you'd never met my family?"

"It's not fair of you to ask that."

"Just answer the question. Would you have married me if you'd never met my family and if September eleventh had never happened?"

She stared at the floor.

"Answer me!"

She looked up and met my gaze. "Probably not."

"That's what I thought."

"What is so wrong with me loving your family? Sometimes I think I love them more than you do. How much time have you spent with Caleb and Emma lately?"

"I have a business to run."

"I can't be with you when you're like this."

She left me to go talk to my mother and Marilyn. I knew she'd tell them everything and that they'd end up on her side. And that made me furious, especially after all I was trying to do for the family.

In a fit of rage, I began to dump everything into trash bags as fast as I could.

A few minutes later, when my mom and Marilyn and Cheyenne entered the room, the place was empty except for ten trash bags.

"I'm done here," I said. "I'll start in the bathroom."

"There are some things we'd like to keep," Marilyn said.

"It would have been nice if you'd told me that before I started in here."

"We didn't know you were just going to throw everything into trash bags."

"What do you want to keep? Tell me, maybe I'll remember which bag I put it in."

"We need to see what's in each bag," Marilyn said.

"It's all just junk. There's nothing worth keeping."

"This junk, as you call it, is the only thing we'll have left to help us remember him," Marilyn said.

"You're not his daughters. He's only in your family by marriage."

"He was always good to us, Ben, and we loved him."

"Fine, then, have it your way!" I picked up each bag and dumped its contents on the floor and then stormed out of the apartment and got into my car and drove away.

Driving helps me sort out my feelings, and I had a lot to sort out. I kept going most of the night. I ended up going north on I-87 and then west on I-90. I'm not sure what I planned to do. If I could have easily taken up a new identity and forgotten everything that had happened, I'd have gladly done that.

I didn't blame Cheyenne for my problems, but in the deep recesses of my mind I felt she was always comparing me with Justin, her missionary. I could imagine her thinking to herself, *Justin would never do that.*

Around two in the morning, I passed a sign for the Hill Cumorah. It brought a flood of feelings, not so much about the Church but about Cheyenne. The first time I met Cheyenne, she was the Church. And, to a large extent, she still was. I couldn't think of the Church without thinking about her. That had drawbacks because when I was mad at Cheyenne, I was also mad at the Church.

I'm not sure why I took the Palmyra exit, but I did. I drove out to the Joseph Smith home and parked and soon fell asleep.

I woke up the next morning when a minivan pulled beside me and parked and a family from Utah climbed out and started down a path. They appeared to be heading into a pasture. I was curious, so I followed them, not close enough for them to pay much attention to me, but close enough that I could hear their conversation.

They entered a path leading into a grove of tall trees. I

240

followed them at a distance. When they stopped, I sat down on a bench so they wouldn't know I was, in a sense, stalking them.

"Is this where it happened?" a boy, maybe nine years old, asked.

"Yes, somewhere around here," his dad said. "This is where God the Father and his Son Jesus Christ appeared to a farm boy named Joseph Smith, who wanted to know which church to join. And how grateful we are that he offered that prayer."

"And that Father in Heaven answered his simple prayer," his wife added.

Of course I'd heard the story in the discussions, but I hadn't thought about it much since I was baptized.

The dad asked his twelve-year-old daughter to say a prayer. I could hear every word, and I could tell she was sincere—that she believed that God does answer prayers.

I wasn't sure I believed it, but I was glad this girl believed it.

They started singing as a family.

I felt embarrassed for them. I'm not sure why. I'd never known any families who sang church songs in a grove of trees.

I remember thinking that this was the kind of family Cheyenne would have had some day if she'd married Justin. She gave away a good portion of what she'd dreamed would be her future when she agreed to marry me.

She'll never live close to her family, I thought. *She'll never have in-laws who are descendants of Mormon pioneers. She'll never have what her mom and dad have wanted her to have. She's given up everything for my family because she loves them.*

I've got to go back and try to do better. I've got to try to be the kind of man this father is with his wife and children.

241

I hurried back to my car. A few minutes later I was on my way back.

Back to my family.

♦   ♦   ♦

I'm not sure what I expected when I returned later that day. I guess I assumed I could just start over again. After my experience in the grove and the long drive home, I felt like a new man, more committed to making my marriage work, more willing to be understanding when it came to the way Cheyenne devoted her time and energy to help Emma and Caleb deal with their loss.

Maybe it happened to Scrooge, but it doesn't happen in real life.

I had hurt Cheyenne deeply by running out on her and not letting anyone know where I was or what I was doing for almost twenty-four hours.

She listened to my explanations. I tried to turn it into a spiritual quest by putting in the fact that I'd decided to come back while in the Sacred Grove, but she was tentative from that point on. I felt like she didn't really expect me to change and that she was just waiting for enough bad marks in her account book so she'd be justified in leaving me.

My mom and Marilyn didn't help much. They were clearly on Cheyenne's side.

"We had no idea where you'd gone or if you were even alive," my mother scolded.

"I called."

"You called a day later. Do you have any idea what that poor girl went through last night? The least you could have done is call and tell her where you were."

"Yes, that's what I should have done, all right."

"Without Cheyenne I don't know where we'd be right

now. If you ask me, she's an angel sent from God," my mother said.

Marilyn was no less condemning. "If my husband went into a rage and left me without a word of where he was, that would be the last time he'd do that. I'm not sure why she stuck around. If I had been her, I'd have been on the first plane home."

"She stayed because she loves you and Mom and Caleb and Emma."

"She loves you, too."

"Does she?"

"Yes, she does, and I'm sorry you can't see that."

Eventually, though, Cheyenne and I patched things together.

The patch must have worked because a month later Cheyenne became pregnant.

♦   ♦   ♦

We sold my mother's house in March. I was not asked to help her move. They hired movers to do it. And they did it while I sat idly in the catering office with Hazel, waiting for some business.

In the privacy of our bedroom, I mildly complained to Cheyenne. "We could have saved a lot of money if we'd rented a truck. I could have loaded it, driven it here, and unloaded for a fraction of what my mother paid to have a moving company do it."

"We talked about it. We thought it would be better this way."

End of discussion.

When Cheyenne first got pregnant, I was very happy about it because I thought it would bring us closer. And it did at first, but as this creature began to take on life, I could see a

243

change in Cheyenne, subtle at first, but it definitely put our relationship on a different plane.

She no longer had to worry about just herself. Now she had a responsibility to this yet unborn child. I felt that now she looked at me, not as her friend and lover, but as the father of her child.

And I could tell she wasn't sure I had what it would take.

I never said anything to her about it because I was afraid she'd tell me my worst fears were justified, and then we'd get into an argument and she'd leave me and go back to Idaho.

◆　　◆　　◆

For the next three months I worked night and day to breathe life back into Morelli and Sons Catering. We did some clever ads on cable TV that brought in some business. Old customers who had loved my dad and Eugene and my grandfather came to us when they had a party or reception or dinner to put on.

After weeks of catering small receptions and making hardly any money, we finally got a break. We were asked to cater a retirement party for C. R. Cazini of Cazini Enterprises, a Fortune Five Hundred company.

Two hundred people would be at the sit-down banquet in Cazini's mansion, in Port Washington. The one-hundred-year-old castle was on the top of a bluff, overlooking Long Island Sound.

It was to be a gala evening, and we hired all my dad's old regulars for the event. It was exciting to see so many of the people I'd grown up with working together to make this a big success.

Naturally, I wanted everything to be perfect. Some of the most successful business leaders in the area would be there. It alone could bring in additional business for years to come.

On the day of the retirement party, I'd worked through

much of the previous night with a crew preparing food, and so by the time we were serving the food, I was a little strung out.

At the end of the meal, Caleb was working with about fifteen others, putting out the desserts. Just as Caleb was moving one of the desserts to the table, a guest slid his chair back, causing Caleb to drop the dessert on the man's wife's lap.

I saw it happen and rushed over immediately to apologize and try to clean up the mess. "I'm very sorry. Let me help."

"Look at this! My dress is ruined!" the woman said. She was in her midsixties and should have had gray hair and wrinkles, but by the miracles of science had dark black hair and a face that had been tucked and pulled into that of a much younger woman. I had the impression that if she smiled, the strain would be too much and the skin would split into bits and pieces.

I bent down and cleaned up what had fallen to the floor.

I looked up at Caleb. He looked as though he was about to cry.

"Look at what you've done by your clumsiness! You've ruined my dress."

"It wasn't my fault!" Caleb said.

"I assure you, ma'am, this will never happen again. It is an outrage." I turned to Caleb. "You'd better come with me right now!"

I marched Caleb into the kitchen area, out of the sight of the guests. "How dare you ruin this for me, Caleb! You think that woman or any of her friends are ever going to bring any business to me, after what you've done?"

He had tears running down his face.

I should have stopped with that, but I didn't. Maybe because of lack of sleep, or maybe because this was so important to our survival as a company, I went on too long and said some things I shouldn't have said.

And in the middle of it, Cheyenne came in and saw me,

245

heard what I was saying, and hurried over. "You leave him alone!"

"You don't even know what he did."

"What did he do?"

"He dropped a plate of cake on one of the guests and ruined her dress."

"That could happen to anyone."

"Go back to work and let me handle this."

"No, you back off and let him be. It was an accident, that's all."

Now I had two people questioning my authority. I started ranting against both of them.

And then something happened. I happened to see my reflection from a cookie sheet set up on its side. The image was that of my father. I had become my father.

Suddenly, I knew why my father had been so hard on me when I'd been caught with my hand on a classmate's shoulder in a gesture of greeting. He had had no choice. He could not be viewed as condoning such behavior.

The second thing that happened was that Cheyenne stepped in between me and Caleb and led him off to her car and drove away.

Cheyenne and Caleb being gone didn't slow us down that much, but I felt like she'd deserted me when I needed her help the most.

When I got home late that night, she was asleep in the TV room with Caleb.

Emma, who had been with me, joined them.

I went to our room and tried to sleep but ended up tossing and turning for the rest of the night.

I got up at ten the next morning with a headache. Everyone seemed to be gone, so I stumbled into the kitchen and made myself a cup of coffee.

I was on my second cup when Cheyenne suddenly walked into the kitchen.

"Is that coffee you're drinking?" she asked.

How dare you try to make me feel bad for having a simple cup of coffee after you deserted me last night, I thought.

"Yeah, you want some?"

She sat down at the table. "Beady, we need to talk."

"Yes, we do. Let's start with last night. Let's talk about you walking out on me and taking Caleb with you and me having two hundred people needing service. Let's talk about that."

She shook her head. "How could you talk to your own cousin like that?"

"This is a business, Cheyenne. Last night was very important to the survival of Morelli and Sons. I can't have my people fouling up all the time."

"Fine, run your business, but don't ever ask Caleb and Emma to help you again." She stood up and walked out.

We didn't talk much for the rest of the week. I spent most of my time at Morelli and Sons. One of the things I found out was we hadn't made as much money as I'd expected at the retirement party. I'd made a mistake in calculating my expenses. By the time we paid for the food, we had made barely enough to make payroll.

Within a week, I'd made my apologies to Caleb and Emma and Cheyenne. That seemed to make things better between us for a while.

In order to bring in more business, I bought a trailer outfitted to make waffle cones, that I could haul around Long Island on weekends. I talked Caleb and Emma into working for me. They were excited about making some money since things were so tight at home.

Cheyenne wasn't very happy about my working Sundays. She wanted me to go to church with her. She also held it against me that I talked Emma and Caleb into working with me on Sundays.

"It's a way for them to make some spending money," I said.

"They should be in church."

"They're not members of the Church."

"It doesn't matter. They should go to their church."

"They'd rather make money."

"They're a lot like you, then, aren't they?"

"I'm doing this for the family."

"You're not doing it for me, that's for sure, because if you were, you'd stop. How can you expect to receive the Melchizedek Priesthood if you never go to church?"

"I won't have to do this forever."

"Who is going to give our baby a blessing?"

"I know. Why don't you call Justin and get him to come out and do it?"

I knew immediately it was the wrong thing to say. She glared at me, then left the room.

Another check mark against me.

On a sunny Sunday in July, while Emma and Caleb and I were having a great day selling waffle cones, my cell phone rang.

It was Marilyn. "Cheyenne is very sick. We're taking her to the hospital. You'd better meet us there."

"What's wrong with her?"

"I'm afraid she's having a miscarriage."

We closed up shop and raced to the hospital.

By the time we got there, she had been admitted and was in a bed in one of the rooms.

"I came as soon as I could."

"I want a priesthood blessing," she said.

Once again I felt condemned. "I'll call and try to get someone here."

"Hurry, Ben, I need help."

I called our ward meetinghouse and asked to speak to the bishop. He told me he'd come right away.

But before he could arrive, Cheyenne had miscarried.

When they let me in to see her, she wouldn't look directly at me. "I lost my baby," she said quietly.

"I know. They told me. Are you going to blame me for this, too?"

"Is that all you can say?" she asked.

"Well, no. I'm sorry it happened."

"Maybe it's for the best." She turned her face to the wall and wouldn't talk to me.

A week later, she told me she was going home to try to gain some strength.

"Will you come back?" I asked.

She wouldn't answer me for the longest time, and then she said, "I don't know."

I drove her to the airport. Because of the need for beefed up security, all I could do was drop her off at the curb and drive away.

So, she left me.

16

With Cheyenne gone, I had nothing to live for. Well, maybe that's an exaggeration. I still had the New York Yankees.

I felt like a total failure. My wife had left me. I'd stood by and watched as my family's investments were lost. I'd taken charge and personally destroyed Morelli and Sons, a business my grandfather had started when he was about my age. To avoid complete humiliation, at the end of July I sold it to my dad's fiercest competitor, who bought the building and equipment for pennies on the dollar.

With that and the money we got from selling Mom's house, Marilyn and her kids and my mom had enough to keep going.

In the middle of August, with no job and no motivation to do much of anything, I moved to the family cabin on Lake Winnisquam. It was for sale, but so far nobody wanted to pay what we were asking for it. I decided to use it while we still had it.

One bit of good news. My mom had pulled herself

together and was doing a lot better. The priest from their parish had spent a lot of time with her and had helped her renew her faith in God. And that seemed to give her greater peace of mind. So I was happy about that.

I took my laptop with me, and Cheyenne and I exchanged emails occasionally. She told me she was doing well. She had a job working at a local radio station in Boise, writing and selling ads. She was very good at it and was making a name for herself in Idaho. (That is, if making it in Idaho actually means anything.)

On the last Monday in August, I was sleeping upstairs in what had been my grandfather's room. I heard the crunching of gravel as a car pulled into our driveway. I looked at the clock. It was a little after one in the afternoon.

I heard a knock on the door. Since I was doing some part-time work for my old boss, Ross, and was expecting a Fed-Ex delivery, I put on a pair of slacks and a T-shirt and went to the door.

I opened the door and there, larger than life, was Cheyenne's father, in jeans and boots and a dull brown, long-sleeved shirt. He was wearing his usual baseball cap advertising a feed company.

My first thought was that he'd come to kill me.

"Are we going to stand here like this all day or are you going to ask me in?"

"Yeah, sure, come in."

He stepped inside. I'd found a pizza place in Laconia that delivered, and so there was a three-foot stack of old pizza boxes in the corner. In the middle of the table was a stack of past issues of *The New York Times*. It's such a good paper, I hated throwing any of it away.

"You were sleeping? It's after one o'clock."

"I was up late last night, working."

"Doing what?"

"Working on an ad campaign for a new brand of soap."

251

He looked around at the mess. "You ever consider actually using the soap?"

"I don't have to use it."

He shook his head. "That's the way it looks to me, too."

"So, why are you here? Did Cheyenne send you with divorce papers? Is that what this is about?"

"Nobody knows I'm here. My family thinks I'm at a range management convention."

"I still don't know why you're here."

"You going to ask me to sit down or not?"

"Yeah, okay, you can sit down . . . if you want." I moved the stack of newspapers aside so we'd have eye contact sitting across from each other.

"You want something to eat?" I said.

He was a man on a mission. "I didn't come all the way back here to eat."

"Let me see what I've got. Maybe I can interest you in something."

I opened the fridge. It smelled as if something dead was in there. I closed the door quickly and went to a cupboard and found a can of beef stew. I showed it to him. "I'm going to have this. You want any?"

He nodded.

I opened up the can of beef stew, washed a bowl, and dumped the jellied sludge into the bowl and zapped it in the microwave.

He waited until I sat back down, then said, "I need to know your intentions in regard to my daughter. You got any plans?"

"I guess it's up to her. She's the one who left."

"You know why, don't you?"

"Probably to start up with Justin again."

One thing I learned that day was never get a cowboy riled up. He banged the table with his fist and yelled, "What on earth is wrong with you, boy?"

The microwave dinged, but I let it go, fully expecting he'd be leaving soon.

"Cheyenne hasn't talked to Justin, and he hasn't talked to her. In case you've forgotten, she's a married woman. She knows it, and Justin knows it. They're not going to be getting together."

"Oh, well, tell her not to worry. Someone else will come along. Look, why don't we cut to the chase? Just give me the divorce papers, and I'll sign 'em and you can be on your way."

With one swoop of his large hand, he angrily swept the pile of newspapers off the table. "You think I came all the way back here to get you to sign divorce papers? Let me tell you something, boy, I flew in an airplane to get here!"

"I still don't know why."

He shook his head, looked out the window, removed his hat and set it on the table. "It's not what you think. It's not what anybody would think."

"Well . . . are you going to tell me or not?"

He ran his work-hardened hands over his face. The way he did it, I could believe it was something he did when he had a hard job ahead of him. He glanced at me quickly and then averted his gaze, finally ending up staring at the strewn out stack of newspapers on the floor beside us. To dramatize what he was about to say, he sucked air between his teeth, then said, "I haven't always liked you."

"That has occurred to me."

"But . . . a few days ago, I got to thinking about how you lost your dad and your uncle and your grandfather all in the same day. So . . ." His voice trailed off, and he avoided eye contact.

"Yes?"

"I started thinking that maybe what you needed was a dad. Being your father-in-law, I guess I'm the closest you're going to get to havin' one. But I got to warn you, I'm not an easy man to get along with."

253

"Really?"

"You remember the first time we talked? And I told you to keep your hands off my daughter? Did you abide by what I said?"

"Well, not after we were married."

"I'm not talking about after you were married! I'm talking about before! Did you go by what I told you before you got married?"

I had to think about it. "Yeah."

"See, I already knew that. Because I asked Cheyenne. That's what she told me, too."

"And we're talking about this because . . . ?"

"If you could keep your hands off my daughter before you married her, then maybe you can do just about anything you set your mind to. Especially if you had somebody who could guide you along the way. That's what got me to thinking I should come back here."

I was still confused. "For what purpose?"

"To help you see what a complete fool you're being to walk away from your marriage and drop out of society."

"This is New Hampshire, for crying out loud. It's part of society, okay? So that's why you came here? To play dad?"

He sucked air through his teeth. "Yep, that's it, all right."

"Well, okay, you came here, you gave your little pep talk. Is that it?"

He shook his head. "I'm staying here with you."

"You are?"

He nodded. "Yep. I'll be here until Saturday."

"That's almost a week."

"I know how long it is."

"Isn't that a waste of your time?"

"I wouldn't do it for just anyone . . . but I would for a son," he said more softly.

I didn't know what to say. I couldn't imagine that either

one of us would last until Saturday. "What are we going to do for a week?"

"For starters, we're going to do is clean this mess up. My barn is cleaner than this place."

We worked most of the rest of the day cleaning up. By the time we were through, we had seven trash bags stuffed in the dumpster. I had even cleaned out the fridge.

"The next thing we need to do is to get some decent food, so let's go shopping."

What does a rancher from Idaho buy when he goes shopping? Steak and potatoes. But he had a problem with the selection of potatoes. "I want to speak to the manager," he told the checkout girl who had the misfortune of working while we were there.

When the manager showed up, my new dad didn't waste much time. "How come you don't have any decent potatoes in your store?"

"We haven't had any complaints."

"I don't see any Idaho potatoes. They're the best in the world. How can you as a manager sleep at night knowing you're not giving the best product to your customers?"

"We can get these a lot cheaper."

"I'm going to send you some Idaho potatoes. Use them in your own home and see if they aren't worth the little extra they cost."

"All right, I'll try them."

I was very glad to leave that store.

We grilled some steaks outside on the grill and fried some potatoes inside and sat and ate and watched the sun setting beyond the lake.

"How come you took over your dad's catering business?" he asked as we cleaned up.

Before I answered him, I said, "I don't even know what to call you."

"Well, my name's Hugh. That'll probably do. Or you can call me 'Dad.'"

"Okay, Hugh, I took over the business because I figured that's what he'd want me to do."

"If it were my son, I'd rather have him do what he was good at instead of what I was good at. All my sons got college educations so they wouldn't have to take over my place."

"I've pretty much ruined everything my family had built up over the years."

"At least you tried. That's better than most would do. The day I die is the day my sons put my ranch up for sale."

"So what are you saying?" I asked.

"I'm saying there's no reason for you to hang your head because you couldn't make it in the catering business. Work on what you're good at, not at what you don't enjoy."

I stole a glance at this rugged rancher, who was at that moment wearing my mom's flowered apron.

"Thanks for the advice."

"I've got a lot more, but this is all you're going to get today. Where do you want me to sleep?" he asked.

"I'll put you on the first floor next to the bathroom. I usually sleep on the second floor."

"Is there a bathroom on the second floor?"

"No."

"So why do you sleep there when you're the only one here?"

I started to blush. "Because the bedroom on the first floor is where Cheyenne and I stayed when we were first married."

"So?"

"The room reminds me of her."

"I guess the mind does play tricks on us sometimes."

I washed up and went upstairs and crawled into bed. A few minutes later, he climbed the stairs and stuck his head in the room. "We didn't have family prayer. I guess it must have slipped your mind."

I sat up. "Where do you want to have it?"

"Ordinarily, it wouldn't matter. But tonight let's have it downstairs in the kitchen because I got a few things I need to teach you."

So we went downstairs to pray, me in my boxer shorts and him in his "Idaho potatoes" pajamas, featuring a creamy white background overlaid with hundreds of photos of actual potatoes, with the dirt still clinging to them.

"Is that what you wear to bed?" he asked me.

"I was about to ask you the same question."

"These are pajamas."

"It's a good thing it's been a mild day. When it's really hot, I don't wear anything to bed."

He gave me a disgusted scowl. "Okay, let's get through this. This is your place, so you're in charge. That means you ask someone to give the prayer. You can say the prayer or you can ask someone else to give it, but you always take charge. None of this having your wife take over. All right, go ahead."

"Would you give the prayer?"

"I'd be happy to."

It was a very long prayer and covered his wife, every one of his sons and daughters, and all his grandchildren by name. He spent a lot of time asking blessings for Cheyenne and me, that we'd be able to make our marriage work.

And then, finally, it was over.

"You'll want to do that every night, and, if possible, every morning. The main thing to remember is you are the priesthood leader in your family, and so you're to take charge. Is that understood?"

"Yes."

"All right then. Let's hit the sack."

The next morning at seven-thirty, I heard him in the kitchen. And then I could smell bacon frying.

He hollered up to my room. "Breakfast is ready."

I washed up and came down to eat. He had me do the morning prayer routine. This time I called on myself.

We began to eat and then he said, "I'm still on Idaho time. That's why I got up so late."

"This is late?"

"I usually get up at five-thirty."

"In the morning, right?" I asked.

We finished eating and then did the dishes.

"Do you have some work you need to do today?" he asked.

"I need about four hours to finish up a project I've been working on."

"What will you do with this work once you're done with it?"

"I send it as an email attachment."

"That's it? You don't have to mail it or anything?"

"No. I send it, and if they like it, then they electronically deposit some money in my account."

"I wonder if I could send my cattle as an attachment when I'm ready to sell them. That'd save me a three-day cattle drive."

I worked all morning. He left me alone. In fact, he went to town.

When he came back, he was all smiles. "Guess what? I got some gear so we can do some fishing."

"Fishing?"

"How can you stand to be living next to a lake and not fish?"

"Because I wouldn't know what to do if I caught one."

"I'll show you everything you need to know. It'd be a lot better if we had a boat."

"There's a boat in the garage. It's just a rowboat though."

"That's all we need."

We spent the afternoon sweltering in the hot sun, trying to get a fish to take our bait.

A little before five, he hooked a fish and managed to bring it into the boat. "What kind of a fish is that?" I asked.

258

"It's a sucker," he said. "We'd better be very careful because this is an extinct fish. Let's call this lake a federal reserve and tell all the folks who have homes here that they'll have to move so we can save this rare endangered species."

"What are you talking about?"

"Don't get me started, Son, don't get me started."

I didn't.

That night he gave me another lesson. "You need to get yourself worthy to receive the Melchizedek Priesthood, so let's see what's holding you back."

He gave me an interview similar to one I would have when applying for a temple recommend. And when it was over, he sucked air between his front teeth and said, "Well, it could be a lot worse. Basically, you got to start going to church, start paying tithing, quit drinking coffee, and quit watching R-rated movies. Think you can do that?"

"I guess I could try."

"A steer can try."

"Cheyenne says that."

"Says what?"

"A steer can try."

"So?"

"Nothing. The first time she said it, I thought it was strange for a girl to be saying that."

"She learned it from me."

"I know."

"What about putting your life in order so you can receive the Melchizedek Priesthood?"

"I'd have to think about it."

"Take all the time you'd like." He sat there waiting for a reply.

I went outside for a while and then came back in. "Okay, I'll do it."

"I'm proud of you for making that decision."

He stood up and said it was time for bed, then waited for

me to take charge. Because I didn't want a long prayer, I said it.

On Wednesday he let me sleep until nine. When I went downstairs, he was at the table, writing.

"I worked up something for you this morning. It's called 'Things Every Husband Should Know about Marriage.'"

"You want to read it to me?"

"Nope. I'll give it to you one at a time as we go along."

He gave me the first one after breakfast.

"Okay, here's the first one. Most of the time when your wife asks you a question, she doesn't actually want an answer. So don't make the mistake of giving her an answer."

"Give me an example."

"Suppose it's Sunday and you come in the kitchen dressed for church, and your wife asks, 'Are you going to wear that tie to church?' Your first thought is to say, yes, right? I mean you wouldn't have put it on unless you intended to wear it."

"Yeah, right. So what do I say?"

"You say, 'Is the color wrong?' Most of the time that'll be it. She'll tell you what tie to wear, and you go make the change."

"What if I really want to wear that tie?"

He shrugged his shoulders. "It's just a tie. Let it go. Do you want her scowling at you all the time you're in church?"

"No."

"Then go along with what she wants."

"I get it."

He gave me the second piece of advice in our boat that afternoon, fishing. He pulled his list out of his shirt pocket. "Okay, here's the second one. If your wife says, 'We need to talk,' then you got to realize she's going to do all the talking. And, you also need to know you're in deep trouble."

"So what do I do?"

"Just listen. Don't even try to defend yourself by telling her

260

what you were trying to do. I've butted up against that, and it doesn't do any good."

"What do I do when she's done?"

"You say, 'What can I do to make things better?'"

"That's it? I could do that."

"But then you actually have to try to make it better. Otherwise, me telling you this is a complete waste of time."

"How many more of these do you have?"

"I'll keep giving them to you until you tell me to shut up."

I didn't write down his list of ten things, but I can still remember some of them.

"Okay, here's a for instance. You get home and Cheyenne's upset because the washer or dryer quit working. Okay, remember this, don't fix it right away."

"That doesn't make any sense. Why wouldn't I fix it?"

"Oh, you'll fix it, all right. What I'm saying is, not right away. First thing you got to do is say, 'Oh, that's awful. You must have had a terrible day.' And then she's going to unload on you, tell you in great detail how bad it was. Well, you just listen, and every once in a while, you say, 'I am sorry things didn't go well.' And then you give her a big hug and you tell her you love her. And then you sit down with her and let her talk some more. I'd say, give it . . . oh. . . . I don't know, maybe ten, fifteen minutes."

"That long?"

"Yep, that's right, until she's all talked out. And then, when she's not looking, you go downstairs, flip the circuit breaker, which is what it'll be nine out of ten times, and then go back up the stairs and you say, 'Guess what, Honey, I fixed it!'"

I had to think about that for a long time, but finally I asked, "Why can't I just fix it right away?"

"Because she'll be mad at you if you do. Believe me, I know. Women aren't like us. You want to know something?

261

I don't fix anything right away anymore. I just listen and let her tell me how bad it was before I even try to go fix it."

"This is very tricky," I said.

"You have no idea. I'm giving you the benefit of a lot of mistakes I made. Women have got to vent their feelings. And they don't want you to give them a solution to their problems. But that's what men do most of the time. Whatever they say, you've got to listen. I know it's tough not to try to fix it right away, but that's the way you got to work around 'em."

Later that day, he gave me another hint. "Okay, let's suppose Cheyenne is about to decorate a room. It could be a living room or a kitchen or a nursery, you know, whatever. And she comes to you and says, 'I can't decide whether to paint the room periwinkle blue or apricot peach.' What are you going to tell her?"

"I'm going to say, 'I don't care one way or the other.'"

He shook his head. "You got a lot to learn! I know because that's basically the answer I gave when my wife asked me that same question right after we were married."

"So what should I do? Pick a color?"

He shook his head. "Nope. Don't do that, either."

"I have no clue, then."

"I didn't either when it happened, but I've worked it out, so pay attention. What you do is put your hand to your chin, like this, like you're thinkin' real hard, and then you say somethin' like, 'Hmmmm. . . . that's a tough one. I can see where the soft tones of periwinkle blue would be good. But, on the other hand, I can see where apricot peach would be good, too. Kinda brighten up the room.' Then you pause like you're thinkin' real hard, and you say, 'What do you think?' And she'll give you an answer. Let's say it's periwinkle blue. And then you say, 'You know, I really think that *is* the best choice.' And, then, once again, you got yerself through the pasture without steppin' in somethin'."

On Saturday, just before we had to leave to go to the

airport, as we were reeling in our lines, he said, "There's one more thing I need to say before I go."

"What is it?"

"You were right about one thing. We should have been there for your wedding. I should have never let my foolish pride get in the way. So, I'm apologizing to you for that."

"Accepted."

"Thanks. It's always hard to eat crow." He paused. "But you're goin' to find that out soon enough, when you go to visit Cheyenne."

At the airport, we stood there, looking at each other, not knowing whether to shake hands or hug.

"Thanks," I said.

"No problem. When you come to visit, remember, I was never here. I was at a range meeting all week."

"Right. It never happened."

"Good luck with Cheyenne. She can be as stubborn as a mule sometimes."

"I know. She's a handful, all right."

He shook my hand, then pulled me in and threw his other arm around me.

"So, I'll be seeing you around, okay?"

"Okay."

He turned and started for the terminal.

"Hugh?"

He turned around and looked at me.

"Thanks . . . Dad," I said.

He nodded, then continued on his way.

17

In the middle of September, after working my way through a long list of self-improvement tasks Cheyenne's dad had given me, I flew to Boise. Her dad had warned me I had to actually go there. "Don't think that some fancy email attachment is going to do this for you. You got to sit down face-to-face with her and let her look you in the eye and see for herself that you've changed for the better."

I didn't tell Cheyenne I was coming because I was afraid she'd tell me not to bother.

When I picked up my rental car at the airport, I got a map and directions to the radio station where Cheyenne worked.

Half an hour later, a secretary took me to her. Cheyenne was sitting with her back to me in a tiny sound booth, working up a commercial for a new herbicide. I was able to watch her through a small window in the sound booth door.

She'd cut her hair since I'd last seen her. It made her look efficient and focused and business-like and far less approachable. She looked good, though, just not the same. Of course, I wasn't the same, either.

I figured she must have written the commercial because it was clever, in a small-town, small-budget kind of way. It featured a conversation between two weeds. The only trouble was both weeds sounded the same because they were both being done by Cheyenne. So it sounded like a weed with a split personality.

I listened to a run-through and then opened the door and let myself in and sat down next to her. "I think it will be better if I take the part of the second weed."

She stared at me in disbelief and then turned her gaze to the script.

"Unless you'd rather be the second weed," I added.

"No, you can be the second weed."

We did a run-through. It was much better.

"You want to do it again?"

"No, that's good enough." She forced herself to make eye contact. "Why did you come?"

"To try to save my marriage."

She sighed and shook her head. I knew that was a bad sign.

"Look, I've got my old job back at the advertising firm. I've even got the Great American Cereals account. Saddlemier wants you, too, but I told him you wouldn't be working once we had kids. He's okay with that, if you are. I've quit drinking coffee and started going to church. I've been interviewed to receive the Melchizedek Priesthood. My bishop says I should be ready by the end of October. As soon as that happens, and it's been a year since we got married, we'll be able to go through the temple and be sealed."

She looked stunned. It was too much to take in at one time. "You have a lot of nerve, waltzing in here out of the blue. Did you think I'd just drop everything and sail off with you into the sunset?"

"No."

"What did you expect to accomplish by coming here?"

"I expected we'd have a chance to talk."

"What do we need to talk about?"

"We need to see if there's any hope for us."

She kept her eyes on the script. "How many minutes are you going to give me before you rush off to bigger and better things?"

"I'll stay here for as long as it takes."

"Really? And are you expecting to stay with my family?"

"I'll do whatever you want me to do."

"I'd feel much better if you stayed in a motel in town."

I was disappointed, but I tried not to show it. "You know what? I wouldn't have it any other way."

She told me she didn't want me around while she was working, so I found a motel, took a shower, changed clothes, and watched TV until it was time for me to meet Cheyenne at the station.

"Now what?" she asked when we met in the parking lot by her car.

"Can we take a walk?"

She drove us to Boise's river walk. We walked together along the Greenbelt but didn't hold hands and kept our distance. It was her choice, not mine.

"How are Caleb and Emma?" she asked.

"They're good. They want to come to Idaho and visit you."

"I'd like that very much."

"I'll tell them when I go back."

"When do you have to go back?"

"I'm supposed to start work on Monday."

She nodded.

"I bought a ticket for you, too, if you decide to come with me," I said.

"I hope the ticket is refundable."

"It is. Totally," I lied.

"Good." She stopped walking and looked into my eyes.

266

"Do you actually expect me to make up my mind about us in four days?"

"Well, we are married . . . so you don't have to decide if you want to marry me."

"No. All I have to decide is if I want to stay married to you."

"That's right."

We were coming to a picnic table just to the side of the path we were on. "Can we sit down and talk?" I asked.

"I suppose."

I sat down opposite her at the table. It was painful for me to be looking directly at her. It was like looking at something precious I'd lost for a long time, but when I found it again, it was no longer mine.

"I've thought a lot about what happened," she said.

"I've thought about it, too. I'd really like to know what you've come up with."

"The reason I married you was because . . ." She stopped. I could see in her eyes that she didn't want to say it because she knew it would hurt me.

"Go ahead, it's okay, I can take it."

"The reason I married you is because I loved your family more than . . ." She stopped.

I finished the sentence for her. "More than you loved me."

She nodded. "That's a terrible thing to say, isn't it?"

"Not if it's the truth."

"I loved Caleb and Emma, and I always will. And they were going through such a hard time, and I felt like I was actually helping them. And your aunt and your mom were having such a hard time, too, and, well, being there for them seemed like the most important thing I could do."

"And I was just part of the package, right?"

"I don't know, Ben. I thought I was in love at the time."

I tried to hold her hand, but she pulled away. "Listen to me," she said. "All my life I'd dreamed of marrying someone

267

who loved the Savior. So, after we were married, the difference between what I'd dreamed about and what I'd settled for became more and more obvious. With each flare-up, with each argument, it became more and more clear I'd made a mistake in marrying you. When I got pregnant, though, I thought it was a sign from God that I should stay in the marriage."

"But when you had the miscarriage, all bets were off, right?"

"More or less."

"So you came back here."

She glanced up at me. "In case you're wondering, I didn't come back to see Justin. We haven't even talked since I got home."

"I know that."

Her eyebrows raised. "How would you know that?" she asked.

Whoops. I'd learned that from her dad. "What I mean is, I believe you."

"So that's where we are," she said.

"Thank you for telling me."

"Where are you in all this?" she asked.

"I'm mentally healthy now. I have a job. I'm working to be worthy to go to the temple."

"Those are good steps, whether or not we stay together."

"Cheyenne, I love you, more now than ever before."

"I wish I could say the same thing, but right now I'm sort of numb. You hurt me, Ben. You hurt me so much."

"I know I did. I'm sorry."

She drove me back to the radio station so I could pick up my rental car.

"Can I take you to dinner?" I asked when she pulled alongside my car.

"Not tonight, but thank you for asking."

"How about tomorrow night?"

"I don't know. We'll see," she said, then gave a pained sigh.

"Is it always going to be this way?" I asked.

"What way?"

"Me trying to win your love, and you resisting my every move."

She shrugged. "I guess we'll just have to see, won't we?"

"I haven't been with any other women since you left. I mean, if you're wondering."

"You didn't have to tell me that."

"You have a right to know."

"Why do you say that?" she asked.

"Because we're still married."

She glanced away. "I suppose that's true. I haven't really thought about it much."

"You haven't thought about the fact that we're still married?"

She shook her head. "Of course I have. I don't know why I said that."

"Maybe to hurt me?"

She looked away. "I suppose that's possible."

"Hurt me all you want, Cheyenne, if it will make you feel better."

She rested her elbow on the steering wheel, shielding her face from my gaze with her hand, and began to cry.

I didn't know what to do or say, so I did nothing. I'd learned from her dad not to defend myself or try to fix it.

A few minutes later, she asked me for a small box of tissues in the glove compartment. I gave them to her.

"I'll do anything you ask to try to make it up to you," I said.

"What if I want a divorce?"

That's when I wished I'd never come out.

"Ben?"

"Of course. Whatever you want."

"I'm sorry it didn't work out."

I got out of the car, then leaned forward to look at her through the open door. "You want to know what I'm sorry about? I'm sorry you're not willing to put forth any effort at all to see if maybe we might have been able to make our marriage work. That's what I'm sorry about." I closed her car door and got into my car.

I was halfway out of the parking lot when she started honking like crazy.

I drove back into the parking lot, pulled alongside her car, and ran my window down. She looked at me through her open window. "It's possible, I suppose, that my dad would expect me to ask you to supper."

"Your dad?"

"Yes, he's softened a little in his opposition to you. Yesterday, he actually said something nice about you."

"I'd like to see him again. And your mom, too."

"Don't expect much from my mom. Do you want to follow me out?"

I nodded.

My supper with Cheyenne and her folks was torture. Cheyenne had told her mother everything. Not even an occasional positive remark from her dad could alter the mind-set of mother and daughter.

But over dessert, her dad did say, "I can't believe you're staying in a motel. You should be staying with us."

"He's already got himself a motel room," Cheyenne said.

"Actually, I would rather stay here."

"You can stay in the barn. We haven't washed the sheets since the last time you were here," he said.

"That's not true," Cheyenne's mother said.

Since all my things were in my motel room in Boise, her dad rummaged around and got me a new toothbrush and some toiletries. He even gave me a brand new pair of "Idaho potato" pajamas, which I accepted out of courtesy.

One more word about the pajamas. They were a brain-child of the Idaho Spud Producers. They were so ridiculous looking that not even potato farmers would wear them. They ended up in a half-price bin at one of the malls in Boise a few Christmases before. Cheyenne's dad bought ten pairs and had been trying to get rid of them ever since.

That night in my room in the barn, I couldn't get to sleep. It was difficult, knowing that my wife was less than a hundred feet away in her room. But for all practical purposes, we might as well have been a thousand miles apart.

The next morning at six-thirty, Cheyenne's dad knocked on my door.

"Come in."

"Let's get rolling. We have a lot of work to do."

I didn't even stop to ask. I was glad to have some time with him. Maybe he'd have some ideas of what I could do.

We drove around the ranch.

"How's it going?" he asked.

"I think I'm too late. Cheyenne is talking about wanting a divorce. I'm not sure anything I can do will be enough."

"She's sizing you up. You've just got to give it some time."

"I've told her about getting my old job back and how I'm preparing to go through the temple, but none of it seemed to have much of an effect on her."

"You're not going to all this effort just for her, are you?"

"Well, in a way, I am."

"Wrong answer. If you're just doing it for her, then you'll go back to the way you were after she comes back. She's got to be wondering if this is just another advertising blitz you've worked out to get her back. She has to be convinced the changes you're making are rock solid. Then maybe she'll believe you're on your way to becoming the man of her dreams."

"It might be easier for her to just get a divorce and then marry the man of her dreams."

271

"No girl ever marries the man of her dreams. All brides think they have, and then, as time goes on, they see that their husband has some flaws."

"So what do they do?"

"They do what my wife did. They work on their man to see what they can make of him."

Cheyenne had to cancel the dinner date I'd made with her because she sang in a choir and they were practicing, so I had supper with her mom and dad, and later I went next door to visit with Cheyenne's sister and her husband. That was painful. The bad news about me had gone out to them, too, so I soon left because I didn't feel welcome in their home.

The next day I was at a loss as to what to do. I didn't think I could stand to drive around playing rancher with Cheyenne's dad, and Cheyenne had no use for me at work.

Cheyenne's mom gave me a suggestion after breakfast, just after Cheyenne had left for work. "Why don't you go to the stake Family History Center and work up a TempleReady file for your father and your uncle and your grandfather?"

I decided that was a good idea. It would keep me from doing ranch work.

The Family History Center was at the stake center in town. There was only one other car parked in the lot when I arrived. The rest of the building was locked, but the library had its own separate entrance.

I walked in and was greeted by an old man, who at that moment was using his pocketknife to remove the peeling from an apple. He looked to be in his seventies.

"Mornin'. Can I help you?" he asked.

"I'm not sure. Is this the Family History Center?"

He chuckled. "If it isn't, we're both in the wrong place."

"I want to work on my family history."

He cut the white apple into wedges with his knife and set them on a folded piece of paper towel. "What have you done so far?"

272

"Nothing. I'm a convert. I joined the Church last October. I'm from New York."

"City?"

"Yes."

"Were you around the towers on September eleventh?"

I looked away, not sure if I wanted to open my soul to this stranger. It was always painful to talk about what had happened. But, because I had come to help the men I'd lost on 9/11, I decided to let him know.

"My dad and my uncle and my grandfather were in the World Trade Center when it happened. They didn't make it out. I want to go to the temple and be baptized for them."

He set the apple aside. "Jean? Come here. We got work to do. Come and meet this young fellow."

She had white hair and walked with a cane.

"This is my wife, Jean. My name is John. We're the Beesleys. You can call us Brother and Sister Beesley. That's what people call us when we're here."

We shook hands, then he said to his wife. "This young fella lost his dad and his uncle and his grandfather on September eleventh in the World Trade Center. He wants to prepare some TempleReady slips for them."

"Yes, of course. Let's get started on it. We'll help you all we can."

They needed birth dates and places. I got on my cell phone and called my mom.

"Mom, I need to know some family history from you and Marilyn."

"What for?"

It was a difficult question to answer, and I was afraid if I didn't give them what they needed to hear, they'd refuse to help me. I said a silent prayer and began. "You know, when you and Dad were married, it was until death do you part. Well, the Mormons believe you and Dad can continue your marriage forever."

273

"That's what I believe, too."

"Then help me."

"You're talking to me about marriage lasting forever, and I'm sitting here wondering if your marriage will last another month."

"I'm working on that, too. Will you help me?"

"What do you need from me?"

"When was Dad born? Where was he born? When were you and Dad married? Where were you married? I need the same information on Granddaddy and Grandmother."

"I can do that, I guess."

"I'll need Marilyn to get me the same kind of information, too."

"I'll tell her. Give us half an hour and then call us back."

I set the cell phone on the counter.

"Let's start with you," Brother Beesley said.

We sat down in front of a computer. These people were so old and so obviously farm folks who'd probably never traveled out of Idaho, I couldn't believe they'd even know how to turn a computer on. They did, though. In fact, it was amazing how much they knew.

It took most of the day to work up PAF files and GEDCOM files and whatever else they kept talking about all the time.

They told me I would not be able to go to the temple to do work for my dad and uncle and grandfather until a year after their date of death. Also, my dad and Eugene could not be sealed to their wives unless my mom and Marilyn were members and went to the temple. But it would be possible to have my grandfather and grandmother sealed to each other. They explained that being sealed means their marriage will go on forever. I was sure they would both like that to happen.

At supper time, when I returned to Cheyenne's folks' place, I was on fire with excitement with what had been accomplished in just one day. In addition to my immediate family, we had found ten names for whom I would be able to do temple work, as soon as I had a temple recommend and could go to the temple.

During supper I couldn't contain myself. "You see, the thing is you got your PAF 5 software and then from there you make yourself a GEDCOM file. That's what I've got here in this floppy. And then from that you go to TempleReady. When you go to the temple, you give 'em the floppy and they give you a pink or a blue slip for every ancestor. Brother and Sister Beesley showed me some of theirs. I'll use those slips when we do work in the temple for my family. Brother Beesley says I'm a real natural at this. You know, you can just keep going from one generation to another, all the way back to Adam. Isn't that great?"

Cheyenne was staring at me as though I had come from another planet.

Her mom and dad were excited for me. They took me to their own computer and did a little GEDCOM magic of their own. In our searching, we found a common ancestor on my mom's side.

"We're related then!"

Cheyenne stood at the door watching this scene play out in front of her.

I put my disk in their computer and showed them what we'd done that day. "When the men in my family died, I felt so bad, not just because they'd gone, but because I couldn't tell them how much I loved them. For me, doing this is a way to let them know how much they mean to me . . . still."

It was one of those rare moments in my life when I felt good about what I was becoming.

Finally, Cheyenne sat down. She didn't say much. I think she figured this was just a very clever ad campaign I'd cooked up. I felt like she was trying to find a flaw in my delivery or an inconsistency in what I said that would expose me for what she thought I was, and would always be—a man without any beliefs who says and does whatever he needs in order to win over his target audience.

Which, in this case, was her.

"Why would you do this for your father, when you and he didn't get along when he was alive?" she asked.

"I learned a few things after taking over Morelli and Sons. I could see why my dad got so mad at me sometimes. I did the same thing to Caleb when he spilled the cake on that woman's dress at the Cazini banquet."

"The way you yelled at Caleb and me was very wrong," Cheyenne said.

"I know that. I've apologized to Caleb a hundred times."

"So, you've learned to apologize. That's good, I guess, but does it go any deeper than just words?"

It was a good question. I knew myself well enough to wonder if this was just smoke and mirrors I'd concocted to get Cheyenne back. I mean, after all, that's what I do for a living.

Cheyenne was expecting a quick comeback, but that's not what she got. I had to think it through. I wasn't sure either.

I went back in my mind and remembered the feeling I'd had while doing Family History work.

The excitement had been real and genuine.

"This was one of the most amazing days of my life," I said softly.

She looked at me like she was seeing me for the first time.

"It's late," her mother said. "Can we have family prayer now?"

We knelt down. "Ben, would you offer our prayer?" Hugh asked.

Cheyenne glared at her father.

"Father in Heaven . . ." I began.

I can't remember all I said, but I do remember thanking God for being able to prepare TempleReady slips for my family. "Please help me to be worthy to go to the temple and do this work so they'll know we have not forgotten them and the good they did while they were on the earth."

After the prayer, I stood up and told them I could hardly wait to go back to the Family History Center in the morning to see what other ancestors I could find.

Cheyenne followed me outside on my way to the barn. "Can I talk to you for a minute?" she asked.

I stopped halfway between the house and the barn. She stayed on the porch.

"Of course."

"I'm proud of what you've accomplished today, Ben."

"Thanks. It's been pretty exciting."

"Yes, I can see that it is."

"Well, good night," I said, giving her a half-hearted wave and turning toward the barn. I had taken a few steps when she called out, "What would you think about inviting me to your room later tonight?"

I stopped and turned to face her in the darkness. "Is that allowed?"

"We're still married, aren't we?"

"Yeah, we are . . . but . . . uh . . . well . . . that is . . . actually, this is kind of unexpected."

"It is kind of a gamble, isn't it? It could be setting us both up for more heartache."

"It could do that, all right."

"I would want an invitation from you, though. I don't want to just barge in on you in the middle of the night."

She probably could see the silly grin on my face. "I know what you mean. That would such a bother, having you wake me up in the middle of the night when I'm trying to sleep."

We stared at each other.

"So, are you going to invite me or not?" she asked.

"Yes, of course. Would you please come and visit me tonight?"

She gave me a fake frown. "Of all the nerve. What do you take me for?"

After a long pause, while I tried to decide how to answer that question, I finally said, "I take you for my wife."

"Good answer. What time will be convenient?"

I laughed. "Are you serious? As soon as your parents are asleep, come and see me. Run as fast as you can, too, okay? I am most anxious that such a meeting take place."

She laughed. "Well, some things haven't changed, have they?"

"That's very true."

"I can speed this up if you'd like," she said.

"How?" I asked.

She opened the screen door. "Mom? Dad? Can you both come here?"

They appeared a minute later at the doorway. "Is anything wrong?" her mom asked.

"No, nothing's wrong. I just wanted you to know that I'll be spending the night in the barn with Ben."

Her mom's mouth dropped open.

Her dad's face broke into a huge grin.

And I did my best to look calm and under control.

Cheyenne went and packed a few things and then showed up in my room a few minutes later.

When I opened the door to the bedroom in the barn, she took one look at me and cried out, "Oh, my gosh, I can't believe it! You're wearing Idaho potato pajamas! And a cowboy hat?"

"Howdy, ma'am. Come on in and make yerself to home."

♦ ♦ ♦

In November 2002, Cheyenne and I received our endowments in the Boise Idaho Temple. Her whole family was there with us. Also that same day, Cheyenne and I were sealed to each other. Later that day, I was baptized for my dad and my uncle Eugene and my grandfather. Cheyenne was baptized for my grandmother.

The next day Cheyenne and I did the rest of the temple work for my grandparents. The biggest thrill was for the two of us to act as proxies for them as they were sealed to each other.

My mom and my Aunt Marilyn and Caleb and Emma have not joined the Church yet, but they're taking the missionary discussions.

Cheyenne and I live just ten minutes from where Marilyn and my mother and Caleb and Emma live. We visit them several times a week. We often invite Caleb and Emma to come over on a Friday night, where we sprawl in our sleeping bags in front of the TV and watch movies and eat. And then, because my father-in-law took the time to coach me in priesthood procedure, I take charge and tell everyone it's time for family prayer. And then I call on someone to say the prayer.

As I look back on the events of 2001, it seems so incredible that in a few brief seconds on September eleventh, my family was torn apart, devastated. And even more incredible that, through the gospel of Jesus Christ, we have been able to put the pieces of our lives back together again.